✔ KU-513-176

KINDLING THE DARKNESS

JANE KINDRED

MILLS & BOON

First Published in Great Britain 2018
by Mills & Boon, an imprint of HarperCollins*Publishers*
1 London Bridge Street, London, SE1 9GF

Kindling the Darkness © 2018 Jane Kindred

ISBN: 978-0-263-26686-3

0818

Printed and bound in Spain
by CPI, Barcelona

For the freaks who suspect we could never love anyone…and just need someone to save us from ourselves. (With thanks to Aimee Mann, who expressed it so eloquently.)

Chapter 1

A timeless monument to spiritual devotion—and a 1950s architectural marvel that somehow managed not to insult the majesty of the burnished sandstone buttes into which it was wedged but to grace them—Sedona's Chapel of the Holy Cross wasn't where you might expect the gates of hell to open. But open they did, for a few brief moments on one gorgeous midnight last spring. On Lucy Smok's twenty-fifth birthday, to be exact. Funny thing, though, about opening the gates of hell to let something in: stuff got out. And it was Lucy's responsibility to round up the wayward "stuff" that escaped and put it back in. Cleaning up after Lucien. As usual.

Not that it was really his fault this time. It was their father who'd traded her twin's soul to the devil. And when Edgar Smok died, the bill had come due. Lucien's transformation into an infernal being had opened the gates until his descent to rule the nether realm closed them. In that brief interim, the path between the nether realm and this one had been a two-way street.

Dozens of hell beasts were now running amok.

The one she'd tracked this evening—or rather, early this morning—wore a female skin suit: a haggard-looking twentysomething waitress at a greasy spoon, dishwater-blond hair slipping out of a limp ponytail and into her eyes as she took Lucy's order. She was such a cliché that she had to be infernal.

Lucy had tracked the fugitive with a little help from the thousand-year-old Viking who happened to be dating Lucien's sister-in-law. Leo Ström was the chieftain of the Wild Hunt, and the instincts of the Hunt wraiths under his command functioned like a metaphysical GPS, homing in on any vicious killers in the area. As much as Lucy hated the idea of them, connections among the not-quite-human came in handy for her present mission. And Theia Dawn, Lucien's wife, had an entire family of not-quite-human connections. The Carlisle sisters, who claimed the demoness Lilith as their ancestor, seemed to attract it.

Lucy had other means of finding infernal fugitives, of course. As the CFO of Smok International and its subsidiaries, Smok Biotech and Smok Consulting—as well as its acting CEO in Lucien's absence—she had access to the world's most sophisticated database for tracking and logging unnatural creatures. But the fugitives from hell weren't in any database, and those that hadn't made themselves obvious through their sheer audacity in attacking humans right out of the gate, so to speak, were extremely good at blending in with the human population and keeping a low profile.

The stop at the coffeehouse had been serendipitous. After losing the trail, Lucy had taken a break to refuel, and the little downstairs café was the only thing open this early in the morning. She hadn't been sure until the waitress brought her order. A telltale flick of the woman's tongue at the corner of her mouth accompanying a rapid eye blink had given her away as a reptilian demon. Anyone else would have missed it. The demon saw Lucy's recognition in the same instant, eyes widening with alarm.

Before it could make its escape, Lucy grabbed it by the wrist and pinned its hand to the cool wooden tabletop.

"Let go of me." The eyes narrowed to reptilian slits with an unnerving clicking sound, like a muted camera shutter.

"You're out of your element."

The demon bristled, a reptilian reflex beneath the borrowed skin. "And you're about to discover how far you are out of yours."

Lucy smiled darkly. "You'd be surprised how far my element extends." She'd been banking on the fact that the demon wouldn't want to make a scene in the middle of a brightly lit coffeehouse with a small but decidedly human audience. She hadn't counted on the demon's desperation.

A hissing sound provided an instant's warning before the demon spat, giving Lucy the chance to duck and dodge, narrowly missing a face full of demonic acid. Unfortunately, the evasive action also loosened her grip, and her quarry was off in a flash.

Lucy catapulted over the counter into the short-order kitchen in pursuit of the creature, startling a busboy and a tired cook. The demon flung the busboy across the kitchen as a distraction, but Lucy wasn't here to pick hapless busboys up off the floor. She was here to stop a hell fugitive.

She leaped over him and followed the demon through the back door into the alley. It had given up its pretense of humanity, shedding its skin and leaving the corpse of the unfortunate woman it had been wearing in a heap among the trash bins as it dropped onto all fours and scuttled through a crack between two buildings.

Lucy spared a glance back up the alley to make sure she wasn't observed before using the advantage of her own unnatural blood to scale the back of the building and race over the top. Inheriting some of Lucien's curse came with a few perks. She leaped down onto the unlit street just in time to block the demon's egress as it crept out. The demon reared up on its hind legs in surprise, poised for an attack, as Lucy drew her gun—she'd brought her favorite, the Nighthawk Custom Browning Hi Power 9 mm—and aimed between the thing's inhuman eyes. The skin it had shed evidently wasn't the corpse of a human after all, but a sort of shifter's shell, as evidenced by the demon wriggling to redon the same form like a translucent skin coat, albeit a slightly fresher version. It was an obvious ploy to appeal to Lucy's humanity. Always a mistake.

"Please." The demon held its human-appearing hands in the air. "I have babies at home. I'm a single mom."

"Oh, for God's sake." Appealing to her womanhood was an even bigger mistake. Lucy palmed the slide to chamber a round. "Hope you kissed them goodbye."

Before she could pull the trigger, something barreled into her from her left, knocking the gun from her hands and her to the ground. Her Russian martial arts training kicked in automatically, and Lucy flipped over and onto her feet before her attacker could grab her, swiping his leg with a roundhouse kick from a crouch and incapacitating him with a one-two punch to the neck as he fell. When he hit the ground, Lucy leaped on top of him and dug her fist into the hair at his forehead to slam his head back onto the concrete. He managed to block her as she swung at his jaw simultaneously, trapping her arm inside his with an elbow jab toward her throat. They were deadlocked.

Lucy glared down at her attacker, sizing him up. A dark hood framed salt-and-pepper hair and a tightly compressed, disapproving mouth in a tan face offset by a sharp, muscular jaw. For a middle-aged man, he was in damn good shape. Not an ounce of fat on him.

"That was an escaped fugitive whose rescue you just came to, G.I. Joe. Thanks to you, a violent predator is in the wind."

"From where I'm lying, you seem to be the violent predator." He let go of her arm, and she let him yank his hair from her fingers. "I'd like to see your badge."

Lucy snorted with derision and rose to collect her pistol from where it had spun against the corner of one of the buildings. "I don't have to show you anything."

"Maybe I'll just make a citizen's arrest, then."

Lucy let out a sharp, humorless laugh. "I'd like to see you try."

The demon's rescuer rubbed the back of his head with a grimace as he got to his feet and observed her for a moment with a frown of mistrust. "Exactly what did that one-hundred-pound woman do that's so dangerous?"

Lucy checked her clip. "Killed at least five people last week, for starters. I tracked her here from Flagstaff, where she left a trail of bodies. Two of them kids. I won't go into detail, but let's just say she's got an appetite for skin."

Midlife G.I. Joe frowned and shook his head. "You've got the wrong girl. She's been working at the Mine Café for a month. Hasn't strayed beyond a ten-mile radius since she got here."

"How would you know?"

"I make it my business to know when someone extrahuman is in my neighborhood. And this one's harmless."

So he'd peeked beyond the veil. Lucy studied him. Seemed human. Didn't necessarily mean he was. "My sources say you're wrong."

"Well, your sources are mistaken. I'm part of a neighborhood watch—of a sort—and I'm telling you this girl can't be your perp."

Lucy holstered the gun in her shoulder strap. "You think I'm law enforcement?"

"Not ordinary law enforcement, obviously. But yeah. Aren't you?"

"Let's just say I'm a private contractor. I track things that don't belong in this plane. And I tracked an infernal flesh-eater here."

His eyes had narrowed in a glower at the words *private contractor*.

"Maybe you tracked something here, but it wasn't her." He pulled up his hood as it began to drizzle, warm skin tone reduced to a craggy monochrome silhouette under the flickering sodium streetlight. "And we don't need any private contractors stalking our citizens. The town of Jerome takes care of its own."

"I don't really care what you 'need.' There's a killer

on the loose, and I intend to take it down. Wherever it attempts to hide out."

He glared down at her, trying to use his height to dominate. "If I see you in Jerome again, I'll consider you hostile."

Lucy gave him her best death stare through the now-pouring rain. "Why wait? You can consider me hostile right now." She turned and strode away before he could form a retort, heading through the downpour back toward Main Street, where she'd parked her car.

As she wound down the two-lane highway, the beat of steady autumn rain against her windshield was already slowing, and the sun had made a dismal appearance through the dull steel of cloud cover in the five minutes it took to reach the bottom of Cleopatra Hill. The town of Clarkdale ahead of her was the first sign of civilization—if you could call it that—in the Verde Valley Basin. After that, the somewhat larger sprawling suburban town of Cottonwood laid claim to the title with a population of twelve thousand. Not that her current base, Sedona, was really any bigger, but it felt like a larger town with its hip vibe and nonstop stream of tourists who came for the metaphysical ambience and stayed for the real magic of sun and stream and stone.

After filling up at the Clarkdale Gas-N-Sip, Lucy headed for the restroom outside the convenience store, unwinding her knotted braid and separating the soaking hair into three dripping plaits as she rounded the building.

She sensed the presence in the bushes before it leaped, but there was only time enough to meet its force with a full frontal attack of her own. The creature snarled and went for her throat as she aimed for its solar plexus.

She was taking a guess at where that was, but her left fist landed solidly while she followed up with a right to its jaw. Sharp teeth grazed her knuckles—luckily, she was immunized against lycanthropy—but the blow to its gut had slowed it down.

While its footing wavered for an instant, Lucy drew her Nighthawk Browning and emptied four rounds into it point-blank. It made a sort of furious yelp and snarl and took off so swiftly she couldn't follow. More angry than wounded, it seemed. Which was impossible. She hadn't gotten a clear look at what kind of wolf it was, as it had been mostly fur and blur, but the snout was clearly lupine and the upright frame humanoid. Four Soul Reaper bullets should have incapacitated it almost immediately. It should be writhing in its death throes on the ground in front of her right now.

Though it wasn't the impact of the bullets in Lucy's gun that killed infernal creatures. It was the poison inside. "Soul Reaper," Lucien had nicknamed it, because it obliterated anything not human from within the host flesh, and if any remnant of a human soul happened to remain within the infernal, Soul Reaper sent the remnant to hell.

After cleaning up in the restroom, Lucy paid for her gas and hit the road, grateful that no one else had been outside the Gas-N-Slip. She was bone tired—by her count, she'd been up for nearly twenty-four hours—and ready for a hot shower followed by a stiff drink and bed by the time she got home.

She glanced down at her bloody hand as she unlocked the door. It was a little bit more than a graze. Immunization or no immunization, she had to take care of the bite. With a growl of her own, she went inside, gun firmly in both hands while she made a quick survey of the place. It had become a habit. When she was sure the villa was empty, she took off her jacket and slipped the shoulder holster off and tossed it on the couch along with her piece. She'd meant to find something more permanent and less ostentatious than a villa at an exclusive resort once she'd decided to stick around after Lucien's departure, but apartment hunting took a back seat to rounding up hell beasts.

After cleaning the wound, she decided on a bath instead of a shower. Baths weren't really her thing, but every muscle ached at this point, and Epsom salt was a thing she believed in.

As the tub filled, Lucy wrapped her arms around her knees and rested her forehead on them, replaying the wolf's moves and her own, analyzing what she might have done better. Merciless postmortem had been ingrained in her from Edgar's training since she was a kid. She'd let down her guard because she was tired. Mistake number one. Vigilance was mandatory. But for the most part, she'd followed protocol. It was the creature that was the unpredictable element.

What the hell *was* that thing? How could it have kept moving with four Soul Reaper bullets in its chest? It *was* infernal. It had to be. But it moved faster—and it was larger—than any garden-variety werewolf she'd encountered. And it had seemed somehow less…furry.

The tub had filled, and Lucy shut the water off and leaned back against the built-in headrest. It really was a hell of a tub. She hadn't paid much attention to it when she rented the place, since she'd only intended to use the stand-alone shower. But it was deep enough and wide

enough for her to stretch out both arms and legs and let
them float in the silky water without touching anything.

Eyes closed, she ran through the encounter in Jerome
with the same critical review. The reptilian-demon waitress wasn't in the Smok registry, so, killer or not, it was
definitely a fugitive. But was it possible it wasn't the
killer she was tracking? What were the odds more than
one hell fugitive would be hanging out in Jerome, Arizona? The artsy haven carved into the side of Cleopatra
Hill in the Arizona Black Hills, a former copper mining
boomtown that had turned its colorful history into a tour-
isty cash maker as an active "ghost town," had a grand
total of less than five hundred permanent residents.

The vigilante—which was what G.I. Joe likely was,
given his skulking around in a dark hoodie in the middle of the night on his "neighborhood watch of a sort"—
had been adamant that the waitress wasn't Lucy's killer.
Not that Lucy was going to take his word for it, but he
hadn't struck her as a liar, whatever else he was. He genuinely seemed to believe the girl was harmless. And he
claimed he'd been watching her for a month.

Maybe he was just a perv who liked watching young
women. But he hadn't given off that vibe. And he hadn't
made any typical masculine overtures toward Lucy,
who was just a few years younger than the waitress appeared to be. Honestly, it had kind of annoyed her. She
was used to being noticed by guys his age—just hitting their midlife-crisis stride and hyperaware of any
younger woman in their vicinity to project their inse-
curities onto and gauge their own desirability. Not that
she *wanted* middle-aged dudes creeping on her, but it
was almost suspect when they didn't.

So what was this guy's deal? Middle-aged but in

almost-military shape, living in tiny, artsy Jerome in the middle of nowhere keeping tabs on its "extra-human" population? Maybe *he* was a fugitive. Lucy opened her eyes. Maybe he was *her* fugitive.

The phone rang from the living room. She'd left it in her pocket when she stripped out of her wet clothes. Lucy sighed and climbed out of the tub.

She got to the phone after the call had rolled to voice mail, and she listened to the message on speaker while toweling off. An older woman spoke a bit hesitantly, as though her request was awkward. She spoke on behalf of "the council," which wanted to contract Lucy's services to investigate a werewolf sighting. In Jerome. So much for taking care of its own.

Chapter 2

Whoever this "council" was, they were clearly desperate. Lucy called the woman back to verify the job's legitimacy before agreeing to take it. Despite the unorthodox call to her personal phone, they'd been referred to Smok Consulting through the proper channels. They were anxious to meet with her this morning, in an hour, wanting to take care of the problem before too many residents—or more likely, tourists—became aware of it. This "werewolf" was probably the fugitive she was tracking. She could kill two hell beasts with one stone.

Lucy pushed down the exhaustion. She'd stayed up this long. Might as well go for two days. She couldn't remember when she'd last eaten—she'd left a gorgeous plate of hash browns cooked into a giant pancake, plus a sweet side of bacon, at the coffeehouse—but there wasn't time for a proper breakfast. Maybe she could grab coffee and a muffin somewhere in Jerome before meeting her contact. Lucy sighed. As much as she'd resented Lucien's attitude about Smok Consulting's work, it had sure seemed easier handling these kinds of jobs with two people. Maybe he hadn't been entirely useless.

The road to Jerome, once she'd left Sedona and driven through the flat stretch of valley beyond Cottonwood and Clarkdale, was straight up the escarpment separating the Black Hills from the valley. One thing Lucy hated was driving slow, and driving up between the stacked limestone retaining walls that hugged the mountainside meant driving slow.

Arriving in Jerome with fifteen minutes to spare, Lucy parked in front of an artsy-looking shop in the bottom of a restored Victorian on lower Main Street near the Ghost City Inn, an old miners' boardinghouse turned B and B. A wrought-iron sign hanging over the door declared the shop was Delectably Bookish. She wasn't sure if it was a café or a bookstore, but she thought she smelled coffee brewing inside. She opened the door, pursuing the scent. It looked like a reading room, with comfy mismatched chairs and couches strewn among tables beside stacks of hardback books—and, hallelujah, a shellacked wooden counter at the back bearing an espresso machine and a case of pastries and treats.

Lucy made a beeline for it. Coffee was definitely brewing. But there was no one in sight.

"Hello?" She leaned over the counter, peering into the back through a beaded-glass curtain. "Anyone back there?"

Nothing.

She was running out of time, and she really needed that coffee. She'd been awake for almost thirty hours at this point. "Hey, *hello*? You've got a customer out here."

In frustration, she tossed a five-dollar bill on the

counter and grabbed a lemon poppy seed muffin, stuffing a bite into her mouth while she went around the counter and helped herself to a cup of coffee. There were no paper cups. She'd have to bring back the cappuccino cup after her meeting.

Lucy sipped her coffee as she headed back around the counter and nearly dumped it on herself as she looked up. At the bottom of the staircase that led from the book stacks to the second floor of what she assumed were more book stacks, a ruggedly handsome middle-aged man stood watching her, arms folded—and they were seriously impressive arms packed tight into a white T-shirt—a scowl on his tanned face. It was her G.I. Joe vigilante.

"Find the cash register all right? I hope that pesky drawer didn't give you any trouble. It sticks sometimes."

"Cash register? No, I—just needed a coffee. There was nobody here. I left money on the counter."

"Jerome isn't your personal hunting ground. You might want to learn some manners before someone mistakes you for a thief and treats you accordingly."

Heat rushed to Lucy's face. "Yeah? Well, you might want to be a little more responsive when a customer is waiting. In the real world, baristas don't get tips when they ignore people. Maybe you shouldn't be taking bathroom breaks when you're supposed to be working."

"Maybe you should learn to read." His head tilted toward the words printed in large gold lettering on the outside of the glass panel on the door. "We open at noon."

Lucy tried to maintain some dignity, the stupid muffin crumbling in her hand as she set down the coffee cup. "Why the hell is the door unlocked if you're not open?"

Barista G.I. Joe studied her for a moment, his expression giving away nothing. "We generally trust our neighbors around here. This is the first time I've ever been robbed."

"Robbed?" Lucy picked up the five-dollar bill and waved it at him. "I paid you. But you know what? Forget it. Keep the coffee and the muffin. And the damn change. Maybe you can buy yourself a functioning lock."

She tossed the muffin and the money on the counter and stalked to the door, willing down the prickly heat in her skin threatening to top off her humiliation with a furious blush. She made it all the way to the door— and then pushed instead of pulled.

His soft laughter as she adjusted her grip on the handle followed her out.

Lucy wasn't easily flustered. Years of practice being the "good" daughter under Edgar's strict rules and dealing with supernatural rogues, paranormal entities and therianthropes—or shape-shifters, in layman's terms— of every description had made her preternaturally calm under pressure. Everything was to be kept inside. A Smok wasn't supposed to react with emotion but with a cool head to defuse the most unpredictable situations. And she certainly didn't get embarrassed. What was it to her if some petty wannabe-vigilante barista chose to call her a thief just because he couldn't be bothered to man the counter at his day job?

Normally, she'd have already forgotten the encounter. Maybe it was the lack of sleep—and caffeine—affecting her, but her blood was boiling, and she couldn't shake it off. She wanted to go back and punch the guy in the mouth.

Lucy gritted her teeth and entered the landscape-dominating Civic Center building on Clark Street that housed the town hall, an odd mix of classical architecture and Mission Revival that defied the small-town-Victorian aesthetic.

With a few minutes to spare, she stepped into the bathroom to make sure she was presentable. Charcoal-gray pin-striped suit immaculate, white shirt crisp, nothing out of place. After tucking a few stray hairs into the loose braid that hung down her back, she touched up her Blood Moon lip stain—the dark, dramatic hue was the one concession she made to traditional femininity; the over-the-top color went beyond sexual appeal, making an aggressive statement that made her feel in control—and headed upstairs to her meeting.

The door to the meeting room opened outward—like a respectable door. Lucy pulled it open and stopped on the threshold in disbelief. Among the three council members sitting at the table was Barista G.I. Joe.

His dark brows drew together into a disbelieving scowl that matched the one she was no doubt displaying as he met her eyes. "You have *got* to be kidding."

The elderly woman who'd risen from the seat next to him at Lucy's entrance glanced from him to Lucy and back. "Do you two know each other?"

"No, we don't," said Lucy before he could answer. "We just had a misunderstanding about coffee."

"I see." The woman reached a hand across the table. "I'm Nora Peterson."

Lucy stepped forward with a nod and shook Nora's

hand, trying to ignore the unfriendly glare emanating from beside her. "Lucy Smok."

Nora indicated the chair opposite her. "Please have a seat."

As Lucy sat, she reevaluated her initial assessment of G.I Joe's age. Prematurely graying hair had made him seem older at first glance. He was definitely on the nearer side of forty.

She smiled politely at Nora and the other council member, avoiding the glowering eyes. Even though they were compelling. And an intense deep cinnamon, just a shade darker than amber. Not that she noticed.

"I didn't realize the town council would be here. Generally, people like to keep these matters hushed up."

Nora tilted her head. "The choice of meeting place may have been unintentionally misleading. We're not exactly the town council. We're more like...the para-council." She gave Lucy a slight smile. "We're a volunteer group. But we've taken it upon ourselves to manage incidents that fall outside the normal operations of the town. With the council's blessing. Unofficially."

Lucy took out her phone to take notes. "So they do know about these paranormal occurrences."

"Everyone knows." The man on Nora's other side shrugged. "Jerome is a small town. It's hard not to know things. We just don't talk about them. Except for the ghosts, of course." He smiled. "They're sort of our livelihood."

Lucy nodded, uncertain whether he was being facetious. "I see. Thank you, Mr..."

Nora clucked her tongue. "So sorry, Ms. Smok. This is Wes Mason."

Wes reached over the table to shake Lucy's hand, his dark skin weathered and rough. "How do you do?"

"And Oliver Connery." Nora indicated Barista G.I. Joe.

Lucy turned to him with a bland, polite expression. "Mr. Connery."

He rose to shake her hand, maintaining a similar expression in return. "Pleased to meet you, Ms. Smok." The handshake was firm but not too firm.

Lucy sat back in her chair. "So you said there's been werewolf activity?"

"We assume it's a werewolf," said Nora. "We haven't personally gotten a good look at it."

"You're sure it's not coyotes or stray dogs? And you're certain it's only one?"

"I think we all know the difference between a dog and a werewolf." Oliver Connery wasn't quite as unflappable as he'd pretended. The other two members of the council glanced at him, as if the defensive tone was out of character. He seemed to realize it and dialed it back. "We've spotted tracks matching the profile of wolves that disappear into human footprints. Normally, this wouldn't be cause for alarm. Most shape-shifters just want to be left alone, and we believe in a live-and-let-live philosophy."

"That's not consistent with my experience, Mr. Connery." Lucy calmly met his eyes. Now she was in her element. "Rogue shape-shifters are never benign. Every one I've dealt with has caused chaos and destruction."

"Your experience? Forgive me, but you can't really have much experience. I'm a little surprised, honestly, to find that someone so young is the CFO of Smok International. Or that the CFO herself would take this job."

Lucy fixed her gaze on him. "I've been deeply involved with the company operations—both the biotech side and the paranormal-consulting side—since I was fifteen, and I started working as a consulting agent when I turned eighteen. I spent the last five years traveling Europe and the eastern states as Smok Consulting's premier field agent before my father turned the business over to me prior to his death. And I am telling you—from *experience*—that shifters who aren't actively managing their conditions and integrating with normal society are dangerous."

Oliver opened his mouth, but Wes spoke first. "Ordinarily, I'd agree with Oliver, but this is a different breed. We've never encountered any so malevolent. It's been responsible for at least three vicious attacks in the area—official reports are attributing the deaths to a rabid mountain lion, but we have eyewitnesses who claim to have seen a large, misshapen wolf. That's why we've called you in. This is bigger than we can handle. We took a vote." He glanced at Oliver a bit apologetically. "It was two to one in favor of bringing in professional help."

"Well, you've made the right decision." Lucy spared a cool glance at Oliver. "This is my area of expertise."

Oliver's strong jaw was tight. "I'm not sure I care for your use of the word *normal*, but despite my reluctance to bring in an outsider—whose motives are purely mercenary—I concurred with Nora and Wes's assessment that this isn't ordinary. If it's a wolf, it's like no wolf I've ever encountered."

"You can't have encountered many, Mr. Connery. Smok Consulting tracks this kind of activity closely, and we have no previous evidence of any werewolves in Jerome, Arizona."

"You assume every werewolf in existence announces itself to you."

Now, *that* was an odd thing to say. Perhaps Oliver Connery had experience after all. Personal experience.

"You assume all the unnatural creatures in our database are aware that they're in it."

One dark brow, in stark contrast to the silver in his hair, twitched.

Nora made an effort to regain control of the meeting. "So how do you usually approach these matters? Despite the fact that people are aware of certain odd goings-on in Jerome, we do want to maintain some discretion."

Lucy nodded. "Absolutely. I'd like to start with a list of all reported sightings, including times and dates and any physical contact. And then I'll survey each of the sites, interview any eyewitnesses who are willing to come forward and get to work tracking the creature or creatures down."

"I'm not sure how many eyewitnesses will be willing to talk to you." Nora and Wes shared a look. "But I'll give you what I can." She rose and shook Lucy's hand again. "We're very grateful for your help. In the meantime, Oliver will take you to the location of the most recent sighting so you can examine the physical evidence."

Lucy paused as she rose with the others. "Oh… I wouldn't want to put you out, Mr. Connery. I'm sure I can find it on my own."

"Please, call me Oliver. And I'm sure you can't."

"You doubt my abilities?"

"I don't have any idea what your abilities are. It's not about your abilities. It's just that it's not something we can simply write down and give you directions to."

One of her abilities was being able to kick the asses of men twice her size. She supposed she could put that ability to use if she had to. Again.

Lucy shrugged. "Well, if it won't inconvenience you." She nodded to Nora and Wes as they headed out into the hallway before she turned to give Oliver a pointed look as he came around the table. "I suppose you have someone to cover your shift?"

"My shift?" He stopped in front of her, forcing her to look up.

"Aren't you working at the coffee shop?" She smiled darkly. "You did say it opened at noon."

Oliver chuckled, hooking his thumbs into the back pockets of his jeans. "I don't work there."

Lucy frowned, the usual potency of her practiced icy stare diluted by having to look up. "Then what were you doing there?"

"I live upstairs." He smiled back at her as if they were having a perfectly friendly conversation. "I own the place."

"Oh."

"So that coffee and muffin you stole come directly out of my profits."

She didn't normally lose her temper, but there was something about this guy that totally pushed her buttons. "I paid for the food!" Her fists were clenched at her sides as she resisted the urge to punch him in the face. The urge was strong.

His eyes were laughing at her, crinkled at the corners. "A large coffee is two fifty, and the muffin was four seventy-five."

"Four seventy-five for a *muffin*?" Lucy yanked her wallet from her inside pocket and pulled out another five and shoved it at him. "That's two seventy-five you owe me, then. I'm not leaving a tip for such poor service."

Oliver stared down at the bill as if he wasn't quite sure what to do with it or how to respond to her, thumbs still firmly in his pockets. When she continued to hold out the money, he took it at last and tucked it into the pocket of the flannel shirt he'd put on over the T-shirt since she'd seen him in the shop. It gave her the impression she must have caught him getting dressed.

Lucy cleared her throat deliberately. "My change?"

That dark eyebrow twitched again. "I don't keep a cash register on me. I'll just consider this an advance on your next muffin." He rolled up his sleeves and reached to open the door, and Lucy took a broad step past him to get it herself.

As she pushed it open and went through, he chuckled once more behind her. "I see you figured out how doors work."

Chapter 3

Oliver studied Lucy Smok's profile as she followed his directions and drove toward the Gold King Mine & Ghost Town attraction just outside the town proper. When he'd clashed with her the night before, he was focused on her militant intrusion into his world, her unwarranted attack on poor Crystal Harney, an "undergrounder" who was just trying to get by.

Crystal belonged to a certain class of the not-quite-human who were shunned by those who ran in elite circles like the world of Smok International. Oliver had seen his fill of vulnerable undergrounders being victimized and demonized among the paranormal-aware community, and he'd vowed to watch out for them when he could, since no one else would. Lucy's arrogant insistence that Crystal was a killer rubbed him the wrong way, the sort of attitude he'd seen from law enforcement types all his life.

Then, today, when Lucy had appeared in his shop after raiding his kitchen, Oliver took her for a spoiled brat. In the dark and the rain the night before, he hadn't noticed how young and slight she was, and it was hard to reconcile the two versions of her. But discovering she was Lucy Smok, the high-powered twenty-five-year-old CFO of Smok International the council had brought in to deal with their problem, had thrown him for a loop. How all three things could exist simultaneously in one compact—and highly opinionated—person was difficult to process.

She was also one of the most visually striking women he'd ever seen.

Pale aquamarine eyes and porcelain skin contrasted sharply with almost-ebony hair, and the deep red lipstick she wore—like the stain from a beet—enhanced the effect. The paleness of her eyes made her seem like a dangerous wolf. He might have suspected her of being a shifter herself if she hadn't been so adamantly bigoted against them. She also possessed a sharp cockiness he didn't see in most women, the kind of confidence a woman would need, he supposed, to run a multimillion-dollar corporation—especially at such a young age.

He kept coming back to that. Because, beyond her puzzling contradictions, he was having trouble reconciling his own powerful attraction for a woman almost ten years his junior. It wasn't the image he had of himself. Later in life, ten years wouldn't matter so much. But a man in his midthirties chasing after a woman in her twenties was just embarrassing. Not that he was chasing after her. He didn't chase. And he wasn't interested in any kind of intimate involvement. He was done with that. But the attraction was undeniable.

It was almost visceral, like he'd been waiting for her, his senses pricking up in anticipation as if his body recognized her. And not in a sexual way—though he couldn't deny there was that, too—but with a sense of familiarity, of knowing, that he couldn't explain and didn't particularly care for. Her scent seemed made for him, a blend of cardamom and amber, something both earthy and exotic at once. And he didn't think she was wearing perfume.

"Now where?"

Oliver blinked. "What?"

She glanced over at him, annoyance drawing her ebony brows together. "Where do I turn?"

They were at the crossroad where Jerome-Perkinsville Road split off in two different directions, one toward the rustic museum of antique mining machinery and the other up into the hills.

"Oh, sorry. To the right. You can pull over by the gate."

Lucy turned a bit too swiftly, tires kicking up dirt and gravel, and drew up in front of the rusted barrier chaining off the private road. "It says No Trespassing."

"We're not going in. We're just heading up the forest road a bit. We could drive in farther, but I don't think your car is made for dirt-road driving." Her expensive convertible two-seater looked like it was designed more for show than for sport.

He noticed the dress boots with a two-inch block heel under her tailored suit as she stepped out of the car. She was even shorter than she seemed. He could probably pick her up and carry her under one arm like a caveman claiming his mate. Not that he approved of cavemen scooping up and claiming women. Or that he considered her a potential mate.

Oliver swallowed and reined in his idiotic thoughts. Sometimes it seemed like his brain took pleasure in going off on tangents that would make him uncomfortable. At any rate, how such a slight-looking woman could possibly be one of Smok Consulting's premier field agents was beyond him. Going after someone small and defenseless like Crystal was one thing. And Lucy obviously had some kind of martial arts training. She'd briefly overpowered him with the element of surprise on her side. But what was she going to do when she tracked one of these things down? Call animal control?

Lucy was eyeing him with a mixture of impatience and annoyance. "Well?"

"This way." Oliver strode past her, hands in his pockets, up the dirt and gravel road, not waiting to see if she'd followed. Her expensive, unscuffed boots crunched on the gravel behind him. They weren't going to be unscuffed for long. He led her around the bend, where he veered off the road and headed downhill over the remains of old mining spoil, only to realize she was no longer behind him.

He turned to find her standing at the top of the hill with her arms folded, watching him. "Too steep for you?" he called up to her.

Lucy uncrossed her arms and rested her fists on her hips. "Mr. Connery, is there a point to this little trek?" Her ability to project was impressive. She must have had stage experience.

"It's Oliver," he yelled back. "And yes."

After regarding him with suspicion for a moment longer, she finally headed down the side of the hill with a sigh—extremely sure-footed on the damp earth despite the boots that didn't look like they were made for hiking. It occurred to him as she came closer that perhaps it looked like he was leading her out into an isolated area for nefarious purposes. He'd forgotten to put himself in her shoes—not that he'd fit them—which was a large part of his meditative practice.

"Sorry about that," he said when she reached him. "I should have told you what we were doing. This is where we tracked the creature after it was spotted lurking around the Ghost Town. The lupine tracks disappear here, to be replaced with human footprints."

She looked where he was pointing, and Oliver stepped aside and moved off a few paces to let her examine the area without him hovering behind her. Lucy sank into a crouch, perfectly balanced on those thick-heeled boots, and took out her phone to snap some pictures before straightening and walking around the prints to get some shots from another angle. After walking farther down the hill to follow the now-human prints for a ways, she turned and headed back up.

"I see what you mean. The animal tracks aren't standard wolves. I've never seen any quite like that. Certainly not that size. But those are definitely human prints leading away from them, with no sign that anyone else was out here until they appeared." She glanced at Oliver's footwear—a much more utilitarian pair of old brown work boots. "Except you, evidently. And now me, of course."

Oliver tilted his head and studied her, amused. "You think I'm the werewolf?"

"Are you?"

"Would I tell you if I were?"

Lucy shrugged and headed back up the hill. Oliver followed, and they walked in silence until they reached her car and got in.

"I'm not," he said as she started the engine.

"Not…?"

"The werewolf. For whatever my word is worth to you."

"Exactly as much as any man's is worth."

He had the distinct impression that meant "zilch."

She turned the car around and pulled back out onto the paved road. "Besides, I don't think we're dealing with a werewolf."

"Oh?"

"Lycanthropic transformation isn't instantaneous and smooth. The creature would have struggled and fallen, and the human shape would have been on all fours before the footprints began. There's no sign of any transition at all with these tracks. It's as if the creature simply chose to be human at that moment."

"What kind of shifter could do that?"

Lucy was quiet for a moment before she answered. "None that I know of. So where to now?"

"Haunted Hamburger."

She looked over at him. "Haunted…what?"

"Best burgers in town." He smiled. "I think I owe you a meal."

The outdoor seating overlooked the entire Verde Valley—the hundred-mile views the restaurant boasted of along with burgers, brews and "boos." The distinctive red-rock formations that defined the Sedona landscape, made blue and soft by distance, marked the horizon like the rim of another world. Lucy gazed out across the panorama while they waited for their food, wondering how much of this territory might "belong" to the creatures she was hunting.

"It's a pretty great view, huh? The ghosts seem to like it here, anyway."

She turned toward Oliver, who was sipping his porter. "Hmm?" Lucy glanced at the valley once more. "Oh. Yeah, it's nice. I was just thinking about the direction this thing might have gone. The tracks we looked at must have been made within the last few hours since the rain stopped."

"That's right. We got the report of the sighting about an hour after I caught you harassing one of our citizens."

Lucy ignored the bait. "And what makes you think the tracks were made by the same creature responsible for the 'mountain lion' attacks?"

"Because similar tracks were seen at the sites of those attacks. And a kid was found close to that spot yesterday with his throat torn open and his intestines missing."

The same MO as the beast she'd been tracking from Flagstaff.

Oliver grimaced as the burgers arrived. "Sorry. I wasn't planning to talk about that while we ate."

"Why not? Isn't that why you brought me to Jerome? I didn't come for a social visit."

"No, of course. And to be clear, *I* did not bring you here. I was outvoted, if you recall. But don't you ever take a break?"

Lucy shrugged. "I'll take a break when they do." Which seemed like it was going to be never. She dug in to her burger, having forgotten how hungry she was until now. "So, where were the other attacks?"

"A hiker was killed in Deception Gulch near the old mine at Hull Canyon, and a couple of campers were torn to shreds near Woodchute Trail. And there was one more sighting recently at Hogback—the Old Miners Cemetery just south of town. But no contact there."

"So it's staying close to Jerome." Lucy washed down her burger with a sip of root beer. "I wonder why."

Oliver gave her a wry smile. "Some people like it here."

"No, I'm sure they do. I mean, why, specifically, would it gravitate toward a small town with limited hunting and few places to hide in an area that's neither urban nor wooded. Werewolves tend to prefer hunting grounds near large groups of people where they can blend in and stalk at night, or they isolate themselves and hide in undeveloped forestland and hunt small game. But this one—if it is indeed just *one*—has gone a few miles out, perhaps to hide, but then returned to the center of Jerome, where it made a brazen kill that it could have been caught at."

"Maybe it isn't afraid of being caught." It was an unsettling idea.

While they both concentrated on their food, Lucy pondered where to start her hunt.

After a moment, Oliver set down his burger and took a drink of his porter. "So, how do you intend to catch it?"

"I don't intend to catch it. I intend to kill it."

His hard jaw was set even harder. "So you're judge, jury and executioner."

"That's right. That's what people like you pay me to be. What did you expect me to do, put it in a zoo?"

"Doesn't your biotech company develop drugs to help shifters lead 'normal' lives?"

"We have certain promising pharmaceuticals in development but none on the market yet."

"Isn't that your brother's bailiwick? You both inherited the company, didn't you?"

Lucy breathed evenly. "Lucien has a lot of responsibilities that keep him from the day-to-day operations. But yes, Smok Biotech is Lucien's particular area of interest, and the anti-lycanthropy project is one that he's spearheaded."

"There are rumors about him."

Her hand remained perfectly still around her glass, and she kept her expression neutral. "Rumors?"

"That he's actually at some swanky rehab center in California, and his addiction is being quietly covered up."

She made a dismissive sound and emptied her glass. "Lucien isn't an addict. Rest assured, the company is in very capable hands. My brother just happens to be a rather private—and busy—person. You can spread *that* around your rumor mill." Lucy set her napkin on the table and pushed her plate away. "I'll take a drive out to Hogback and see if I can spot anything unusual. In the meantime, a sketch of the creature would be useful in determining what we're dealing with. Did you get a detailed description from any of the eyewitnesses?"

"I'm afraid not. We have fairly limited resources at our disposal. But I do have this." He took out his phone and displayed the photo, turning it toward Lucy on the table. "The eyewitness at the Gold King Mine got a picture of it before it took off. I'm afraid it's not very clear."

Lucy studied the blurry image, like a photo of Bigfoot through the trees, only this was a large, dark, doglike shape on its hind legs, its muzzle caught in midsnarl. As unclear as it was, there was something unsettling about the image. The creature seemed fully aware it was being photographed, as if it was posing for the camera, the snarl a ghoulish grin.

And it was a dead ringer for the thing Lucy had shot this morning.

Chapter 4

Lucy studied the photo on her phone while she waited for dark. It was blurred—as her glimpse of her attacker this morning had been—but she was certain that if it wasn't the same creature, it was one of its kind.

After seeing the picture, she'd changed her mind about the sighting in the cemetery. What this creature wanted was prey, and it seemed to prefer getting as close to populated areas as possible. It was likely to try again closer to town. And the creature that had attacked her this morning was intelligent and had sought her out on purpose. She needed to begin thinking the way it would.

Most likely, it knew she was here. And it was probably proud of its kill. It would return to the site of its latest victory to gloat, knowing she'd be there.

As dusk fell, she got out of the car and walked down the embankment where they'd seen the tracks before climbing up the other side of the hill into the area marked No Trespassing. Full dark had hit. It was a new moon. But Lucy had no trouble seeing in the dark. Her cycle was perfectly aligned with the lunar month—and with PMS came the weakening of the drug that suppressed her condition.

Lucien's anti-lycanthropy compound had come in handy after their twenty-fifth birthday ushered in the transformation. There had been just one little problem with Edgar's calculations when he'd sold his firstborn son's soul to the devil: he hadn't figured in the fact that Lucy and Lucien represented a rare occurrence of opposite-sex monozygotic twins—genetically identical except for an extra X chromosome—and the curse had affected both of them. Lucy's change was only partial, but partial was enough. She'd become sufficiently practiced that she could use her infernal enhancements when she needed them, but Lucien's compound kept her from being a slave to them. It was "shift control." And like birth control, it only effectively balanced her hormonal cocktail about twenty-one days out of the month, leaving her vulnerable to accidental transformation during that critical week.

Lucy scanned the darkness for movement. She didn't have to wait long. Along the perimeter of a tailings pond— the slurry from leftover mining waste—something was skulking. It crouched on all fours, stepping out slowly into view, before rising on its hind legs to face her, letting her know it saw her, too. If it was the same creature, it showed no sign of being injured. And this time it laughed. The unnerving sound carried unnaturally, echoing across the hillside, and Lucy made the mistake of reacting, a slight recoil, a barely perceptible shudder. In that split second of reaction, the creature sprang into motion, striking her as it pounced and rolling with her over the ground with its claws slashing.

She couldn't reach for her gun from this angle. She

should have had it ready. Her reflexes and instincts were shit when she was this tired.

Lucy scrabbled left-handed for the knife in her boot while defending herself from the creature's claws with one arm, her fingers closing around the handle just as the massive jaws clamped onto her left shoulder. With a primal shriek, she grasped the knife firmly and punched upward with it between her attacker's ribs. The thing howled with outrage and stumbled back, sheer hatred in its eyes.

It was readying for another attack, but this time Lucy was prepared. The shriek and the punch had been impelled forward on the strength of the infernal component in her blood, and as the creature came for her, she jerked the shifting bones at her shoulder blades to unleash her wyvern wings and leaped into the air to meet the creature's advance head-on, talons extended as they grew from her nail beds.

Weakened by the knife in its gut, it couldn't match her ferocity, and a final kick to the knife itself drove it in deep. The furious creature snarled and howled again at the dark of the moon before turning tail and loping away into the brush. As it disappeared among the foliage, she saw the distinct shape of a fully clothed man.

Ordinarily, she'd have flown after it, but she'd reached the limits of her second—or maybe third—wind. With the rush of adrenaline fading, Lucy wobbled on her feet, wings and talons retracting. The compound was still working for the most part, but she'd have to get another dose soon or risk transforming at an inopportune moment—and being unable to shift back on her own. In the meantime, she needed to clean up her new wounds and get some goddamn sleep.

Climbing back up to the car took a monumental effort. Lucy leaned back in the driver's seat and closed her eyes just for a moment. When she opened them, the stars visible through the windshield had shifted significantly. The clock on the dash read two in the morning. Her muscles ached, and her shoulder was killing her. She touched her fingers to the torn cloth over the bite; it was soaked with blood. There was no way she was going to make it home like this. And she knew the address of exactly one person in Jerome. He'd said he lived in the building his shop was in, which meant the upstairs must be his residence.

Lucy drove back to Main Street in Jerome and managed to find parking in front of Delectably Bookish once more. Her head swam, and the ground dipped and swayed as she got out of the car. Lucy gripped the post beside the entrance of the shop to steady herself and pounded on the door.

A light came on above, followed by the lights in the shop a moment later. Oliver Connery appeared, shirtless, salty hair askew and glaring furiously out of those cinnamon-brown eyes as he unlocked the door.

"What the hell is—" He stopped, staring openmouthed as he took in her appearance. "Jesus. What happened? Come inside." Oliver put an arm under hers and led her in to sit on one of the couches. "The werewolf?"

"I'm even more sure now that it's not a werewolf." Lucy rubbed her brow with the back of her wrist. "It's incredibly fast and resilient—and strong—and it shifts with the wind, like it just decides when it wants to be human."

Oliver had gone to the café counter to grab some

towels, and he returned with them, shaking his head as he pressed one to the shredded shoulder. "I knew this was a bad idea."

"I assure you, I'm perfectly capable of handling this thing now that I know what I'm up against." She was sure of no such thing, but she wasn't about to listen to more of his criticism of her age and experience. Or implicit criticism of her sex.

"So you didn't kill it."

Lucy grabbed the towel from his hand. "It wasn't for lack of trying. You need to get over this idea that all lycanthropes are misunderstood people who need to be given a chance. This thing is a monster."

"That isn't what I meant." Oliver frowned down at her. "You're going to have to take that suit off. We need to disinfect the bite, and you're probably going to need stitches." He held out his hand. "Come with me."

Lucy bit back another retort about being fine and not needing any help and instead took his hand to let him pull her up from the couch. Because as much as she hated to admit it, right now, she was not fine.

Upstairs in the bathroom of Oliver's apartment, Lucy peeled off the torn suit and blood-soaked white shirt—both of them ruined by her transformation before the creature's teeth had even sunk in—and sat begrudgingly on the covered toilet to let Oliver clean the wound and sew her up. "I can do that myself," she complained between gritted teeth. "I know how to stitch up a wound."

"Oh, for God's sake, stop trying to impress me. I get it. You're experienced. You're tough as nails. You're a total badass."

"I'm not trying to—"

"That wasn't sarcasm." Oliver glanced up, his cinnamon eyes dark with concern. "I am impressed. I'm also very worried about this bite. If it's a werewolf—"

"It's not a werewolf. And… I happen to be immune."

Oliver's dark brows drew together. "Immune?"

"One of the perks of owning a biotech firm that specializes in parapharmacology."

"I see. I don't suppose that particular pharmaceutical is on the market for ordinary folk?"

"It's part of a limited trial."

Oliver's jaw tightened, but he said nothing else.

As he tied off the stitches in her shoulder, Lucy became acutely aware of the fact that she was sitting here in his bathroom in her bra and underwear while he was wearing nothing but a pair of flannel pajama bottoms. One of the other aspects of her heightened senses at this point in her cycle was unusually intensified sexual desire.

After putting the first aid kit away, Oliver glanced up and seemed to realize her state of undress, as well. "Let me get you a robe." He slipped out of the bathroom and returned with one in blue-and-black flannel that matched his pants.

"Thanks." Lucy rose and attempted to slip her left arm gingerly into the sleeve and nearly pitched forward into him.

Oliver steadied her, instinctively avoiding her arm and shoulder, instead catching her about the waist. His hands nearly circled her. Lucy looked up into his intense russet eyes. There were similar-colored highlights in the salt-and-pepper hair, and what she'd thought of as a tan was a matching cinnamon-bark undertone in his skin, evenly warm…everywhere.

Her spine twitched as she resisted a full-body shiver.

This was no time to indulge her overactive wyvern hormones. It would be a disastrous mistake. She breathed in his scent—a damp, dusty smell like the desert after rain when the creosote bushes released their resin. She could swear she felt one of her ovaries dropping an egg.

"No, no. Hell, no." Lucy pushed his hands away and pulled on the rest of the robe, tying it with a jerk. Her hands were sweating.

Oliver blinked and took a step back, his expression mortified. "That wasn't a move. I was just trying to make sure you didn't crack your head on the basin."

"I know it wasn't a damn move. I wasn't talking to you."

He blinked again. "Who…who were you talking to?"

Lucy's head was starting to throb. She groaned and clutched it in both hands, unconsciously rubbing the spots at her hairline where a pair of ruby dragon horns had protruded just hours ago.

"Are you all right?"

Lucy shook her head and regretted it. "I need to go home."

"You can't drive in this condition."

"Don't tell me what I can do."

Oliver sighed patiently. "Your injuries aside, when was the last time you slept?"

"I don't sleep."

"You don't *sleep*."

"I don't have time. I catch a power nap when I can." The truth was that she couldn't sleep at this time of month. And she really had to stop smelling his desert-dusty-rain smell right goddamn now.

Lucy pushed past him and headed for the door. She wasn't sure if it was chivalry or indifference that kept him from trying to stop her as she advanced into the hallway weaving like a drunk. She stumbled and landed on her ass on the carpet runner at the top of the stairs. *Good move. Idiot.*

Oliver stood watching her, arms folded, from the doorway of the bathroom. "Would you like the double bed or the queen?"

She let out a low growl of defeat. "Can I just sleep here? Maybe put a grave marker on it and call it done."

He laughed, his right cheek dimpling in a way that made her want to growl more. "I'll get you a blanket." He crossed to the linen closet and took one out. "Of course, the queen room is right here if you prefer."

Lucy followed his glance to the open doorway on the other side of the bathroom. A high, fluffy-looking bed with a down coverlet posed invitingly beneath a sloped ceiling. "Why do you have so many rooms?"

"It's just three bedrooms, actually. But I've been planning to turn it into a B and B since I bought the place and took over the bookstore. I'm thinking of calling it Bed, Book and Candle."

"Nice." The bed really did look enticing. "Maybe I could catch a few winks." She got to her feet, steadying herself against the wall, and accepted the blanket. With a questioning look, Oliver offered his arm. She wasn't sure what would happen if she touched his bare skin right now, but she knew it wouldn't be good. "Thanks. I think I've got this." Somehow, she managed to pull off a semblance of normalcy, making it inside the bedroom and closing the door before she collapsed gratefully into the downy oasis.

She was almost asleep after all when something she'd been aware of in the back of her mind came to the fore.

Oliver's bare chest had been notable for more than its exquisite form. He had four puckered scars, impact craters with jagged starred edges that looked distinctly like the kind made by bullets. It meant nothing, probably. Maybe he'd been in Afghanistan or Iraq. But they had the pale pink color and sheen of a recently healed injury. And they were placed almost precisely where the shots she'd fired into the hell beast would have landed yesterday morning. And lycanthropes were known for rapid healing.

Chapter 5

Lucy was gone in the morning. Oliver hoped to God she'd gotten some sleep. His sleep, on the other hand, hadn't been good. He couldn't get her off his mind. For an instant last night, when he'd caught her from falling, she'd looked at him with what he could have sworn was naked desire. It had shocked him. And the next instant, the look had been gone, leaving him wondering if he'd imagined it.

He worried the ring on his right hand with his thumb. Vanessa's ring. She'd been gone for more than five years, but he still couldn't take it off. Transferring it from the left hand to the right was the most he'd been able to do. It reminded him not only of his loss but also of his part in it. He was responsible for Vanessa's death.

Oliver imagined what she'd say to him. *You can't take credit for the failures and ignore the successes.* But the raid that day had been more than a failure. Darkrock had no business going into an unsecured nest without doing the proper reconnaissance first. And Oliver had gotten cocky, imagining that despite the disadvantage of not knowing how many vampires were holed up in the meth lab or how organized the vamps were, he had what it took to handle whatever they found. Darkrock had sent him, so Oliver had gone.

Vanessa had been his partner, in life and on his Darkrock team. Their team was first, positioned in a side alley near the den, and Oliver and Vanessa had scaled the fence into the weeds and garbage. Oliver had kicked in the back door while the other members of the team made a frontal assault. They'd expected a handful of meth addicts sharing needles and sharing each other's depleted blood. They'd expected any vampires, at least, to be sluggish with the daytime hour. What they hadn't expected was an ambush.

A very sophisticated operation had been overseeing the nest—a nest of donors, not vamps. They'd fed Darkrock an anonymous tip about the place, one that seemed reasonable on its face. It was a known hangout for meth heads, and meth heads were often mixed up in the trafficking of blood. Because of that symbiotic relationship between addicts and vampires, a house full of addicts often ended up breeding a house full of low-rent, weak vamps. And those that remained donors had only a short shelf life, so the siring vamps would move on once the supply dwindled.

When Oliver and Vanessa and the rest of the team had busted into the house, they'd expected to round up the victims and vamps with little resistance. Instead, they'd been set upon by very healthy, bloodthirsty vampire lords. One of them had Vanessa before Oliver even knew what had hit them, and the rest of the team was dead. The vampire lord holding Vanessa had smiled at

Oliver, reading his mind, knowing what Vanessa was to him, before taking a drink.

Oliver slammed his fist down on the counter, jarring the coffee cups. He didn't need to go down that road again. That was a dead end. In more ways than one. As he got the coffee started for the morning, his phone vibrated on the counter beside him, skittering across the slick shellac. He was on call for the Jerome Volunteer Fire Department this week, and they were calling him in.

After shutting down and locking up, he headed over to the firehouse, expecting some cat in a tree or a kitchen fire at the burger place, but a two-alarm fire was in progress at the newly built storage facility off State Route 89A on the road down the mountain toward Verde Valley. Oliver's crew was assigned to search and rescue while the first crew fought the blaze. The storage units were brick and metal, but the summer had been dry, and maintenance hadn't been kept up to clear weeds and brush from around the facilities. And some clever asshole had thought treated wood-shingle roofing would be a good idea for a storage facility on a mountainside. In a town that had burned down more than once.

Since most of the units were locked up, scanning for occupants was simple enough, but after calling in the all clear on his section, Oliver caught movement out of the corner of his eye. He thought at first that he'd seen a coyote or a stray dog, but it had withdrawn into the shadows among the trash bins at the back of the rear units where the yard ended in a high cement fence. An animal might have been skittish around humans, but animals weren't generally good at hiding—particularly when they were trapped near fire.

"Hey," he called. "Anybody back there?"

Silence answered, but there was movement behind the bins.

Oliver moved closer cautiously. If it *was* a trapped animal, it could be dangerous. And if it was a person, it could be an arsonist. Why else would someone hide nearby during a blaze? He switched on the flashlight on his shoulder strap as he stepped around the industrial bin, illuminating the dark corner. Huddled beside the bin, a wide-eyed, sandy-haired youth stared up into the beam of his light, frozen in terror.

Instinctively, Oliver knew the boy was "family." It was the term he used in his head for Jerome's not-quite-human residents. And just as instinctively, he knew better than to call this in. No one helpful was looking for this boy.

He made sure his radio was off before crouching down to the boy's level. "Hey." He kept his voice neutral, his body relaxed. "I'm Oliver. You need some help?"

The kid's eyes widened a bit farther, as if he hadn't expected kindness. He shook his head, lowering his eyes under Oliver's continued scrutiny.

"You hungry?"

The dark eyes darted up once more, the answer obvious in them, though the boy didn't speak.

Oliver took a protein bar from his pocket and offered it to him. After glancing past Oliver as if to see if this was some kind of trick, he snatched the bar from Oliver's hand and tore it open, gobbling it down in two bites. As the boy looked up hopefully for more, Oliver took inventory of the dirty T-shirt, torn jeans and bare feet. The kid had been living on the street—or in the wild—for a while.

The boy jumped and scrambled back at the sound of Oliver's radio crackling with an announcement from the team leader that the fire was contained.

"It's okay," Oliver assured him. "Everybody's going to be leaving soon. I won't tell anyone you're here."

Looking only slightly less mistrusting, the kid nodded.

"So you can understand my language, yeah?"

Another nod.

"Can you speak it?"

No answer.

"Okay, forget about that for now. Do you have a name?"

The kid blinked at him, understanding but clearly having no words. Whether it was because he didn't have a name or simply couldn't speak at all, Oliver wasn't sure.

"Can I give you one? Just to make it easier for me to talk to you." When the boy didn't shake his head, Oliver pondered it for a moment. "How about Colt?" He reminded Oliver of one, skittish and wild.

The boy considered it and seemed to recognize its meaning, as a shy smile spread slowly across his face, and he nodded.

"Okay, Colt. I have to go right now, but I'm going to come back in a little bit. Will you stay here and wait for me? I can bring you some proper food and some water, give you someplace warm to sleep—but I'm not going to take you anywhere, don't worry," he added as Colt looked alarmed at the last bit. "I'm not going to bring anyone, either."

Colt's demeanor relaxed to his previous level of vigilance, and he hugged his knees, resting his chin on them with a slight, wary nod.

Oliver's radio went off again, his partner wanting to know where he was.

He straightened and responded before nodding to Colt once more. "Be back in a bit."

As he arrived at the front of the lot, a little zing of dismayingly pleasant recognition went through him at the sight of Lucy Smok conversing with one of the other firefighters. When she turned her head as if feeling his gaze on her, he smiled. And then felt like an idiot. What the hell was he smiling about? They weren't friends. He tried to look nonchalant and let the smile fade naturally. Lucy's expression made it pretty clear that he'd only succeeding in pulling off "idiot."

She took in his uniform as he came closer and managed a perfect Spock eyebrow lift. "So now you're a firefighter, too?" The words sounded like an accusation, like she thought he was messing with her.

"It's a volunteer fire department, and I'm a volunteer. So, yeah, I guess. I mean, yeah." *Jesus.* Why was he on the defensive all of a sudden? Something weird had happened last night. With that one little look from her as he'd kept her from falling, he'd lost his own mental footing with her.

The eyebrow was still halfway up. "Okay." She seemed to be waiting for him to say something else.

Oliver cleared his throat. "What brings you here?" *Jesus.*

"The fire. I got a tip that someone had seen a wild dog out here right after the fire broke out. I thought I'd check and see if our…" She paused and glanced at the crew packing up around them. "If there was any connection to the case. Did you see it?"

Oliver had been watching her lips move, the dark

lipstick she favored mesmerizing, and he'd forgotten to listen to the words she was saying. "Sorry, see what?"

Lucy gave him that inscrutable look once more. "The wild dog."

He shook his head, and even as he said no, a certainty struck him in the gut. Of course he had. Colt.

"Well, it sounds like it wasn't big enough to have been…the animal in the other reports, but your chief says this fire looks suspicious. Definitely arson, but I'm getting another vibe. Like the origins don't make sense. No incendiary devices, no clear starting point, just combustion out of nowhere. Which is right up my alley. With Smok Consulting, I mean."

"Smoke." He was just blurting out dumb-ass shit now. So they sounded the same. Smoke/Smok. This wasn't news.

Lucy squinted at him. "Right."

"Well, I've gotta run. I'll see if I can get any more details about the cause." Halfway to the truck, he paused and glanced back. "How are those stitches? You look rested."

"I… It's fine. Yeah, I did. Get some rest." Now Lucy was stumbling over her words, too.

He tried not to smile. "Okay, I'll check in with you later?"

She nodded, and Oliver climbed onto the truck, avoiding looking at her as they pulled out of the lot, because looking at her made him feel warm. God, he was completely regressing to an adolescent state.

He shook himself mentally, remembering that Colt was waiting for him.

He gave it an hour before heading back in his regular clothes, a few boxes and a small rolled-up carpet loaded into the back of his pickup. The storage facility attendant didn't bat an eye. They hadn't had any direct interaction when he was here in uniform, so Oliver hadn't expected him to, but he still felt guilty, like he was doing something illicit. Which, of course, he was. But not because of the fire. At least, he hoped it wasn't because of the fire.

He asked for a unit in back, saying he didn't want his stuff to smell like smoke, and the attendant accommodated him without question. The unit was just two down from the trash bins where he hoped Colt was still waiting.

After unrolling the carpet on the floor of the unit and moving his boxes into it, Oliver unpacked the inflatable mattress and pump and set it up before heading to the trash bins. At first glance, he thought Colt had taken off, but the boy scrambled out from between the bins and the wall after evidently seeing that it was Oliver. It had probably taken Colt a moment to recognize him out of uniform.

"Hey, Colt. So I brought you some stuff, and I've put it in that storage unit over there, see?" He walked back to the opening between the rows and pointed, waiting until Colt moved forward cautiously to see where he was pointing. Oliver held out the key. "You can use it if you want. It's not meant for living in, but you can stay here overnight if you promise to stay out of sight if anyone comes around. Can you do that?"

Colt stared at the key and eyed the open door again warily.

"Come on. I'll show you what I brought." Oliver walked back to the unit, and in a moment, Colt followed, skittish and scuttling, moving in short bursts. He had definitely learned to stay out of sight in however long he'd been on his own.

Inside the unit, Colt gaped at the bed and blankets, but was even more impressed by the cooler of food and cold water Oliver directed his attention to.

"There's more water in here." Oliver showed him the box. "And some hand wipes. And there's a lantern that works on batteries. There's also some stuff to read if you want it. I don't know if you read."

Colt was already busy tearing into the sandwiches and fruit in the cooler. In a few minutes, he'd settled on the little bed, eating his lunch and looking with curious interest at one of the comic books Oliver had taken out of the box. It looked like the makeshift hideout was a hit. Now he just had to figure out a longer-term plan. And determine exactly what Colt was—and whether, as Oliver suspected, he was the cause of the morning's fire.

Chapter 6

Oliver Connery was up to something. If that was even his name. He'd had a guilty look on his face the entire time Lucy had been talking to him. And what better cover would some kind of paranormal arsonist have than being a volunteer fireman?

She loosened the top two buttons on her shirt as she sat in her car outside the Civic Center building after picking up the list of eyewitnesses Nora had finally compiled. For November—or was it December now? That might explain all the irritating lights and decorations she kept seeing around Jerome—it was awfully warm. Except it wasn't the weather. It was her damn wyvern thermostat.

Lucy swore softly. "A fireman? He's a goddamn *fireman*. Firefighter. Whatever." But "man" was the part her stupid hormones were focusing on, for sure. He'd been suited up in a heavy bunker jacket and loaded down with gear. It wasn't like he'd been shirtless and posing for a "Hot Firemen of Jerome VFD" calendar, for God's sake. But she'd already seen him shirtless.

"Dammit." She didn't need this. She should just stop by Polly's Grotto in Sedona tonight, pick up some dumb, harmless satyr with an overactive libido and get her itch scratched.

Except that itch increasingly wanted to be scratched by Oliver Connery. Who was probably a fire-starting were-beast.

She'd phrased it that way in her head to remind herself of the dangerous territory she was heading into and shut off her train of thought, but her libido immediately responded with another spike of temperature. *You know you want a fire-starting were-beast.*

"I do *not* want a fire-starting were-beast!" Saying it aloud didn't help. She was never going to be able to concentrate on these eyewitness interviews if she didn't do something about this nonsense. It was only three o'clock—a little early for drinking, but Polly's had the distinction of being a sort of free-floating alternate dimension. There were always a few patrons inside from other time zones. Lucy could take care of business and be back in Jerome by full dark to hunt.

She stopped by the villa to change into something that would be easy to get out of and back into—a knee-length shift in black stretch velvet—and took her hair out of the braid before heading to the Grotto. Any hope of slipping in under Polly's radar was dashed almost as soon as Lucy arrived.

"That time of the month, is it, darling?"

Lucy gritted her teeth as she turned from the bar where she was waiting for her drink. Polly was sporting lavender locks this evening—and a silk sheath dress in the same color that was so transparent it ought to have been illegal.

"I'd say the same to you, except I'm pretty damn sure you're on the prowl all the time."

Polly blinked matching lavender eyes, an amused smile tugging at her lips. "So you're admitting you're on the prowl, then. That's refreshing. Until your accidental transformation when Lucien ascended—or rather *de*scended to the throne, to be precise—I had the impression you were a bit of a cold fish."

Lucy snorted. "I thought you were the one who was a fish."

Polly looked offended. "I am not a *fish*. Sirens are not *fish*."

Lucy's drink had arrived. She put her money on the bar and picked up the highball. "Honestly, Polly, I don't care if you have a mermaid's tail and scales or slippery shark bits. I didn't come here to socialize with you. I'm on a job tonight, and I have about thirty minutes to—" She felt her skin flush as she realized what she'd been about to say.

Polly laughed. "I have just the boy for you. It *is* boys you like?" She grabbed Lucy's hand before Lucy could move it out of reach and dragged her through the misty club to a set of booths in a dark corner.

"Finn, meet Lucy."

From one of the shadowy booths, a figure peered out—and instantly seemed to create his own bioluminescence. Lucy swallowed. Finn was about as far from human as a creature could get while still maintaining a human appearance—but what an appearance. The glow seemed to be coming from inside his pale green skin. He looked like a ghostly Channing Tatum.

Finn rose and smiled. "Pleased to meet you, Lucy. Won't you sit down?"

Lucy turned toward Polly and murmured, "What am I dealing with here?"

"Finn is a kind of deep-sea undine," Polly said without attempting to be discreet. "An electric mer-eel, if you will. He has a unique talent." She pushed Lucy into the booth. "Why don't you two kids get to know each other?"

Lucy glared at Polly's back as the siren turned and flitted away, trying to retain her dignity as she sipped her drink. "Sorry. I don't know what Polly was thinking—" Lucy's words cut off on a gasp as Finn took her hand while he slid back into the booth. His touch was like a light surge of current that traveled up her arm and over her skin in a tingly ripple. It was as if he'd instantly licked her all over then traced it with a violet wand.

"Is that all right?" Finn's voice was sensual and soothing. "You're unusually receptive. I normally have to ask first before a pulse is received."

"A…pulse?"

"My energy seeks to fulfill desire. Every time I breathe, it sends out a pulse."

Another one went through her. "Oh, shit." Lucy set her drink roughly on the table, sloshing gin and tonic over the rim. "Oh. Wow."

"And the pulse is translated by the receiver into whatever he or she is in need of."

He smiled and exhaled, and Lucy nearly had an orgasm.

But Finn's smile faltered. "Ah, I'm sorry." He looked a little sad as he let go of her hand. "Your need is more specific."

"What…my…specific?" She tried to regain her composure and resist the urge to snatch for his hand like a kid in a candy store grabbing for a sweet.

"Your desire is for an individual." Finn sat back. "If you want my advice, I wouldn't seek to fulfill it elsewhere, and I wouldn't try to resist it. It's not good for your health—physical or emotional—to bottle that up. If he reciprocates that desire, there's no time like the present." He smiled, and the smile seemed to set Finn's skin glowing in a slightly warmer hue.

Lucy downed her drink and cleared her throat. "And if he doesn't reciprocate it?"

Finn's gaze flitted over her with a little shake of his head. "I'd find that hard to believe."

After thanking Finn, Lucy made her escape. Polly winked at her from the bar as Lucy slipped out the door.

She collapsed into the seat of her car once she'd reached it. *What if he doesn't reciprocate it?* What the hell was she thinking? She was *not* going to throw herself at Oliver Connery just because her wyvern hormones had fixated on him. They weren't the boss of her. And they'd subside on their own in a few days if she could just keep her shit together.

Her phone, which she'd tucked into the waistband of her underwear, buzzed, and Lucy nearly jumped out of her skin. *Jesus.* Who needed a…whatever Finn was… when you had a vibrating phone? On second thought, Finn had been decidedly more satisfying. Just not… satisfying enough.

It buzzed again, and Lucy hitched up her skirt and yanked out the phone and answered. "Lucy Smok."

"Are…you okay?"

Oliver's deep voice rumbling against her ear made her wet. "Of course I'm okay. Why wouldn't I be okay?"

"You just sound a little funny. Sorry. I wanted to let you know that we've had another sighting."

Lucy sat up straight. "During daylight?"

"Sort of. It was in one of the mine shafts."

"Did it attack?"

"No, some tourists caught sight of it and got the hell out of there. They're here at my shop now. Do you want to come interview them?"

"I'm in Sedona, but I can be there in forty-five minutes."

It would take too much time to head back to the villa for a change of clothing, but she kept a "go bag" under the seat, a habit from her days of globe-trotting for Smok Consulting.

Lucy stripped off the dress where she sat, ignoring the looks from a couple who'd pulled into the space next to her, and wriggled into the garments she'd pulled from the bag: a pair of soft faded jeans and a comfortable shirt from her alma matter that she liked to travel in. After trading her heels for a pair of white slip-on sneakers, she was on her way. Dusk was just settling over Mingus Mountain as she made her way up.

Oliver did a double take when he came to unlock the door. This was a decidedly different look for Lucy. In a pair of well-worn jeans and a gray rugby shirt that said University of Oxford, she was wrapping her loose hair into a makeshift knot at the nape of her neck as she stepped inside. Her beet-stain lipstick was even more striking with the casual clothing.

"They're in back, having some hot chocolate." Oliver nodded toward the Hendersons sitting on the couch by the counter. "They were pretty spooked, but they've calmed down some."

Despite her uncharacteristic attire, Lucy introduced

herself to the couple with her usual cool professionalism. "I'm Lucy Smok. Can you folks tell me what you saw?"

Mrs. Henderson held her mug between her hands as she looked up. "We found one of those old mine shaft openings out near the park. You're not supposed to go inside, but we just wanted to take a quick look around, and I think we…woke…whatever it was."

Her husband continued. "I thought it was a dog, but it was huge, like a wolfhound. Shaggy."

"And it smelled terrible," Mrs. Henderson put in.

"I figured it must be a stray, and I took a step toward it…and its eyes shot open." Mr. Henderson shuddered. "They weren't…right. We hightailed it out of there, and thank God it didn't follow."

"Tell them what you heard," Oliver prompted.

Mr. Henderson hesitated. "It's going to sound ridiculous."

"It spoke," said his wife.

Lucy had been looking slightly bored and annoyed at the pedestrian encounter, but she perked up at that. "It *spoke*?"

"It's crazy, I know. But I swear—"

"What did it say?"

Mr. Henderson studied Lucy with surprise. "What did it say?"

"You said it spoke. I assume you mean words. What did it say?"

"Sorry. I just didn't expect you to believe us. I mean, Mr. Connery was very understanding, and—"

"What did it say?"

He swallowed. "It said, 'Give my regards to the… the Queen of the Damned.'"

"It had to have been someone in a costume," Mrs. Henderson cut in. "I mean, it was very convincing, horrifyingly realistic, but of course it must have been a person."

Lucy was quiet, obviously thinking intently.

Oliver pushed himself away from the chair back he'd been leaning against. "We really appreciate you letting us know about this, no matter how odd it may seem. Ms. Smok is absolutely the best person to figure this out."

Lucy gave him an odd look.

The couple rose, recognizing that their exit was being announced, and Mr. Henderson shook Oliver's hand. "Thank you, Mr. Connery. Ms. Smok. I'm not sure how much we helped."

"You've been a great help," Oliver insisted as he walked them out. He turned around after locking up and shuttering the door to see Lucy sitting on the couch, staring at her hands poised on her thighs. "Did that mean something to you?"

Lucy's head shot up. "What the hell could it possibly mean to me?"

Oliver tucked his hands into his pockets as he neared the couch. "You just looked pretty startled."

"I was shocked that it would speak to a victim."

"But maybe they weren't intended to be victims. Maybe it was sending us a message."

"Or me, you mean. You think I understood the message."

"Do you?"

Lucy's eyes narrowed. "It means I need to get out there and find this damn thing." She rose decisively. "It's getting dark. I'm going to go check out this mine shaft. Where is it?"

"That thing tore your shoulder open last night. You need to let it heal."

"I told you, I'm fine. I'm a fast healer." She tried to walk past him, but he sidestepped in front of her.

"Let me take a look at it. You should have gone to a hospital today instead of rushing off to wherever hunting things."

"As a matter of fact, I saw my doctor. She took a look and said it was fine. She approved of your stitching skills."

"Is that so? Then you won't mind if I verify that you're healing."

If Lucy's eyes could start a fire, he was sure they would be doing it now. "Are you serious?"

"Very."

Lucy glared at him for a moment. "I'm trained in Systema. Russian martial arts."

"I'm familiar with it. I'm pretty sure I can take you."

"*Take* me?" Lucy's stance seemed to turn instantly rock hard and immovable, a promised threat emanating from her, though she hadn't moved. "I seem to recall you ending up on the ground under me the last time you tried." After a split second's pause, her skin grew flushed. With anger, presumably. But he was getting a weird vibe.

"I wasn't actually challenging you to a fight."

"You just said you could take me."

"You brought up your Systema skills. Which seems pretty strange, because all I suggested was that you let me look at the stitches and see how you're healing. Is there some reason those are fighting words to you?"

Lucy let out a slow, deliberate breath, as if trying to breathe out her own anger—a gesture he was familiar with. "No, I suppose not." They stared each other down for another few seconds before Lucy unexpectedly crossed her arms in front of her waist, grabbed the hem of her shirt and whipped it up and over her head. She turned her bandaged shoulder toward him. "Well? Take a look. I haven't got all day."

Oliver stepped closer and peeled back the edge of the bandage. The skin was healthy looking. No redness or swelling. Little bruising. And soft. Really soft.

He drew back his hand with a jolt as though he'd touched a hot stove. "You're right. It looks good. Glad to see it."

She turned to face him, the T-shirt still balled in her fist. "Now let's see yours."

"Mine?" Oliver had to check himself from reflexively covering his crotch.

"You have some interesting scars. They looked fresh."

"Scars?" Oliver tried to keep his voice even, his expression believably puzzled.

"On your chest. From bullet wounds."

"*Bullet* wounds?" If he pulled this off, he deserved an Oscar. "I think your sleep deprivation may have gotten the better of you last night. It's understandable if you were a little confused."

"Was I?" Lucy's fists went to her hips. "Then take your shirt off and let's see."

"This is silly."

"It's a little weird that you won't just do it if I'm being silly."

Oliver blinked at her. "Maybe you should just put yours back on."

Lucy swore and yanked the shirt over her head, shoving her arms into the sleeves with two sharp jerks. "Quit stalling and take your shirt off, Oliver. Or I'm going to assume my suspicions are correct."

"And what suspicions would those be?"

"That you're something I should be hunting."

"Oh, for God's sake." His temper threatened to spike. He hadn't meditated yet today. Oliver pulled off his T-shirt and held his arms out at his sides. "Satisfied? No bullet wounds." He tried to keep his breathing steady as she stepped toward him, her nose scrunching with disbelief.

Lucy's fingers settled lightly on the pale thin line beneath his bottom right rib, and Oliver drew in his breath sharply. "What is this?"

"A scar from an accident I had a while back. If you think that's from a bullet wound, you need your eyes examined."

She glanced back up at his chest. She hadn't moved her hand except to relax it against his side. "I was sure I saw them." Lucy shook her head. "Maybe it really was sleep deprivation." She raised her eyes and met his gaze, her thumb stroking absently along the scar.

Oliver looked down at her hand. "What are you doing?" He'd meant for it to sound slightly accusatory, disapproving, a little annoyed. It came out sounding rough and low and hopeful.

"I don't know."

Her thumb was still tracing the scar, and he grabbed her hand. "Well, stop." He moved her hand away from him, which seemed to take a monumental effort. But he hadn't let go of it. It was like her skin was a magnet.

"I don't like you." Lucy's voice was equally throaty.

"You're pompous and…" She seemed to be grasping for adjectives. "Full of yourself."

"Those are the same thing."

"See?"

She'd surprised a smile out of him. "I don't like you, either." His delivery was utterly unconvincing.

"Then let go of my hand."

He was barely holding it. "You let go." She didn't.

Whatever was happening here was a bad idea. His rational mind knew it. He didn't do romantic involvement. Or sexual. He should have meditated this morning. He should let go of her hand and put his shirt back on.

He put his other hand on her waist. *No. No, that is the opposite of letting go. Definitely do not kiss h—*

Oliver swore silently at himself as their lips came together.

Chapter 7

Lucy switched off her brain and let the hormones take over. Oliver was swearing softly against her lips, and she didn't think he was aware of it. It was sexy as hell. As if by silent, mutual agreement, their clasped hands released at the same moment—two seconds too late— and Oliver cupped her face in his hands and deepened the kiss as Lucy put her hands on his chest and stroked the hard terrain, moaning appreciatively.

When her hands moved down over his abs and traced the V of his obliques, Oliver let go of her mouth and cradled the backs of her thighs to lift her off the floor so that she had to wrap her legs around him, hooked behind his ass, and walked her swiftly backward to drop her into a plush, roomy armchair next to a pile of books.

Lucy unbuttoned his jeans while Oliver lifted her shirt from the back. He tugged it over her head as she finished unbuttoning him, and she let go for a second so he could draw the shirt away. His erection pushed against the briefs exposed at his fly, and Lucy tugged down the shorts and freed him while he unhooked her bra.

Oliver groaned as she encircled his cock in her hand, warm and hard like an eminently satisfying stick shift, and stroked upward, letting the bra strap slip off her other arm before trading hands to remove the other and toss the bra aside. She brought her right hand beneath the left. He was easily a two-fister. He swore a little again as he unfastened her jeans and tugged them down. Lucy lifted her butt to let him take them off, kicking off her sneakers, and wrapped her legs beneath his ass once more, using them to jerk him toward her.

Oliver pulled her hands away, locking his fingers in hers, and held her arms against the back of the chair as he dipped in to kiss her once more. The slick heat of his mouth and his tongue made her want to taste his cock.

"Stand up," she murmured against his lips, letting her legs drop.

Oliver paused. "What?"

"Just stand up straight for a minute." She wriggled forward on the seat, and he must have thought she was just trying to get more comfortable because the little strangled yelp as she swallowed him was more surprise than pleasure. But his soft grunts and groans—along with more delightfully muttered expletives—quickly turned into the latter as he gripped the arms of the chair. God, she needed him inside her. She needed to hear those little bursts of sound at her ear as he burst inside her.

Lucy released him and pulled Oliver down toward the chair, wrapping her arms around his neck and putting her mouth to his ear. "Do you have a condom?"

Oliver blanched. "Oh, shit. I don't... I don't think so." What kind of guy didn't have condoms?

She nodded toward the jeans balled up on the floor. "In the little wallet in my back pocket."

With a raised brow, Oliver extricated himself and dug in the pocket for the wallet, which was really more of a coin purse, containing two condoms and two applicator-free tampons. Part of her go bag supplies. Because you just never knew.

Lucy watched him don one of the condoms while she stripped off her panties and teased a finger into her pussy, getting herself ready. Hell, whom was she kidding? She'd been ready for almost twenty-four hours. With his pants still on, Oliver scooped Lucy out of the chair and sat in it himself, pulling her onto his lap and onto his cock. Lucy moaned with relief. Oliver kept his movements inside her slow and sensual, focusing on pleasuring her with his hands, one at her breast and one at her clit, until Lucy was squirming and pushing herself deeper onto him, her moans louder and more plaintive.

When she reached her arms over her head and back around his neck to bury her fingers in the hair at the nape of his neck, he finally let go of all restraint and drove himself into her deep and hard. She knew he was coming when he started swearing against her temple, like a stream of X-rated endearments, and his expert fingers at her pussy brought her to climax just moments after. It was as though they'd been racing to a frantic finish before either of them could back out of the game, and Lucy relaxed into him with happy little noises, whimpers of contentedness, relieved to have made it to the end.

Oliver wrapped his arms around her and kissed the side of her neck. "Still don't like me?" he murmured after a moment, and Lucy laughed out loud. It felt good to laugh; she wasn't in the habit. It felt comfortable. As did his arms hugging her. It was almost as much a relief as having him inside her. Almost. Oliver kissed the underside of her jaw. "You didn't answer."

Lucy grinned. "I like certain parts of you a great deal."

"Just certain parts?" Oliver sighed. "Any in particular?"

Lucy smacked his arm. "Now you're just fishing."

"Just name one part." He gyrated his hips under her. "One big one."

She laughed again. "Your ego."

"Ha. Touché."

Lucy relaxed in his arms and closed her eyes for a bit, almost falling asleep, until her eyes shot open as she remembered where she was. She glanced toward the door and let out her breath with relief. He'd lowered the shades and locked the door after the Hendersons left.

"What's the matter?" His voice was sleepy, too.

"I had a moment of panic thinking everyone could see us."

"Nah, just the ghosts." Oliver grinned. "We could probably get more comfortable upstairs."

Lucy yawned and shook her head reluctantly. "I should be getting back to work. You're not paying me to..." She paused, realizing how awkward that sentence was about to be. Because he was her client. Whom she'd come on to—and whose bones she'd jumped—while in the middle of a very serious job. She scrambled off his lap and snatched up her scattered clothes, trying not to look at him as she yanked them on. What the hell was wrong with her? She'd let her hormones take complete control. This was so unprofessional. This was so *pathetic*.

"Lucy."

She jumped at the sound of his voice and glanced up reluctantly while she braided her hair. Damn. There were two really good reasons not to have looked at him. That rock-hard body glistening with sweat and those deep cinnamon eyes watching her with disappointment. Or was that three reasons?

"You're just going to take off? That's it?"

Lucy sighed. "Your council hired me to do a job, and people's lives are on the line here. This was a mistake." She cringed internally even as she said it. He'd take it the wrong way. Or the right way. "I'm sorry."

If the sexual release hadn't left his body feeling blissed out, his rage would have gotten the better of him. Not at Lucy, but at himself.

Oliver cleaned up bitterly, everything that had been relaxed and loose moments earlier once more tense and tight. "Mistake" was right. He'd just ended five years of celibacy for an ill-advised twenty-minute romp with someone far too young for him. He should have checked himself, knowing his age and life experience tilted the power balance between them toward him, no matter how much professional experience she had or how tough she acted. And he'd betrayed Vanessa's memory.

He glanced down at the ring, toying with it between the thumb and forefinger of his left hand. He hadn't allowed himself the weakness of giving in to sexual desire since her death. He didn't deserve to be alive—let alone indulging in hedonistic pleasure—when Vanessa was dead.

For a long time, every meal he'd eaten, every breath he'd taken, had felt like a betrayal. With his daily meditation, he'd finally moved beyond that, but he didn't indulge his passions, like decadent foods and spirits. And he certainly didn't indulge in sexual intimacy.

And with Lucy Smok, of all people. Someone who made a living persecuting the paranormal.

Damn. He could still smell her. She was all over him, like she'd marked him. He was never going to be able to sit in that chair again.

Oliver went upstairs and undressed with angry jerks. He needed a shower. He needed to wash her out of his brain. But all he could think about under the almost-scalding water was how soft her skin was and how she'd sounded as she came. And how pale her naked body looked against his, contrasted with the rich darkness of her hair where it tumbled against her neck out of its makeshift knot, while she'd writhed in his lap.

Jesus, this was bad. He'd lost his mind. He had to end their association. Let Wes and Nora deal with her on this case. He was done. If she came pounding on his door in the middle of the night with battle wounds, he wouldn't answer. There was an emergency room in Cottonwood. If she was such a badass, she could get herself there.

But when insistent knocking woke him hours later, Oliver jumped out of bed and hurried downstairs to open the door anyway.

Lucy stood on his doorstep. Not bleeding. Not injured. Just Lucy, in her jeans and Oxford rugby shirt and a black leather jacket, bloodred lips in a pallid face and pale blue eyes boring into him, like the Queen of the Night.

"I don't know what I'm doing here."

He tried to breathe normally. "Are you coming in?"

"No. Maybe."

Oliver took her hand and pulled her inside and kissed her with her back against the door until their mouths ached. When they came up for air, Lucy wriggled out of her coat with a swift, sexy shrug and went for his belt buckle, but Oliver stopped her.

"Upstairs."

Lucy nodded and let him lead the way, both of them taking the steps two at a time, and they were half-undressed by the time they reached the bed. She'd braided her hair again, and he unbraided it while he sucked on her neck and nipped at her throat, and the dark hair spilled across his white pillow like clouds of dark paint in water while he rocked and thrust and drove himself inside her for almost an hour. She came twice before he finally did—once underneath him and once on top—and he was almost sorry to come because he had to stop fucking her. Almost.

Oliver collapsed onto his back, exhausted and dripping with sweat. He hadn't had an aerobic workout like this in ages. Lucy curled up against his side and promptly fell asleep. He didn't realize she'd done so until he'd been talking for ten minutes—about politics and the messed-up state of the world and about being a widower and how he hadn't been with a woman since and how he was constantly questioning himself and his values and feeling adrift in his own mortal frame. After he'd asked her twice why she'd decided to come back and she hadn't answered him, he finally realized he'd been talking to himself. Thank God.

He played with her hair where it snaked across his chest. It felt like silk. Oliver curled it around his fist and smelled it—crisp and cool, like cucumber or avocado— and wondered what she used to keep it so luxurious.

It was too cold to lie here unclothed, as much as he would have been content to look at her being naked and still, her body for once without its uneasy coil of tension and mistrust. He pulled the comforter up from the foot of the bed and covered them both.

When he woke—more rested than he could remember having been for a very long time—he found himself alone.

Chapter 8

Lucy huddled on the floor of her car in the parking lot outside the villa and cried until she was too exhausted to keep doing it, despite the fact that it hadn't provided her with any kind of release. People always said, "Let yourself cry. You'll feel better." It was bullshit. Crying always made her feel a thousand times worse. And this wasn't how a Smok comported herself.

A Smok didn't sleep with clients in the middle of a case—or with anyone while on the job, for that matter. And a Smok certainly didn't cry about it like a teenage girl in her car for an hour at six o'clock in the morning. She'd gone soft and weak and useless. And she couldn't even really blame it on the wyvern hormones, because she'd gotten her period this morning, which meant the past two days of out-of-control desire had been *after* her hormone levels dipped.

And the underside of Oliver Connery's right rib cage had sported a fading scar from a knife wound yesterday afternoon that had disappeared by this morning. Just like the scars from the bullet wounds that she knew she'd seen had faded in less than a day. And every one of those wounds was identical to one she'd given the hell beast. She was fucking her client. And he was the murdering hell beast she was hunting. So *that* was fun.

Lucy sat in the car for a while longer, trying to get herself together and stiffen her resolve. She needed to take down that hell beast tonight, whether Oliver was aware of his alter ego or not. It didn't matter how she felt about Oliver. It didn't matter how decent a person he seemed to be. His infernal form was a dangerous monster, and it was Lucy's job to remove dangerous monsters from the earthly plane and send them back to hell.

It was ironic that she'd criticized Lucien for years for his secret campaign to rid the world of as many unnatural creatures as he could before he became one. It hadn't been part of the Smok Consulting business plan at the time to eliminate supernatural predators. Their loyalty was to their wealthy clients who paid handsomely to have paranormal events kept quiet. But now that Lucien was effectively out of the picture, the circumstances that had taken him out of it had made his former hobby Lucy's number one job.

Regardless of why, she had to get this thing done. Now. Which meant she had to figure out how to kill it. Soul Reaper bullets hadn't worked. Maybe Lucien's special exploding-tip arrows that delivered the Soul Reaper serum directly into the bloodstream would do the trick.

Lucy set up for the hunt, familiarizing herself with the arrows and testing the draw of Lucien's crossbow. After last night, she knew she didn't have to look for the hell beast. The hell beast would find her. Satisfied that her weapons were battle ready, she headed into the bathroom and ran the water for a soak in the tub. It was becoming a habit. Her muscles still ached from her two encounters with the beast—and now she had the added tenderness from last night.

She stared at herself in the bathroom mirror as she undressed. He'd left a mark on her neck and another on the side of one breast—and one on her inner thigh. She closed her eyes, trying not to remember the moment he'd given her that last one, flipping her over after the first time she'd come and licking her pussy while she lay on her stomach before he fucked her from behind. He hadn't seemed the least bit interested in coming himself, just wanting to find as many ways as he could to pleasure her so he could prolong the experience.

Lucy opened her eyes and focused on her disheveled hair. He'd kept running his hands through it, wanting it loose and long. Who the hell was he to decide how she should wear her hair? The long waves seemed like a symbol of her unprofessionalism, her foolishness in letting herself get carried away by her own selfish desires instead of keeping her head in the game. She yanked open the drawer and found the scissors, and with a hank of hair in her hand, she lopped it off at fist length. With a few violent motions, she'd chopped off the rest, jagged and crude. Lucy stared at the wild mess. The scissors still clutched in her fist tempted her to do worse.

She hadn't done it in years, but the temptation to cut herself had never been stronger. To maybe just keep cutting until she severed an artery. The tub had finished filling with steaming, fragrant water. Just a couple of nice matching cuts, and then step in and lie back and relax.

Lucy gripped the blades of the scissors until her hand was shaking. With a wordless scream, she swung her fist in an arc across the bathroom vanity and swept everything onto the floor, cosmetics and bottles of facial cleanser and liquid soap and lotion—all of it scattering across the bathroom rug and shattering on the tile. She dropped the scissors and opened the cabinets and the drawers in the vanity and emptied everything, smashing and screaming until she'd punished everything she could reach besides herself. The urge was still strong as she stood among the wreckage and looked up at her reflection once more.

Her eyes were reptilian. She'd partially shifted. Lucy forced out her wings with a howl of pain and fell on her knees, wrapping her wings around herself. What the hell was she anymore? She wasn't infernal royalty like Lucien, she was earthbound and half human and nothing mattered, and she was so fucking tired. Mr. Henderson's words came back to her, the alleged taunt from the hell beast—*Give my regards to the Queen of the Damned.* It couldn't have meant her. Maybe her sister-in-law. Maybe it was time to try to contact Lucien and Theia and get help.

Lucy let out a choked laugh. Maybe it was *really* time to get help. "Siri, call Dr. Delano." She hadn't expected the mic to pick it up. It was more of a joking plea to the universe. But her phone replied cheerfully from the pile of broken glass and powder, "Calling Dr. Delano."

She scrambled for the phone and shut it off, but not before Fran had answered. The phone rang immediately, Fran calling back, and Lucy hit the button to decline it. She probably should have just answered and pretended it was a misdial. But now Fran knew something was up.

The knock on the door came while Lucy was floating in the immense bathtub, her tucked wings keeping her from going under. Fran let herself in when Lucy didn't answer. *Dammit.* She'd forgotten she'd given her a key. Lucy plunged her head under the water and came up just as Fran arrived at the doorway.

She took in the scene and Lucy's appearance and shook her head. "Sweetheart. Why haven't you been taking your meds?"

"Sweetheart" wasn't what Fran usually called her. Their familial relationship went unspoken. Fran had abandoned her babies after trying unsuccessfully to live with Edgar, and she'd signed a nondisclosure agreement promising never to reveal that she was their mother. She worked for Edgar, just the company and family doctor, as far as they knew—kind but impersonal. But Lucy had figured it out from the way Fran reacted when Lucy was assaulted by a high school boy who asked her out on a date when she was thirteen. It was Fran who'd taken care of her, angry and tearful in turns as she got the story out of Lucy. And it was Fran, Lucy was certain, who'd paid someone to break the little asshole's arm, because Edgar had never found out.

"The pills don't work the same since the transformation. They slow me down."

"That's part of what they're supposed to do. The transformation speeds up your metabolism in ways that aren't entirely healthy. I adjusted your meds to work with the anti-transformative compound. Which I see you haven't taken this month, either."

"I was about to, but… I don't know what I'm doing anymore. The fugitives just keep coming, and now there's a hell beast stalking me. And I can't kill it. And I think I slept with him."

Fran sighed. "Lucy. Honey, come out of the tub. Let's

get you warmed up, and you can tell me all about it. Have you eaten?"

"I don't know."

Fran kicked the shards of broken glass out of the way and set a bath mat on the floor, holding her hand out to Lucy. "Come on. You're going to eat something."

Reluctantly, and mostly because she really was getting a bit chilly at last, Lucy took Fran's hand and climbed out, accepting the bath sheet Fran wrapped her in.

After taking a mild sedative to help suppress her shift, Lucy put on a robe and sat cross-legged in front of the fire while Fran made coffee and whipped up eggs and bacon and fluffy cinnamon toast that she'd evidently brought with her—because Lucy's fridge sure as hell didn't contain any unexpired food.

Fran brought the plates to the living room and sat with Lucy on the carpet. "So what makes you think you slept with a hell beast?"

"He has the same scars—and then he doesn't."

"He?"

"Oliver Connery. He's a client—I know, don't even say it."

"I wasn't going to say anything."

"He's part of some paranormal Jerome town council— Oliver owns a bookstore and café there. They called me in because of werewolf sightings, which turned out to be the same thing I've been hunting. It's big, and it's vicious, and I'm not sure what it is. And I've shot it with Soul Reaper bullets and stabbed it, and nothing even slows it down." Lucy took a bite of toast. "And he's a volunteer firefighter."

"The hell beast is a firefighter?"

"Oliver, I mean. But he's also the damn hell beast, so, yeah. Firefighter hell beast. Can I pick 'em or what?"

Fran poked at her eggs. "You're sure he's the beast?"

"How else would he get those scars?"

"Maybe it's a coincidence. Hear me out. It just seems highly unlikely that this beast would have been hidden all this time, hanging out in Jerome living the life of an upstanding citizen, no reports of attacks until hell happens to be left open and a bunch of demons spill out."

Lucy ran her hand through the damp, shaggy wreck of her hair. "But I saw the scars, and they healed in a day. He's enhanced in some way."

"So are you."

"That was hardly my choice."

"Lucy. Honey. It is almost never anyone's choice. Maybe you should ask him."

"Like he's going to tell me the truth. He lied about having the scars in the first place. And he's lying about something else. I just don't know what. He claims to be some kind of self-appointed 'protector' of inhuman creatures in Jerome, and he's got some kind of law enforcement or military training." Lucy's fingers caught in her hair, and she swore as she yanked them out.

Fran set down her coffee. "Okay, we're going to fix that right now. You have a board meeting this afternoon—"

"Oh, shit."

"And you are Lucy Smok, steel-spined CFO of Smok International."

Lucy laughed as Fran pulled her to her feet by both hands. "I don't think that's correct."

"That is how people see you, my dear, and I know how important it is to you to present a sharp, professional image. You're like your father in that regard.

Your appearance is part of your arsenal, so let's make it precision weaponry."

Lucy sat in a kitchen chair in front of the mirrored bedroom closet doors and submitted to Fran's grooming. The damage was bad. Lucy had hacked within inches of her scalp in places and left other ragged locks hanging. Fran turned it into a softened version of a men's business cut, close to Lucy's head and a little long above the ears, with a side part offset by a curve of eye-level bangs on the right. With a bit of hair wax to smooth the sides and emphasize the point at the nape of her neck, it looked both sophisticated and a little funky.

"Wow, Fran. I had no idea you were a barber *and* a doctor." Lucy ran her hand over the final product. "How Wild West of you. Thank you."

Fran smiled. "I think it suits you." She brushed the loose hair from Lucy's neck and took the towel from around her shoulders to shake it out in the bathroom. When she returned, she watched from the doorway as Lucy added some wax to the bangs to sculpt them into a wave that matched her hair's natural inclination. "Was there something in particular that led to this? I mean, I'm glad you didn't do anything worse, but attacking your hair is pretty specific."

Lucy's cheeks went slightly pink. "It was because he liked it. I know. It's stupid. But I just felt like such a fool, letting myself get caught up in, in being…" Words were eluding her.

Fran gave her a fond, somewhat reproachful smile. "Human? You're allowed, you know. You've been working yourself so hard, trying to do everything on your own at Smok. For that reason alone, I may never forgive Edgar. You deserve to have some pleasure once in a while. Did you at least have a good time with him?"

The heat in Lucy's cheeks became more pronounced.

Fran grinned. "That good, huh?"

Oliver waited as long as he reasonably could to check on the boy. He'd given Colt the key, so if the kid had locked the unit and taken off, he'd have no way of getting inside to verify. His initial knocks on the metal door yielded only silence, but a quick tug on the handle showed that it was unlocked.

He knocked again, not wanting to violate Colt's privacy. "Hey, Colt? It's just me, Oliver. I'm alone. I brought you some more things."

A slight rustling followed from inside, and in a moment the door slid upward a crack. Oliver pulled it up halfway and ducked inside. Over his dirty clothes, Colt was wearing the sweatshirt Oliver had left him in one of the boxes. The boy scuttled into the corner, still untrusting.

Oliver set the bag of dry goods and fruit next to Colt's bed. Luckily, he'd thought to bring more water, because from the looks of the empty bottles scattered about the floor, Colt had drunk nearly all of it.

"Sorry I didn't think about the bathroom situation. I take it you managed to slip inside the office and use theirs?"

Colt shook his head and pointed outside. Whatever worked.

Oliver glanced at the empty bottles once more. That was a lot of water for a kid who couldn't weigh a hundred pounds soaking wet. "Mind if I sit down for a minute?" Colt didn't seem to, so he sat. "Can I ask you a question? And I want an honest answer."

The boy hesitated, looking suspicious, before nodding reluctantly.

"Did you start that fire yesterday?"

Colt's eyes widened, and his gaze darted back and forth as if he was looking for a chance to bolt.

"It's okay. I just need to know. You won't get in trouble."

Colt scooted back against the wall and hugged his knees, staring up at Oliver with a haunted expression. After a moment, he gave a sharp nod and lowered his eyes.

Oliver sighed. "I'm going to guess it's something in your nature. That's why you're drinking all this water."

Colt looked miserable. He probably thought his brief good luck had run out.

"I'm also going to guess this form you're showing me isn't your natural state. That you aren't human."

Colt's face fell, and he slumped against the wall, letting his legs slide to the floor stretched out in front of him.

"I don't care about that, Colt. I just want to make sure you're safe and that you don't accidentally cause anyone harm. I'm sure you're already aware of how dangerous it is for people like you. That there are people who'd see *you* as the danger and try to hurt you." Like Lucy Smok. "And I don't want that to happen. It also isn't safe for you to stay here indefinitely. It's not healthy, for one, and you're likely to get caught sooner or later. I am *not* throwing you out," he hastened to assure the boy. "I just want to figure out what the best solution is for you. Do you have family? Others like you?"

Colt slowly shook his head. It was a mystery how he'd gotten this far on his own. Whatever family he'd had once had probably been hunted. By someone like Lucy. But Oliver couldn't justify leaving the boy on his own, no matter how self-sufficient he might be. He was a child, and he deserved to be cared for like one, human or not.

"I might know some people who could help you. People like you who are different, maybe in different ways than you, but good people. But it may take me a few days to figure out who the right people are and to track them down. Would that be okay with you?"

Colt's expression was fearful, eyes searching Oliver's face intently, as if he might be able to see in it the people Oliver was referring to. He shook his head uncertainly.

"Okay. I won't do anything you don't agree to. But I still want to find someplace better for you than this. I'm going to talk to the people I know, but I won't tell them where you are. I'll just see what I can find out and come back and tell you what I've learned. Is that okay?"

Colt was still uncertain, his anxious expression trying to convey something Oliver was missing. He'd been hiding when Oliver found him, and he'd probably been living in hiding for a long time.

"Colt…is there someone looking for you? Someone you're afraid of?"

The vigorous nod was unequivocal.

Chapter 9

Maybe Fran was right. Maybe Oliver would have a good explanation for the scars and the rapid healing if Lucy just asked him about it. And maybe Lucy was the queen of England. But after last night, maybe she owed Oliver the question. If he lied straight to her face, that would be an answer, too.

In the meantime, there was one way she could find out more about him. Smok International had access to more intelligence than most government agencies. It wasn't just unnatural creatures they kept track of. She'd start with exactly *who* he was. *What* he was might be more complicated.

Before the board meeting, she initiated the search with her research department, and by the time the meeting was over, the preliminary report was already on her virtual desk. He *had* been in the military, under the name Oliver Benally—a Navajo surname; if it was his real name, he obviously had an Anglo parent. He'd served four years in the Marines before being recruited by an organization Lucy was unpleasantly familiar with: Darkrock Security.

It was a paramilitary contractor that specialized in supplying forces deployed in response to paranormal events. Edgar had contracted some work to them once, cleaning up a series of rogue blood farms—vampire operations where humans were kept as long-term feeders against their will—but Darkrock's methods and ethics were questionable even by Edgar's standards. In the years since, Smok had refused to work with them.

So what was Oliver doing in Jerome running a bed-and-books-and-coffee joint and volunteering to fight fires—while advocating for demons and shifters as if they were simply misunderstood? It seemed to go against everything Darkrock stood for. Unless Oliver was undercover and still working for them. That would explain the assumed name. And in that context, his "paranormal protector" role took on new significance. He might be exploiting the creatures he claimed to defend for Darkrock's own twisted purposes.

Whatever the reason, he'd definitely hidden his identity well. If it hadn't been for Smok's on-staff clairvoyants, the research department might have missed it altogether. As Benally, he'd been reported dead.

Armed with her new information and her crossbow, Lucy drove back to Jerome after dark. Before heading to the mine shaft to smoke out the hell beast, she lingered in front of Delectably Bookish. She could go inside and confront him now, demand to know whether he was the hell beast. But if he was with Darkrock… How could he be both a Darkrock operative and a hell beast? Despite her distaste for Darkrock's business model, she breathed a little sigh of relief. Of course he couldn't be the hell beast. Darkrock wouldn't hire an inhuman creature.

She paused with her hand on the door handle. Darkrock wouldn't hire one…but it might create one. That was the one line Edgar had refused to cross. He might have looked the other way at Darkrock's abusive practices, but the company also engaged in live capture. They were known to experiment on their captives to see exactly what made them tick, and rumor had it their ultimate goal was to create their own custom hybrids as soldiers for hire.

Lucy's grip relaxed on the handle. It made a horrible kind of sense. He was hiding out in a small, deliberately created paranormal community off the larger community's radar, pretending to be a friend and protector. A hitherto unknown breed of wolf shifter that could phase in and out of animal and human form at will arrived in the area, coincidentally timed to be mistaken for one of the fugitives released from the gates of hell. Oliver displayed the same wounds Lucy had given the beast—and healed them overnight.

He was secretly still working for Darkrock. And they had created him.

Goose bumps rippled across Lucy's skin. Darkrock had long been interested in a partnership with Smok Consulting despite being frustrated by Edgar's refusals. Their public relations rep had reached out to Lucy shortly after she assumed control of the company, wanting to discuss how they could work together in the future, but Lucy had instructed her assistant to let them know in no uncertain terms that nothing had changed at Smok with Edgar's death. His policies would survive him.

What if they'd decided to get at Lucy another way? What if it hadn't been mere happenstance that Lucy had hunted the hell beast here, of all places, and had run up against Oliver Connery that first night? She'd thought the beast was targeting her. She had a sinking feeling she'd been more right than she knew.

She started the car and pulled back onto Main. If she was right, Oliver wouldn't be home anyway. He would be waiting for her in one of the lesser-known mine shafts. The incident with the Hendersons had obviously been for Lucy's benefit, designed to lure her to it. The mine shaft near the park where they'd spotted it was too obvious a place for the hell beast to be lurking.

Lucy parked at the base of the dirt road that led into the mountains, the spot where she'd fought it before, and hiked uphill, using a special GPS app Smok International had developed to find access points to some of the abandoned mine shafts in the hills. After surveying the area pinpointed on the app, she found the telltale footprints she was looking for leading to an opening hidden among the rocks. Lucy loaded up the crossbow, viewing the tunnel through the night vision scope, and headed in.

The wolf prints were only in sets of two, as if the beast was walking upright. Lucy followed them along the mine cart rails perhaps half a mile into the shaft before they stopped abruptly and became human footprints. Was Oliver himself waiting for her? A deep twinge of wistful body memory recalled the intimacy she'd shared with him not twenty-four hours ago. What kind of sick bastard would play a game like this? It was the ultimate bait-and-switch of seduction.

Lucy stopped and laughed at herself. She was talking about a hell beast. Of course he was a sick bastard.

A noise in the dirt to her right stopped her laughter instantly. She crouched and turned the scope toward the sound. A brief glimpse of the swiftly moving form of a man was all she caught before he rushed her, faster than any human she'd ever encountered, and knocked the crossbow from her grasp. Without the scope, she was blind. She should have opted for night goggles. The beast paced and circled her, now closer to the ground and growling low in its throat. It had shifted once more.

With her Nighthawk Browning in her hand, she tried to track it. If she missed, who knew what the bullet might glance off? She needed to aim into the depths of the mine, catching the creature when it was framed by the passage walls instead of in front of them. A brush of fur made her jump, and Lucy shot in the thing's direction, but it was already gone. She was sure the little growl that followed was laughter.

It was toying with her. And it was obviously every bit as sentient as she was.

"What do you want?" Her words seemed to thud into the dirt around her, as if no air flowed through the tunnels.

The laugh-growl came again from behind, and the creature leaped on top of her before she could spin and get off a shot, knocking her facedown and grinding her into the dirt and rusted tracks. Its weight was considerable, and it had her pinned. The gun was just beyond her grasp. She could feel the creature's hot breath on her neck. And she could also feel it transform, effortlessly, from wolf to man.

"What do I want?" The whispered words sent a chill

down her spine. "I am Death. I am the Pit. I want to take you into my mouth."

Lucy shuddered as a hot tongue slicked across the back of her neck.

"But I am having fun here. Such a charming playground this world is. So I'm in no hurry." He made a breathing sound behind her that was more like a dog's panting than human breath. "And you have something of mine that I want first."

Lucy tried to keep her voice casual. "What could I possibly have of yours?"

"Don't play coy. The thing you've hidden from me. The thing that escaped."

"What thing? What escaped?" She struggled to breathe under his weight. "From where?"

He laughed with the growling, unnatural cadence of the wolf. "From hell, of course. Your obligation to your foolish rules is to send such things back, but instead you've put this one somewhere I can't find it. And I want it. It's my right." He breathed damply against her ear. "I want to feel its tender neck bones beneath my teeth as the hot blood of its carotid artery spills into my mouth." He licked her once more, and Lucy used the uncontrollable shudder to move her hand closer to the gun.

She almost had it, fingers curling to close around the metal, but his hand came down on hers, and he shoved the weapon away. But to do it, he'd moved his body just enough to free her arm, and Lucy punched swiftly back and up with her elbow, hitting him right in the throat. It bought her just enough time and space to scramble for the gun as he reacted with a surprised, furious guttural outburst. Lucy grabbed the weapon and fired into his shoulder, and he jolted backward with the impact, his head striking the shaft wall. She fired again as she rolled onto her back. No longer close enough for her to see his outline in the dark, her shot went wide.

"I will have what's mine!" The words came out in an inhuman bark. He'd shifted again.

Lucy fired blind toward the sound. It was a waste of bullets. He was already gone. By the time she'd found the crossbow and quiver after fumbling around in the dirt, any chance she had of pursuing it was gone, too.

She swore as she got to her feet, the sound this time echoing through the tunnels where they split off in different directions. She'd managed to have as close an encounter with its human form as she was going to get without becoming its next victim, and she hadn't been able to tell if it was Oliver. She was also furious that it had once again eluded her. She'd never fought and failed to kill the same creature three times in a row.

The walk back to the opening of the shaft was warm and dusty despite the temperature outside and the cool air underground. It was the anger and the energy she'd exerted along with the lingering adrenaline. Plus a bit of anxiety threading through her pulse from being in an enclosed space below the earth. It was the stuff of nightmares, and if she hadn't been following the only exit back over her own tracks, the anxiety might have overwhelmed her.

Outside under the open sky, she was able to breathe again. There was no sign of the beast, not even footprints leading away this time. Lucy sat on a boulder and stared up at the stars. There had to be a way to kill this thing. But right now she was just lucky to have gotten away without being killed by *it*. Orion had just cleared the horizon, its easily identifiable pattern in the sky somehow always comforting and grounding. The hunter with his bow. She clutched the crossbow and shook it in the air in solidarity. And made a silent vow to Lucien in the underworld to finish this.

As she walked back to her car, she wondered what the hell beast thought she'd hidden from it. It had obviously meant something living, another creature that had escaped from hell during Lucien's descent. But why would one hell beast want to kill—or more to the point, feed on—another?

Lucy stopped dead on the trailhead as she reached the spot where she'd parked her car. With his back against the driver's-side door, Oliver stood with folded arms.

She decided not to tip her hand if he was really the hell beast. "What are you doing here?"

"I figured this was where you would go after what the Hendersons told us last night. I wasn't sure how else I could find you, since you haven't answered any of my texts."

"My phone is always off when I'm hunting. It's distracting."

"And did you catch anything tonight?"

Lucy lowered her head as she approached the car, not wanting to meet his eyes and give herself away. "No. It was a bust."

"Funny, you look like you've been rolling around fighting something—" Oliver paused, and Lucy looked up as she reached him to find him staring at her with a furrowed brow. "What happened to your hair?"

Her hand went to the back of her scalp reflexively. "I cut it."

"Why?"

Lucy glared. "Why shouldn't I? It's my hair."

"I'm not saying you shouldn't. I just wondered." He studied her face as if he was trying to get used to it. "It's very different."

"Yeah, well, I didn't do it for you." She reached around him to the handle of the door he was blocking. "Can you please get off my car?"

Oliver pushed himself away from the door but stood where he was. "Are you mad at me?"

"Why would I be mad at you? I hardly know you."

He flinched, as if she'd thrown water in his face, and his expression hardened. "I thought we kind of got to know each other a little bit last night."

"We had sex, Oliver. We fucked. I'd hardly call it a bonding experience."

Wordlessly, Oliver stepped aside to let Lucy get in and drive away.

It was up to Oliver to keep the Jerome undergrounders safe while Lucy was on the prowl. She'd been frustrated in her attempts to stop the creature, and he wouldn't be surprised if she went looking for other "fugitives" to make up for it. His instincts were usually correct. At least as far as her bloodlust was concerned. His instincts about her primal, sexual lust were obviously way off. His attraction to her was as strong as ever. Stronger. Which was all the more reason for him to hit the streets tonight—if you could call Jerome's two main connecting drives and their handful of tributaries "streets"—and occupy his mind with something else.

He'd also promised Colt that he'd talk to his underground contacts about a safe place for him, even if the boy wasn't quite ready to go to one. None of his daytime contacts through the council had been able to offer him anything useful, and he didn't dare reveal enough to let them know he was trying to help a young runaway of dubious origin. That left the shadow people, under-grounders who kept to themselves and only ventured out at night. For most of them, it was because they were nocturnal beings; for others, it was the safest time in a sleepy little artists' town.

He made the usual rounds, walking up to Clark Street from the back of his property to Haunted Hamburger and Wicked City Brew and across the little park steps to Main Street past the Spirit Room under the old Connor Hotel and Paul & Jerry's Saloon—the sum total of Jerome "nightlife." Paul & Jerry's and the Spirit Room were the only establishments open past 11:00 p.m.

Oliver nodded to the regulars inside Paul & Jerry's and stopped in front of the fenced-off ruin of the old Bartlett Hotel on the other side of the gallery beside the saloon. The empty brick skeletons of its remaining rooms beyond the easily scalable ironwork bars made it an attractive place to squat for people who weren't quite human. Oliver blended into the shadows and stood watch until he saw signs of activity within the hotel's remains.

A young half vamp he knew—sired by a vampire who'd abandoned her before sharing his blood to give her invulnerability and the community's protection—materialized inside the iron bars.

She leaned against them, crossing her tattooed arms as she stared straight into him. "If it ain't the old man."

He nodded to her. "Hey, Eva. Though I'm not sure I care for that characterization. You're older than I am, as I understand it."

"And you look about as old as I ought to."

"That's...charming to know." He hoped she wasn't chronologically over forty. She looked eternally seventeen. He wondered if they liked the same music. Might be something to ask her some other time. "Listen, I was hoping I could get some information from you."

Eva bristled. "What kind of information?"

"About a safe house for a—someone who may be in a bit of trouble."

"Well, the latter's a given. Why else would they want a safe house? But I don't think I can help you."

"Why not?"

"We've got enough trouble right now. There's a feral shifter started hunting around here, and some kickboxing bitch tried to take out Crystal the other night."

"Yeah, I know. But if somebody really needed help..."

Eva sighed. "You talking about a kid?"

"Might be."

"I've seen that kid. He's not our kind. He doesn't belong here."

"That's what the normals say about all of you."

"Spoken like a 'normal.'"

He couldn't argue with that. "I'm not sure where he came from, but he can't survive out here on his own for much longer."

"Why don't you take him in?"

"I run a business out of my home. He'd be hard to explain."

"Not my problem."

"Yeah, I gotcha." Oliver shrugged. "I figured it was worth a try."

Eva had lit up a cigarette while they spoke, and she

took a drag on it and breathed in the smoke through her nose. "I've heard about some chick in the valley who'll hide folks for a price. Some kind of nymph or dryad or something. She also has the dirt on anyone in the community. Name's Polly."

Oliver nodded thoughtfully. He'd heard of Polly's Grotto in West Sedona. "Thanks. Maybe I'll try her."

"Don't forget about the price, though. From what I hear, she ain't cheap—and she has zero use for human currency."

On second thought, maybe Polly would be better left as a last resort. Not that he had a lot of options. Oliver opened his mouth to thank Eva, but she was gone, leaving her cigarette smoldering in the dirt.

A quick scan of the otherwise deserted street gave him the reason. An unmarked black van with tinted windows had parked on the opposite corner. He felt his blood freeze. It couldn't be. It was Darkrock's signature "inconspicuous" mode of transport.

Chapter 10

Maybe they were just here looking for people like Eva. He'd hoped to keep the underground community off their radar, but with the public sightings of the wolf, he supposed it had only been a matter of time.

Oliver picked up the cigarette to avoid calling attention to the disappearance of the person who'd been smoking it and took a drag, trying not to cough with distaste. It had been years since he'd smoked—to impress friends when he'd been young and stupid—and he'd never really been a fan. He started walking away from the Bartlett, keeping tabs on the van out of the corner of his eye. It followed. Slowly. And obviously. They were here for *him*. How the hell had Darkrock tracked him after all this time?

Oliver tossed down the cigarette, feeling sick, and ground it out with his heel, pulling his hood close and shoving his hands in the pockets of his sweatshirt as he picked up his pace.

It was pointless. They knew who he was. The window slid down as the van pulled up alongside him.

The driver leaned his arm on the window frame. "Well, well. Chief Benally, in the flesh."

Oliver paused and stared ahead down the sidewalk. He shouldn't take the bait, but it wasn't like he was fooling anyone at this point. He could run for it, but he'd be on the run forever, and everything he'd built in Jerome would have been for nothing.

He turned slowly on his heel and faced the window. "Don't fucking call me Chief."

Artie Cooper, his flat-top crew cut the same as he'd had for a dozen years, grinned and turned to his passenger. "Ya see, Finch? I told you it was ol' Chief." He stuck his hand out the window, expecting Oliver to shake it. "Great to see ya, man." Cooper and Finch had both been in his unit.

Oliver kept his hands in his pockets. "What do you want, Artie?"

"What kind of greeting is that?" Artie withdrew his thick arm with a put-on frown. "Is that any way to talk to an old friend?"

Finch leaned across the seat to peer out, the light from the streetlamp falling on his dark skin. "It really is you." He seemed genuinely surprised, and actually looked pleased to see Oliver. "Well, goddamn. I thought you were dead."

He was beginning to think he might be. "Nah, you know me. I'm not that easy to kill."

Finch laughed. "What are you doin' here, man? I thought Artie was pulling my leg."

"Cap says he's running a damn artsy-fartsy inn or some shit."

"It's a book-café and B andB. Or it will be."

"Aw, shit!" Finch broke out into incredulous laughter. "Shut the fuck up."

Oliver shrugged. "So what do you want, Artie? I take it Captain Blake sent you to spy on me for a reason."

"Who's spying? We're just looking for a cup of coffee. It's supposed to get below freezing tonight. Why don't you lead the way to your place and we'll get caught up?"

Reluctantly, Oliver directed them to Delectably Bookish, though he knew they were aware of where he lived. As they made themselves at home, Finch investigating the book stacks with frequent exclamations of amusement, Oliver opened up the counter in back, making coffee for the three of them.

"I can't get over this." Finch accepted the coffee Oliver brought him and took a seat in the armchair that Oliver and Lucy had occupied just yesterday. Oliver made a concerted effort to put that out of his head. "Ollie Benally, puttering around with books and bedsheets in a little tourist trap in Arizona like an old man."

"I needed a change."

Artie stood drinking his coffee, significantly less amused. "You know you're still under contract."

"You can tell Blake that I'll be happy to buy out the rest of my term at whatever fair price Darkrock determines."

"It doesn't work that way. You made a commitment, and Darkrock expects you to honor it."

Oliver folded his arms. "You know I can't do that. You know why I left."

"You made one bad call."

"One bad call that cost Vanessa and two other men their lives."

Artie studied him. "Interesting thing is, it should've

cost you yours. We're all curious how you walked away from that inferno."

"Because I was the one who burned that shithouse down." Oliver could feel his pulse pounding in his temple. "Vanessa and the others were dead. We'd been ambushed. So I threw a CS canister into the nest and got the fuck out."

"And we all felt for you, man, but that's the job. You knew it going in. Vanessa knew it. She was prepared to face the danger every time we went into a hostile situation. Every time, you take a chance you aren't coming back."

"Yeah, well, that's the deal. I'm not coming back. I'm done."

Artie set his cup on one of the tables. "I think you're aware of what's been going on in the area. Some vicious monster's been having a field day, leaving bodies in its wake. We understand it's here. And we need you to help us find it."

"What makes you think I can find it?"

"Because you've got yourself a little help, don't you?" Artie smiled. "Very attractive help, in the form of one Lucy Smok of Smok Consulting."

Oliver tried to keep his expression neutral. "A local group hired her to hunt the thing, yes."

"And you belong to this local group."

Oliver didn't answer.

"Well, I'll tell you what, Benally. We'll give you twenty-four hours to decide how you want to do this. If this Smok girl is everything she's rumored to be, she should have this in the bag. It's your job to make sure she captures the creature alive. Darkrock has plans for it."

"For God's sake." Oliver tried to tamp down his

mounting outrage. "Do you have any idea what you're dealing with here? This is nothing you've ever seen before. Lucy's gone up against it twice now, and she still doesn't know what it is, but from what I can tell, it's nearly killed her both times."

"So it's *Lucy* already." Finch grinned. "Nice."

"From what you can tell?" Artie frowned. "Are you saying you didn't see it yourself?"

Oliver cleared his throat. "She's not big on keeping me in the loop. Both times, I've just seen the damage after the fact. I've tracked it, but I haven't seen it personally." He paced away from them, realizing they were already sucking him into Darkrock's orbit. "This isn't what I do anymore. And Darkrock's making a huge miscalculation if they think this thing is something they can just capture and put to their own use. It's intelligent and malevolent. And very powerful." Somewhere in the past two days, he realized, he'd come around to Lucy's point of view. The creature needed to die.

"Which is precisely why Darkrock is interested in it. This is an unprecedented opportunity to catalog a new species. Rumor is it can change form at will. That kind of ability could prove extremely useful. Revolutionary, in fact."

"It's not going to be terribly useful if it kills everyone in the facility. If you can even tranquilize it long enough to transport it there."

"You just let us worry about that. You make sure Lucy Smok doesn't kill it first. We want you to stick to her like a rat in a glue trap. No more of this 'after the fact' bullshit. The Smok enterprise has gotten in our way before. If she destroys this thing before we have a chance to study it, Darkrock leadership isn't going to be happy. There's talk of eliminating that problem."

"Is that a threat? If I don't take care of Lucy, Darkrock will?"

"It's whatever you want it to be, Benally. If the prospect of something unfortunate happening to Lucy Smok seems like it's a threat to you, well…that's for you to figure out, isn't it?"

And just like that, he was in again. Even if he managed to disappear, he'd be leaving Lucy at Darkrock's mercy. Not to mention the undergrounders. And Colt.

As soon as Artie and Finch had gone, Oliver headed back out on his "beat."

His earlier instincts proved to be right. As he circled back around toward the Bartlett, he caught sight of her watching from the shadows across the street. He'd probably made a mistake keeping close. He'd only drawn her attention to it.

She saw that he'd seen her. Even though he couldn't see her face in shadow beneath the hood of her jacket, he knew she was staring straight into him, as if she had night vision. There was something about her that seemed slightly to the left of human, now that he thought about it. Could Smok Biotech be doing the same kind of work Darkrock was? Was Lucy biologically enhanced?

"What do you think you're looking at?" Her voice carried across the empty street. Oliver almost laughed. It was such a film noir kind of moment. The femme fatale watching him watching her. The dialogue straight out of a movie from the 1940s.

"You tell me," he murmured. And he was certain from her posture that she'd heard him.

Lucy took her hand out of the pocket of her leather

jacket over the dark hoodie—she was holding a cross-bow in the other—and crossed the street. "A little late for you to be out prowling, isn't it?"

"I wouldn't call it prowling. Is that what you're doing? Prowling?"

Lucy's eyes were inscrutable within the hood. "I'm doing the job your council is paying me to do."

Oliver wanted to be objective about her. There were too many variables he wasn't sure of. What Smok International was about. How Lucy might be enhanced. Whether she meant real harm to the people he'd come to think of as "his" undergrounders. But Darkrock's implied threat had gone straight to the heart. She meant something to him. Already. And Darkrock knew it. They wouldn't have been able to manipulate him without that knowledge.

"Maybe you'd like some help with that."

"Help?"

"This thing seems to be pretty elusive, even for you. Maybe the two of us together would have more luck."

She was quiet for so long that he almost asked her if she was okay. "I thought you wanted to give it therapy."

Oliver burst out laughing. "Therapy?" Where had that come from?

"You were pretty adamant about shifters being these misunderstood creatures that didn't mean anyone harm."

"I never said this thing didn't mean anyone harm. It's pretty clear that it does. That's why we called you in."

"So you're prepared to do things my way? You're not going to get in the way when I try to kill it?"

Oliver had walked right into that one, because keeping her from killing it was precisely what he had to do.

"Have you considered that maybe it can't be killed? I mean, you said you hit it with lethal force and it just kept going. Did you hit it tonight?"

"One shot, yeah. I didn't get to use my arrows." She indicated the crossbow at her side. "They're Lucien's actually. They may be more effective than the bullets." She looked thoughtful for a moment. "Maybe I could use someone to distract it long enough for me to get off a shot."

"You mean someone to act as bait."

Lucy shrugged. "Sure. Call it bait."

He couldn't quite figure her out. Was she mocking him or offering to work together? Either way, he needed to buy some time to come up with an alternative to killing the beast that would make sense to her.

Oliver studied her. "So, do you still not sleep?"

Despite her otherwise relaxed body language, her fingers curled and uncurled around the barrel of the crossbow in an unconscious gesture of conflict. "Why?"

"I'm wide-awake, and I have a feeling that's not going to change in the next few hours. I thought we could discuss some strategy over coffee."

She gave him another of those noncommittal shrugs. He took it for agreement.

At the shop, he realized he'd left the coffee cups sitting out from Darkrock's visit. As he scooped them up, he felt Lucy's eyes on him, but she didn't comment. While he started up the coffee maker, Lucy sat on one of the ottomans. The crossbow was still clutched in her hand.

Oliver glanced up from the counter. "You expecting to need that in here?" He nodded at the weapon.

Lucy looked down at it. "I suppose not. My case is

in the car." She set it on the couch next to her. After a moment of watching him brew the coffee, she finally pulled back her hood. The shock of her cropped hair struck him all over again. It highlighted a change in her since yesterday that he couldn't put his finger on. She'd been stoic and hard to read before, but it was like she'd gone deeper. They'd been intimate—extremely intimate—and afterward she seemed to have revoked a level of trust.

The coffee was ready.

Oliver poured two cups and brought them on a tray with cream and sugar to the table next to Lucy. "I wasn't sure how you took it."

"Black."

Of course she did.

As he sat on the edge of the couch opposite, Lucy watched him over the rim of her cup. "You had company tonight."

He stiffened. Had she been watching him? *Oh, right.* The dirty cups. "Yeah, some old service buddies dropped by."

"You were in the service?"

"Marine Corps. *Semper Fi.*" He raised his cup in a salute.

"How long ago was that?"

His mouth twitched with a sardonic smile. "Are you trying to guess my age?"

"Why would I want to guess your age?"

Oliver drank his coffee, starting to regret that he'd suggested this. But there was a reason he had. "So, about the creature, I know you're set on killing it, but maybe we should rethink that, given how hard it's proving to be to kill."

"So therapy, then."

He smiled despite himself. "Not therapy. But doesn't Smok have some heavy-duty drugs that could knock it out first? We could hunt it like big game, hit it with the trank, then track it and wait for it to go down."

Lucy leaned forward on the ottoman, resting her elbows on her knees, the coffee cup still in her hand. "Is that what Darkrock wants you to do?"

Goddamn. Oliver swallowed a mouthful of too-hot coffee. How did she know about Darkrock? Unless…

He set down his cup carefully. "It was you. You told them where I was."

"Told whom?"

"Are you kidding me right now?"

"You expect me to believe Darkrock didn't know where you were?"

"I don't expect you to believe anything. I *would* like to know what you know about it, however. How did you learn about Darkrock?"

"I'm the CFO of Smok International. Of course I know about Darkrock."

"I meant…" Oliver paused. Was Darkrock part of Smok's operations? Had Smok, in fact, created it? Could they be simultaneously working for Lucy and working against her? "How long have you known who I am?"

"Since this morning. I ran a check on you through my research department. Standard operating procedure." Standard operating procedure after she slept with someone?

"And your research department shared that information with Darkrock."

Lucy's jaw was tight. "We don't share anything with Darkrock. If your people found out I was looking into you, it's because of their own flags on such searches. It's not like we're using Google."

"They're not *my* people."

"Are you denying that you work for them? You just admitted you were Oliver Benally. And they were obviously the 'service buddies' who dropped by tonight. Was that before or after you stalked me?"

Oliver got up and paced away from her, trying to employ his breathing technique. "I haven't worked for them since 2012. Since…" He turned to face her, thumbing the back of his ring. "Not since my wife was killed."

Chapter 11

Lucy's stomach dropped, and she straightened, resting her cup on her thigh. "Your wife?"

"We worked together at Darkrock. The last mission we worked was a disaster. Some vamps took out every member of my team. Including Vanessa. That's when I left the operation." Oliver's expression was grim. "I should have left earlier."

"I'm sorry." Lucy's eyes were drawn to the ring he was playing with on his right hand. It was a wedding band, and she hadn't noticed.

"Not as sorry as I am." He seemed to realize he was playing with the ring and moved his hand away, smoothing his palm along the hair at his temple.

"So you just walked away."

Oliver shrugged. "You don't exactly walk away from Darkrock. I burned down the vamp nest and let people think I'd died in the fire with the rest of the team. And they had no idea I was still alive until today. So... thanks for that."

She studied him, trying to decide whether this was

part of his cover. Maybe the whole story had been invented for this very eventuality. If it had, he was an excellent actor. His eyes looked haunted. Whether the rest of his story was invented or not, she decided there had definitely been a Vanessa.

Lucy dismissed an odd little twinge at the idea that he'd loved someone so deeply that he still wore his wedding ring. What was it to her? Nothing. *He* was nothing to her. If anything, he was a threat to her. Which did nothing to dissuade her body from tossing her brain a little reminder of how intimately it now knew his. She needed to focus on the problem at hand. Despite what she'd told him, if Darkrock knew she'd run a search on him, it probably wasn't because of a flag. Her research department's searches were undetectable. Which meant she had a mole at Smok Biotech. The prospect was chilling.

"So you're not working with Darkrock."

There was a slight hesitation before he answered. "No. And they aren't too happy about it." He was holding something back.

"Do they know about the creature I'm hunting?"

"I have to believe they know something about it, but the subject wasn't discussed."

"And you just happen to have come up with the idea for us to team up and try to subdue it instead of killing it right after they came to see you."

"You know I was never a fan of killing it. But I'm becoming a fan. I just don't know if it can be killed, based on everything you've said. If only we could figure out exactly what it is and where it came from."

Lucy had been thinking the same. She wasn't going to make any headway with the hell beast until she had more information about it. And the only way she was going to get that was from Lucien. The problem was reaching him. Only Theia could bring him out of the underworld, and Theia spent most of her time in the underworld with him. It was time to talk to the Carlisles. If anyone knew how to reach Theia, it would be Theia's sisters.

Lucy set down her coffee. "I might know someone who could give us some answers. I'll see if I can track them down." She stood and picked up the crossbow.

"Right now?" Oliver looked surprised. Had he actually thought she'd come over here to have sex with him again? Unbelievable. A couple of orgasms—admittedly above-average ones—and he thought he'd be irresistible to her. He had delusions of grandeur.

"By the time I get back to Sedona, it'll be almost four, and I need to get cleaned up and put on something more suitable." She'd worn jeans again to hit the mine, and she was beginning to feel like a schlub.

"So you're really not going to sleep."

"With you? No."

She'd left him speechless for the moment, but he recovered by the time she reached the door. "I wasn't offering."

Lucy spared him a look over her shoulder before she went out. "Yeah, you were."

Oliver stared at the closed door. *Damn.* She was something else. He couldn't help smiling to himself, as infuriating as she was. It was just as well. He had business to take care of, too. Now he had two reasons to visit Polly's Grotto. To find someplace for Colt and to find out what Polly might know about the connection between Smok International and Darkrock. Because he was convinced there was one.

He headed upstairs to shower, pausing as he undressed to peer closer into the mirror. There was a fresh mark on the skin below his left shoulder. A knot of scar tissue from a close-range bullet wound. Lucy had gotten off one shot—in the beast's shoulder. It was just as well she hadn't stayed the night.

As he'd expected, the Grotto was still open from the night before when he arrived. Apparently, the 2:30 a.m. last call didn't apply here. Oliver wasn't sure what the protocol was for getting the hostess's attention, but he didn't have to wonder for long. Something about him had already put him on her radar.

As he hovered by the entrance, a little overwhelmed by the underwater theme of the place and its fluttering blue-and-green light patterns that moved in waves across the walls and patrons alike, a partially shifted were-tiger approached him.

"My mistress requests your presence in her booth." The voice was deep and raspy through the tiger's larynx.

Oliver followed the were-tiger's glance to a woman in a sequined green gown, with hair that looked like seaweed spun from pure gold that somehow floated about her head despite it being not in water but in air. She lifted her champagne glass to him with an inviting smile.

He made his way to her booth, where a second glass was waiting for him. "I take it you're Polly."

"And you are positively delectable. Welcome to my grotto, son of Gwyn."

"Sorry, son of whom?" Maybe they'd mistaken him for someone else after all. "The name's Oliver Connery."

Polly twirled her hand in the air as she sipped her champagne. "Who cares? The more important question is what are you? And the answer to that, of course, is something nobody expects."

He was beginning to think this wasn't her first bottle of champagne. "I was told you might be able to answer a question or two for me. I'm prepared to offer a fair price for—"

"My ears!" Polly set her glass down and pressed her hands to the sides of her head, screwing her eyes shut. "You have absolutely no manners. Were you born in a bog?" After a dramatic pause, she peeked at him and moved her hands carefully away from her head. "I provide information for people who need it. Grateful recipients bestow me with *gifts*."

"My apologies."

"You said a question or two. The second, I suspect. The first, I'm absolutely in the dark about. I might even give you two answers for a single gift because I'm so curious about what that first question might be and because I'm in a generous mood." She reached across the table and squeezed his left biceps. "And you are just scrumptious. So what's question number one?"

Oliver was having trouble keeping a straight face— and keeping the heat out of it. "I'm looking for a safe house for a boy. A boy who fears for his life."

Polly raised a golden eyebrow. "Aren't there agencies for that sort of thing among the mortal world?"

"There are. But he's evidently not of the mortal world."

"I see. So he's a danger to others, no matter which world. And you want to foist him off on one of our kind rather than deal with him yourself."

"Uh…that's not exactly…" It was, though. Oliver sighed. "Shouldn't he be with his own kind?"

"You tell me, son of Gwyn." Polly laughed at his bemused expression. "At any rate, I'm afraid you're on your own with that. I'm not running an orphanage. Now, on to your second question. You want to know about a certain raven-haired beauty and her connections. Am I right?"

"You are, in fact." He wondered how she could know that. "Specifically about her company's connections with a group called Darkrock."

Polly's expression went from flirtatious to threatening, and she leaned toward him, her hand sliding down to his forearm in a hard grip. "Let me tell you something about Smok International. I happen to be old friends with the new CEO, and he would never tolerate those insidious mercenaries. As for his sister, I can't speak for whom she chooses to associate with, but I would be very surprised to find her in league with such an underhanded operation. She *is* the chief financial officer, however, and I'm absolutely baffled by all things monetary. Perhaps if there's enough money in it, she might compromise her principles. But it *would* be a compromise. And for future reference, do *not* mention that name in my grotto again."

"I…see. My apologies. And thank you for being so candid." Not that he was entirely sure what she was getting at, but it seemed she was at least trying for candid. "What do I—What would be an appropriate gift to show my appreciation for the information?"

Polly's hand was still on his arm, and she squeezed his wrist with a mock expression of remorse. "Goodness, you're adorable. I ought to feel bad accepting a gift for telling you next to nothing." She smiled brightly. "But I do like a good gift." Polly tilted her head at him. "Perhaps in your case, a kiss would do."

"A kiss? That's it?"

"Darling, if you do it right, a kiss is everything." She leaned close, expectant.

What could it hurt? Oliver leaned in to meet her lips. They were surprisingly cool and damp. Not cold, by any means, but lower than normal body temperature—and salty, like she'd been swimming in the ocean. A prism of color seemed to swirl over her skin, flowing outward from her lips where they met his, and the color encompassed her hair, which shifted through multiple hues like a color-changing LED candle. She made the kiss a great deal more intimate than he'd planned before pulling away and breathing in deeply with her lips parted and a smile on her face. He had the distinct impression she was breathing something *out* of him.

Polly put her fingers to her lips and extracted what looked like a perfect pearl from between her teeth, holding it up in the dim light. "Marvelous. Aren't you just the sweetest thing?" She dropped the pearl into her champagne glass and took a sip, the pearl glowing golden at the bottom. "I feel like I owe you a little more for such a lovely gift. Perhaps I'll answer the question you didn't think to ask."

Oliver was still fixated on the pearl and wondering where the hell it had come from. "What question would that be?"

"This is not to go beyond this room, you understand. Not to be whispered to anyone else. Least of all those nasty little friends of yours."

"Of course. And they're not my friends."

"Lucy Smok has a number of weighty responsibilities—incredibly weighty for a woman of her age, though she seems well equipped to handle them. And one of those responsibilities is protecting her brother, Lucien."

"Protecting him?" This was getting interesting. Perhaps he was about to get confirmation of the rumors about Lucien's drug addiction problem. Or worse, maybe Lucien was mentally unfit to manage a multinational corporation.

"Lucien presides over more than just Smok International. He also presides over the underworld."

Oliver's brows lifted in surprise. "You mean mob connections?"

Polly laughed and touched his hand lightly. "You're delightful. Not the mob. *The* underworld. In local parlance, he's the reigning Prince of Hell."

Oliver blinked at her, not sure he'd heard correctly. "The Prince of…"

"Hell. Or at least the underworld of medieval Christian interpretation. It's more complicated than that, but let's just say he presides over a great many things—*beings*—that don't belong in this world. By way of comparison, take a look around you. There are lots of people here who aren't human. But they do belong in this world. Things that cross over from that world to this, however, can be far more dangerous than those inhuman creatures who choose to prey on their human cousins."

It was a little much for Oliver to take in. "I'm not sure what this has to do with Lucy."

"It has everything to do with Lucy. She shares Lucien's blood. She may have avoided his inheritance—his place on the throne—but she's not entirely unmarked by the cursed strain. And her role as an infernal public servant is the guardian of the gates."

He barely had time to absorb the word *infernal* before he registered the latter half of the sentence. "The gates? Of hell?"

"If that's what you want to call it."

"What I want to call it? You're the one who's talking about hell."

"You're cute, sweetie, but I'm starting to get bored now." She emptied her champagne glass, the pearl still glistening at the bottom, and stared at him pointedly. "You're welcome."

It took him a moment to realize he was being dismissed. "Oh. Well, thank you very much for taking the time to answer my questions." Oliver rose, and Polly ignored him, reaching over the side of the booth to greet someone the were-tiger had brought by.

As he left the grotto into the surprising light of day, Oliver realized she hadn't really answered either of his questions. She'd just given him more.

Chapter 12

Lucy tried Theia's number just to cross it off her list. As she'd expected, the number was unavailable. Theia was about as out-of-range as you could get. The next best means of reaching Theia was her identical twin, Rhea. The call rolled directly to voice mail. Rhea had obviously gotten tired of Lucy using her as a go-between. That left Ione and Phoebe, the two older sisters. In Lucy's experience, Phoebe was the most approachable, even if her husband was a bit overprotective.

Phoebe answered on the first ring. "Hi, Lucy. Theia's still out of range."

Lucy was evidently becoming predictable. "I know. I've tried her number. And Rhea's. I just really need to get in touch with Lucien. It's not about the company," she added. "It's…infernal business."

Phoebe was quiet for a moment. "You don't mean some kind of infernal deal? If someone needs help with a shade or a ghost, Rafe and I are happy to offer our aid, but I'm not comfortable helping you get people to sign away their souls."

"No, it's not about getting more people into hell. It's about what's gotten out."

"Gotten *out*?" There was a pause and a muffled side conversation. "Hang on. I'm putting you on speaker. Rafe is here with me."

"Hello, Lucy."

"Rafe."

"What's this about something getting out of hell?"

"Do you remember when Carter Hamilton kept the gates open before Lucien descended?"

Phoebe groaned. "Not that bag of dicks again. Tell me he isn't back."

"No, he's safely locked away."

"You mean when Hamilton was trying to absorb hell's power," said Rafe.

"Exactly. He delayed Lucien's descent before you and Leo showed up to help. And during that delay, the gates were open both ways." Lucy realized this was the first time she'd admitted this to anyone. It felt like her own personal failing, somehow. Because she'd been susceptible to Carter's necromancy, he'd been able to control her through a step-in shade to lure Lucien into his trap.

"And things got out," Rafe said.

Phoebe cut in. "What kind of things are we talking about here?"

"Demons of various assortment. Hell beasts, in short."

"Hell beasts?"

Lucy tried to keep from sounding curt. "I can't go into all the kinds of things that are relegated to the underworld right now, but there are some things that are relatively benign and others that are absolutely antithetical to this world."

"How long have you known about this?" Rafe asked.

"Pretty much since the gates were opened. And I've been tracking them down and returning them, which is why you haven't heard about it. But there's one thing I haven't been able to catch."

"Why didn't you let anyone know?" The irritation was unmistakable in Phoebe's voice. "We could have been helping you."

"Because it's not your job." Lucy cringed at the harsh way that had come out. She hadn't wanted to snap—particularly when she was asking them for help—but her fuse was just too short right now for her to be civil. "This is what it means to be a Smok. You may not agree with our methods, but it's the job your ancestor saddled us with. Madeleine Marchant's last act was to curse our family with the responsibility for managing hell."

"Maybe Philippe Smok shouldn't have denounced her as a witch and had her burned at the stake." Phoebe was always quick with a comeback.

"Point taken. But regardless of how it came about, it *is* our responsibility, and we take that responsibility seriously."

"Some of that responsibility is Theia's now, too," Phoebe reminded her.

"Which is why I'm hoping you can help me contact her."

"She's been away for a while, so I expect she'll be surfacing before too long."

"I can't really wait for her to surface. People are dying. Is there anything at all you can think of? Maybe a spell Ione could do?"

"I don't think it works that way. Why not just have

Polly open her infamous door for you like she did for Theia when Lucien first descended?"

"I have a policy of not being indebted to my brother's ex."

"Even if people are dying?" Rafe pointed out. Maybe he was right. If it was her only option, what was a drop of blood or a tear for Polly's trinket collection next to saving lives?

"Maybe," she began.

But Phoebe interrupted. "There might be one thing."

"Yeah?"

"Theia's been known to dream-walk."

"Dream-walk?"

"She's entered Rhea's dreams a few times while she's been below, to check in on her and pass on information."

"And Rhea can do this, too?"

"Well…not exactly. But she might know how to attract Theia's attention in a dream so that she'll enter it herself."

It sounded like a long shot, but it was better than being beholden to Polly if she didn't have to be. "Could you call Rhea for me? I think she's blocking my number."

"I can do better than that." Phoebe said something muffled, as though she'd covered the mic. "Rhea just walked in the door. Hang on a minute." The phone went silent as Phoebe put her on mute.

When the sound returned, the phone no longer had the echoey quality of being on speaker. "Hi, Lucy. It's Rhea. Phoebe says you need to get in touch with Theia. How do you feel about a semipermanent tattoo?"

"A what?"

"An inkless tattoo. It causes some scarring, but it usually fades in less than a year."

"And why would I want that?"

"Because I assume you wouldn't want to permanently mark yourself with the symbols that would get Theia's attention in the dreamscape."

What Rhea proposed was a series of archetypal symbols that she would tattoo without ink onto Lucy's skin. The images were commonly used in dream interpretation, which Rhea thought Theia would be drawn to while Lucy was sleeping. Apparently, a tattoo had worked once for Rhea when she'd been trying to reach her twin. As a tattoo artist, Rhea was constantly adding ink to her skin, so permanence hadn't been an issue for her.

The idea of using scarification on her body even temporarily wasn't something Lucy was wild about—and tattoos were definitely not her thing—but it was almost certain to fade, especially if she didn't bother the wounds. Unlike tattoos with ink, inkless tattoos used as semipermanent body modification called for the opposite of meticulous follow-up care, since scarring was the goal. So if she did the careful follow-up, she would minimize the scars.

It seemed likely to be less permanent than bargaining with Polly. Lucy agreed. Rhea penciled her in for the end of the day at her tattoo shop. Lucy would have preferred to do it immediately, but Rhea insisted on honoring her existing appointments. It was just as well, since the second step of this communication method required going to sleep. Something that might prove more difficult for Lucy than getting a tattoo.

Rhea's Viking chieftain boyfriend was there when Lucy arrived. The two of them always made a striking picture together, his tall, brawny physique somehow perfectly complementing her diminutive spunk.

He gave Lucy a pointed look. "So that child-killing demon I pointed you toward—that was a hell's gate escapee."

Rhea's dark brows drew together in consternation as she pushed a wayward spike of bleached blond streaked with blue out of her eyes. "You helped her find a demon? When was this?"

"Four days ago. She said it was routine."

"I didn't actually say it was routine." Lucy shrugged off her overcoat and handed it to him. "I said it was right up your alley. It's a killer, and you track down killers that belong in hell."

"Náströnd."

"Same difference."

"I'm not so sure about that."

"At any rate, your instincts were a little off. I ended up going after a reptilian diner waitress who apparently has never hurt a fly." Lucy paused. "Well, probably definitely a fly. But nothing bigger."

"That doesn't sound right."

Lucy shrugged. "Anyway, the hell beast I was looking for found *me*."

"What is this hell beast?"

She had to fight not to roll her eyes. "That's what I'm trying to find out by contacting Theia. I need more information from Lucien."

Rhea stepped between them and steered Lucy to the back room. "You can grill her while I work, Leo. We need to get this started."

Leo followed them in to hang Lucy's coat on the coatrack and leaned back against the counter as Rhea prepped Lucy's skin. "Do you mind if I observe?" He glanced at Rhea. "You're not going to need her to disrobe, are you?"

Rhea glanced up with a patient smile. She was prepping Lucy's forearm, and Lucy had worn a T-shirt. "No, Leo. I can get to her arm just fine." Leo Ström wasn't the sharpest crayon in the box. Good thing he was so easy on the eyes.

Lucy drew back her arm. "Maybe the arm isn't the best idea after all." She didn't relish having to make sure she kept it covered for a year. She pulled her shirt up to the band of her bra. "Can we do it here, below the navel?"

"Might be a little more uncomfortable if you're sensitive there."

"I'm not sensitive anywhere." Lucy glanced at Leo. "And you can stay." Anything for a little distraction, as far as she was concerned. She could handle pain just fine, but having dozens of little needles jabbing into her skin repeatedly wasn't exactly her idea of a good time.

She and Rhea had settled on the simplest possible symbols that could convey the meaning Lucy sought, things that would call to Theia's subconscious: the Lilith mark, a crescent moon with a simple cross descending from it that both Theia and Rhea had tattooed on themselves as descendants of the demon goddess; a serpent twined around an apple to represent Lucien as the archetype of the devil; and two overlapping infinity symbols to signify twinship. With Rhea's magical ability to read tattoos like tarot cards, she could impart more details than just the symbolic meaning as she created them, a sort of reverse reading for Theia to unravel.

Getting tattooed turned out to be more uncomfortable than Lucy had imagined. She'd heard people talk about the endorphin rush, but hers never kicked in. It was only afterward that Rhea mentioned the lack of lubrication from the inkless needles being a possible factor in the level of discomfort.

Leo's pestering helped to keep her mind off it. "The information I gave you from the Hunt was that the killer you were seeking had traveled to Jerome."

"That's right." Lucy tried not to react as Rhea went over a particular spot on top of her pubic bone for the third time.

"Sorry." Rhea gave her a sympathetic shrug. "Without ink, I have to make multiple passes to make sure the scarring will be deep enough."

"I thought we didn't want it to scar."

"Not long-term, no. But the lines have to be solid and deep enough for Theia to be able to pick up the image. Otherwise, it just looks like scratches."

"So the creature wasn't in Jerome?" Leo prodded.

"No, it was, but it wasn't the only one. Apparently, Jerome is a secret haven for paranormal outcasts."

"Well, there are no other killers. You asked me to point the way to a killer." That was good to know, anyway. Maybe Oliver wasn't so far off about the community he was protecting. "You didn't send the diner waitress to hell, did you?"

"No. I was interrupted."

"But you found the killer eventually. Or it found you."

"Yes."

"But you don't know what it is."

Rhea took her foot off the tattoo machine pedal and poked Leo's calf with the toe of her shoe. "Leo, will you leave her alone?"

"It's fine." Lucy looked up at Leo while Rhea returned to her work. "I've tangled with it three times now. I've never dealt with anything like it before. It looks like a huge wolf, but it's like no werewolf I've ever encountered, and it's able to shift without effort."

Leo frowned. "And you're sure it's from hell? Because it sounds a bit like Fenrir, the monstrous wolf brother of the serpent Jörmungandr." He drew up his sleeve and flexed his arm, making the knotted serpent tattoo around his right biceps undulate.

"Leo, stop posing," Rhea said without looking up. "She's not interested in your snake."

"It told me it was from hell," said Lucy. "Or at least, that it's hunting something that escaped hell, and it's not of this world. If I manage to reach Lucien, hopefully I can find out more definitively."

Leo nodded thoughtfully. "Let me know what you learn. I'd be interested to know what has those qualities."

Rhea released the foot pedal and lifted the needles off Lucy's skin. "All done."

While she cleaned up, Rhea gave Lucy instructions on how to use the tattoos. "It'll be easiest to reach Theia if you're experienced with lucid dreaming, but as long as you keep her name in mind as you fall asleep, you should make contact even if you lose track of the dream thread. She'll be able to pick it up from the tattoos."

"The dream thread?"

"It's like a story. If you're directing the story, the flow of the dream follows the thread you spin. Maybe a better way to think of it is as a tapestry. The picture takes shape on the tapestry as you weave the thread. All you need to do is give it your intent, that you need to reach Theia so you can speak to Lucien."

Lucy wasn't experienced. She barely even remembered her dreams. But Smok Biotech had developed a drug just for the purpose of lucid dreaming. It had the added benefit of being a powerful sleep aid.

"What do I owe you?" she asked as Rhea started to close up shop.

"Nothing. Lucien's family, and that makes you family. And I don't charge family."

Lucy thanked her awkwardly, never quite sure what to do with unearned generosity. Before heading home, she drove up to the lab in Flagstaff and picked up a sample of the dreaming compound.

It was almost midnight by the time she was back home and ready to try it out. She lay staring at the ceiling in her bedroom, convinced the sleep aid was faulty. Maybe she was just immune to them. Her wyvern hormones had wreaked havoc with her metabolism. *Think of Theia*, she reminded herself, and yawned. What was the point of thinking of Theia if she never fell asleep?

Something flicked at her ear, a moth or a mosquito that had gotten in when she opened the door, and Lucy brushed it away only to hear what sounded like a sigh beside her.

Warm breath exhaled against her ear, and something whispered in the darkness, "Shall I huff and puff and blow your house in?"

Lucy sprang from the bed and turned on the light, but nothing was there. All this stupid drug had done was make her hallucinate. And the raw flesh on her belly where Rhea had tattooed her was starting to burn. She pulled up her shirt to take a look and gasped. A bright orange glow began to trace over the lines as if molten lava were flowing through them. Instead of the images Rhea had tattooed, however, they were rearranging themselves and forming new lines, spelling out in a stylized script, *Veni, vidi, vici—I came, I saw, I conquered.*

Had Rhea's magic animated the tattoos somehow? And what did the glowing letters mean?

They began to change once more. *I huffed, I puffed, I blew your house down.* What the hell?

She realized she was reading the words even though they ought to have been upside down and backward from her vantage point. Lucy went to the large bathroom mirror. They were readable there as well, as if they weren't in reverse.

"Of course they aren't in reverse," her reflection said to her in a tone of irritation she was all too familiar with using. "You're dreaming."

"I'm dreaming." Lucy let the shirt fall back over the glowing tattoos. "Holy shit. It worked." Now what was she supposed to do? Weave the dream thread. What tapestry was she trying to create? What was the story she was trying to tell? She was already losing track. Lucy used the burning sensation of the tattoos to ground herself for a moment and think. She needed to find Theia and ask her to bring Lucien home so she could find out what the hell beast was.

Her reflection disappeared from the mirror in front of her, leaving her in the dark. Something growled behind her, and the hairs rose on the back of her neck.

There was just one problem with this lucid dream. The hell beast was in here with her.

Chapter 13

The bathroom disappeared, and Lucy was running through a dark, overgrown forest, with the hell beast's warm breath at her back. She managed to stay just ahead of it while it panted and snuffled behind her on all fours, but the grade changed, the forest sloping uphill, and Lucy tripped and caught her shirt on the thorns of a briar as she threw her arms out to steady herself. As she yanked the fabric away from the thorns, the hell beast leaped and knocked her onto her back, standing over her with its tongue lolling in a grotesque grin.

"Did you really think you could outrun me?" He shifted into human form in the blink of an eye. Lucy's heart sank. It was Oliver. She hadn't wanted it to be him. Oliver licked her throat and grinned down at her. "You're supposed to say, 'My, what a long tongue you have, Grandmother.' And then I say, 'The better to eat you out with, my dear.'"

"You're disgusting."

"Am I? You're the one who threw yourself at a hell beast. You knew it was me."

"I did not throw myself at you."

"I notice you're not contesting the second half of that assertion. You sought me out, not because you wanted to do your job, as you keep insisting, not to return me to hell, but because you wanted hell itself inside you. You couldn't be the mistress of hell. You're always going to be second-best, second-rate, the second sex. That one little pesky chromosome, and Lucien stole it all from you."

"What do you know about it?" She'd never told him anything about Lucien. "Get the hell off me." Lucy kneed him in the groin and rolled out from under him as he doubled over onto his side. She scrambled to her feet, but he grabbed her by the ankle and yanked her back down to the ground. Taking advantage of the fact that he was still compromised by the pain radiating from his groin, she kicked upward with her free foot as he tried to climb over her, landing a solid kick to his jaw while she brought her fist and forearm to the back of his elbow. The joint made a nauseating pop as she dislocated it.

His face transformed into the wolfish snout as he roared with pain and fell back. Lucy got to her feet and stood over him. This wasn't the hell beast. As confident as she was in her own abilities, she'd been no match for it physically in the waking world. She was letting her own subconscious get the best of her when she should be concentrating on the dream thread.

"You think you have this whole dream figured out, don't you?" the Oliver-wolf growled. "The problem with you is that you think you're smarter than everyone else."

"That's not a problem, you ass. It's just true. And

right now I'm getting in my own way. I'm not here to psychoanalyze myself. I'm here to talk to Theia Dawn."

The rest of Oliver transformed into the massive shape of the wolf, eyes glowing red, salivating as it rose onto its haunches and came toward her. "I am Death. I am Sex. And I am going to devour you."

Lucy stood her ground. "Good luck with that. I'm just going to wait here for Theia."

The hell beast paused in its low, stalking stride and began to convulse, its underbelly splitting down the center as if a sword had sliced it, and a female arm and leg emerged from the wound. Lucy watched with slightly nauseous fascination as Theia climbed out of the empty carcass.

"Lucy!" Her sister-in-law threw her arms around her but seemed to remember in short order that Lucy was *not* the hugging type and let go. "What are you doing here? I thought I was dreaming of Rhea, and the whole wolf thing confused me, because Leo has a wolf-dog aspect, but it's nothing like this."

"So you thought you'd do a classic Red Riding Hood entrance."

Theia grinned. "Like it?" She brushed a little bit of wolf viscera from her checked skirt. The naturally dark chestnut bob that made her look as different from her twin as it was possible to be and still be identical peeked out from beneath a classic red hooded cape.

"Very nice."

The grin faded, and Theia hooked arms with Lucy beneath her cape, walking her away from what now looked more like a cartoon corpse. "But you wouldn't have gone to these lengths to reach me if something wasn't really wrong. What is it? What's happened?"

"I need to talk to Lucien. The breach Carter Hamilton took advantage of when he was trying to absorb hell's power has had unintended consequences."

Theia nodded. "Lucien has been having a hell of a time—pardon the pun—keeping the books straight. We've noted all the creatures you've sent back, and it's very much appreciated."

"There's one so far that I can't handle—the one I was dreaming of just now—and I need to know how to kill it."

Theia slowed and glanced back at the hell beast. "A werewolf?"

"It's not an ordinary werewolf. It shifts form without effort, and Soul Reaper bullets don't do a thing."

"You've shot it?"

"At least four times point-blank."

"That's not good."

The menacing woods landscape Lucy had dreamed up was starting to lose stability around them, unraveling at the edges. The wolf's body was gone, and trees were disappearing.

"You're waking up," said Theia. "I'll see you soon." She skipped away down the disappearing path in her red hooded cape.

Lucy opened her eyes and found herself on her bedroom floor. In her struggle with the Oliver-wolf, she'd apparently fallen right off the bed. After a moment, she realized the sound of knocking had woken her. Someone was at the front door.

She picked herself up and smoothed her hair with a glance in the hall mirror before opening the door to find Lucien and Theia on her doorstep.

Lucien gave her his lopsided James Spader smirk

that he didn't think anyone knew was carefully cultivated. "Theia thought you might be hungry after all that dreaming."

Theia held out a basket covered in a red-and-white-checked towel.

Lucy looked under the towel as she let them in. "Cupcakes and lattes. That's a modern twist on the fairy tale."

Theia grinned. "It was all we could get on short notice."

"How did you guys get here so quickly?"

"It wasn't that quick. Did you just wake up? It's been several hours since you left the dream."

Lucy shrugged. "I guess I needed the sleep." She took the basket to the kitchen table and passed out the lattes, taking a cupcake for herself.

Lucien sipped his coffee as he sat, studying Lucy for a moment. "Something's different. Are you wearing makeup?"

Theia shoved his arm playfully. "Stop teasing. It looks great, Lucy. When did you cut it? It was still long in your dream."

Lucy's hand went to the back of her hair self-consciously. "Yesterday. I just got tired of washing it."

"Ah." Lucien nodded sagely. "That's what's different. You've stopped washing your hair."

"Very funny, Lulu."

"Don't call me Lulu. I'm the King of Hell."

Lucy raised an eyebrow. "Oh, you've been promoted, I see."

"Only his ego," said Theia. "So, Lucien, tell her about the list."

Lucy sipped her latte. "The list?"

"I've been keeping a list of all the hell fugitives still at large," said Lucien. "There's nothing like the thing you described to Theia. There's a pack of hellhounds missing, four of them, but they're juveniles. They wouldn't be able to cause this kind of trouble. In fact, they're usually quite gentle unless someone's directing them to attack. And I'm pretty sure even a regular bullet would do some damage given how young they are. Four Soul Reapers and it walks away? Not a chance."

She'd gone to all this trouble of sitting through an uncomfortable tattoo and scarring her skin and subjecting herself to an untested psychotropic drug for nothing.

Lucy set down her cup forcefully. "Then what the hell is it?"

"Don't get bitchy. I came all the way from hell to try to help you. But I need some more information if I'm going to be able to figure this out. Tell me everything you know about it. Everything it's done so far."

Lucy described her encounters and the incidents reported in Jerome but left out her suspicions about Oliver. "I thought maybe the Soul Reaper serum would work better with the crossbow, so I took that with me yesterday to the mine, but the thing moves too fast for me to line up a shot."

Lucien's head shook as he swallowed a sip of coffee. "I don't think the arrows would be any more efficient than the bullets, to tell you the truth." He scratched his head, considering. "I would almost think this thing isn't physically in this plane if it weren't for the fact that it's obviously having physical effects on the living."

"Why do you say that?"

"The way it shifts when it chooses to and appears where it wants to when it wants to—it's almost like this thing operates purely on will."

"You mean a projection," said Theia. "Like Carter's

little trick of crashing Phoebe's wedding last spring and his stunts in luring you to the Chapel of the Holy Cross to take advantage of your transformation."

Lucy frowned, watching the paper cup as she rotated it slowly on the table. "You don't think Carter could be behind this?"

"Projecting his will from the underworld?" Lucien shook his head. "No. That isn't possible. And if this thing is interacting with the physical world, then the method of magical projection Carter was using before wouldn't apply."

Lucy ate a bite of her cupcake, pondering how much more she wanted to tell him. "What about Darkrock?"

His eyes narrowed. "What about them?"

"Could they have manufactured something like this?"

Theia glanced from Lucy to Lucien. "What's Darkrock?"

Lucien's jaw was tight. "They're opportunists. Paramilitary contractors that specialize in the paranormal." He studied Lucy. "What makes you think they could be involved?"

"I had a run-in with a guy who claims to be ex-Darkrock, but I have a feeling he's not so ex. He's on the secret Jerome town council that hired me to track the creature. When I found out about his involvement with Darkrock, I got to thinking…what if they created it and released it at the same time the gates were open?"

"How would they have known the gates would open?"

"Carter," said Theia with a sigh.

Lucien nodded thoughtfully. "It's a possibility. I'd be surprised if their research had progressed to the point where they could do that kind of gene manipulation—

and frankly, I'd be a bit disappointed that Smok Biotech hadn't beaten them to it."

"Lucien." Theia glared at him.

"I mean the ability, of course. Not that we'd do it."

"But they experiment on the creatures—and people—they capture," Lucy reminded him. "So if anyone were to have progressed to that point, it would be them."

Theia shuddered. "That's horrifying."

"That's why we don't do business with Darkrock," Lucien snapped. He grabbed Theia's hand and gave it a reassuring squeeze as soon as he'd done it. "Sorry. I just loathe their business model. They're despicable." He nodded at Lucy as Theia stroked his fingers with hers in an irritating newlywed PDA. "I'll try to find out more about what kind of creature might be capable of all this and get back to you—through Theia if I'm not able to get away myself. In the meantime, see if you can find out more about this Darkrock guy. If Darkrock is behind this, his role in bringing you to Jerome is very concerning."

Lucy nodded, focusing on her latte so her face wouldn't give away anything more about him. "I'm already on it. And thank you—both—for coming when I needed you." Something in her face or her words must have betrayed her anyway. Lucien knew her too well.

"Theia, can I have a minute with Lucy before we go?"

Theia smiled quizzically. "Sure. I'll just take a little walk around the complex and give you guys some time together."

Lucy tried to look nonchalant as Theia stepped outside. "What's up?"

Lucien frowned. "Lu. This is me. What happened?"

"What?" She gave him an irritated squint. "Nothing happened."

"Then why did I find a message from Fran on my phone when I arrived this morning?"

Lucy groaned and dropped her head forward on her crossed arms on the table. "She swore she wasn't going to tell you anything."

"She didn't. But you just walked right into that one."

"I hate you, Lucien," she said into her arms.

"That sounds a little more like you, but it's too little, too late. So out with it. Does whatever happened have something to do with your new look?"

Lucy raised her head. "You don't have any idea what you left me with, do you?"

"What I left you with?"

"The Smok legacy. Madeleine's curse. For you, it was a onetime deal. This isn't your true form in this plane. It's only with Theia that you can walk around in human skin."

"It's not exactly a party being a monster in the world of the living, babe."

She fixed him with a piercing look, letting her eyes shift. "You don't say."

Lucien's face registered surprise. "I thought Fran had you on a management regimen with the anti-transformative. Are you still shifting?"

"She does, but it's cyclical. Monthly, to be precise. And my hormones are all messed up, and I jumped a guy I barely knew, and he's Darkrock, and I think…" She stopped just short of saying she thought he was the hell beast. "I don't know what I think anymore."

"You…wait. You slept with the guy from Darkrock? The one who lives in Jerome?"

Lucy growled in answer and lowered her head to her arms once more.

"And what does this have to do with your hair?"

She stayed silent for a moment until frustration hurled it out of her. "I hacked it all off because I'm a *horrible* person, Lucien, and it was less drastic than cutting myself."

"Lu." His hand rested on her shoulder, and Lucy shook him off. "You are not a horrible person."

"Oh, come on. I'm the CFO of Smok International, and I've spent my life convincing people to sell their souls for some temporary peace, and I'm self-centered and arrogant, and I hate people. And they hate me."

"Lucy. That's not true. You do not hate people."

An unexpected ripple of laughter escaped her. "You suck, Lucien."

"I know. It runs in the family. Will you please stop talking to the tabletop and look at me?"

With a sigh, she straightened and met his eyes.

"I know you want everyone to think you're some cold, unapproachable bitch. That's the persona you've built, and that's fine. You don't have to let people know you. But when you start buying into the fiction you project to everyone else, you're not doing yourself any favors. Take it from me. I had everyone so convinced I was a lazy, arrogant asshole that I almost became one until Theia saw through my act. You and I didn't exactly get a lot of positive reinforcement or affection growing up. But we are decent human beings—even if we aren't entirely human." Lucien sighed. "Look, I know I'm not going to convince you to like yourself with a little pep talk. But at least cut yourself some slack. And take your damn meds."

"Ha!"

"And incidentally, I think the haircut looks great."

"Fran fixed it."

"Will you promise me something?"

"What?"

"Don't do anything Fran can't fix."

Chapter 14

Regardless of Lucy's existential crisis, Oliver knew more than he was saying, and Lucy intended to get some answers out of him this morning. After Lucien and Theia departed, she took her time rebuilding the physical presentation of her "public persona." Lucien was right that she needed to come off like a cold, unapproachable bitch. Given her age—and her sex—it was the only way to be taken seriously in her role, whether as corporate mogul, soul negotiator or infernal exterminator. To that end, she needed the proper attire. The sloppy jeans-and-T-shirt look had been an outward sign of her slipping control, and her tailored suits were the opposite.

She'd been wearing them since her senior year in high school, refusing to wear the little pleated skirts and knee socks of her school uniform. She had also refused to buy women's suits, because somehow when the word *woman* was added, it was no longer a business suit but a "pantsuit," as if pants were understood to be a form of playing dress-up as a serious person—in other words, a man—and straying from the proper feminine attire in a way that wearing pants without a matching jacket wasn't. Women's suits also had useless pockets and cheap stitching and idiotic cuts. Instead, Lucy commissioned all her suits from a bespoke men's tailor.

Oliver wasn't in when she arrived—some young blonde Lucy had never seen before was working the counter—and Lucy offered to wait. Her professional look evidently convinced the girl at the counter that whatever business she had with Oliver, Lucy must be too important to waste time sitting in a coffee shop waiting for him. Lucy was about to tell her not to worry about it when the girl told her where Oliver had gone.

"He had some boxes he needed to drive out to his storage unit, if you want to try to catch him there. I'm not sure how long he'll be or if he's coming straight back."

"Is that the facility over on Dundee Lane? Where the fire was the other day?"

"It must be. That's the only one around, unless he has a unit in Cottonwood."

It seemed a little odd that Oliver would suddenly be spending time at the storage facility. He'd been acting peculiar when she saw him there, and it wasn't just because she'd encountered him unexpectedly in firefighter mode.

Lucy thanked the girl and drove down the side of the mountain toward Clarkdale, the autumn light gorgeous on the stacked-rock walls lining the road. At the storage facility, the attendant didn't even balk at giving such an official-looking person a map to a customer's unit. Lucy left her car parked in the lot in front of the office and walked to it. A pickup truck was parked outside it, and the roll-up door to the unit was half-raised, as if someone didn't want passersby to see inside. What was Oliver hiding in there?

She ducked quietly under the door, expecting to catch him bending over crates of black market weapons or drugs. It took her a moment to process the scene. Oliver was seated on the corner of a storage bin talking to a skinny kid eating a sandwich on a makeshift bed.

Before she could even say Oliver's name, the boy had leaped to his feet with a look of abject terror and scrambled toward the door, and as he ducked to scuttle under it, his appearance changed swiftly. A skinny boy in baggy hand-me-downs crawled under the door, but a half-starved juvenile white wolf with red-tipped ears loped away on the other side, leaving the clothing behind.

"Colt, wait!" Oliver threw the door upward and ran after it, but the wolf had already scaled the wall and taken off into the hills. "Goddammit!" Oliver slammed his fist into the metal wall of the nearest unit and hissed another expletive as he wrung out his hand. "Do you realize what you've done?"

"Looks to me like I scared off a werewolf you've been protecting. How long have you been hiding him here?"

"He's a child, goddammit! And I swear to God, if you do anything to hurt that boy, I will hunt you down myself. Our working truce will be over."

"What the hell makes you think I would hurt a child?"

"Because he's not a human child, and to you, apparently, that makes him prey."

Too furious to respond, Lucy walked away from him.

Oliver pursued her. "Are you going to tell me you don't think he's a menace to decent human society? That he doesn't need to be put down?"

Lucy whirled on him. "How the hell would I know whether he's a menace? You've been keeping him here like a pet. How long has he been here? You think keeping a child, human or otherwise, in a five-by-ten metal box is some kind of magnanimous gesture?"

"Oh, so you're just concerned about his welfare? Seems a little out of character for you and your *vast experience*. According to you, rogue werewolves are never benign. They only cause chaos and destruction."

Lucy opened her mouth and closed it again, thoroughly irritated to have her own words quoted back at her—and a bit impressed that he'd apparently memorized them.

"Nothing to say to that, I see."

"This clearly isn't a werewolf, and I doubt he's gone rogue."

The angry heat in his eyes cooled for a moment. "What makes you think he isn't a werewolf?"

Lucy folded her arms. "Because he shifted at will, just like our killer wolf."

His outburst of laughter was genuine. "You think Colt is our killer wolf?"

"Of course I don't. He's a boy."

"I see. So you think he'll grow *up* to be the same thing. May as well just put him down now to save time, then, right?"

"No, I think he's a hellhound."

Something seemed to click behind his eyes. "And you'd know, I suppose."

"Just what is that supposed to mean?"

"Well, you're Lucien Smok's sister. And Lucien, as I understand it, is the head demon currently reigning in hell."

Prickling cold raced over her skin. She'd been extremely careful to control the flow of information about Lucien. "Who told you that?"

"Are you going to deny it?"

"I'm not obligated to confirm or deny any such absurdity to you. I want to know who's spreading this rumor about my brother."

Oliver glared at her wordlessly and yanked down the door of the storage unit before turning to step up into his truck.

"So you're just not going to answer me."

Oliver slammed the truck door and started the engine. "I'm not obligated to confirm or deny where I heard it. Have a nice day."

Oliver spent the better part of the day driving through the hills around Jerome and down into the valleys on either side looking for any sign of Colt, but the boy had obviously had plenty of practice avoiding humans in the time he'd been on the run. He hadn't seen Colt shape-shift before today, but Lucy was right, he'd simply shifted from one form to the other as he ran, like a chameleon donning camouflage. Was Lucy also right about him being a hellhound? Goddamn, she was frustrating as hell.

He laughed at the inadvertent pun. She was frustrating and infuriating and self-righteous, and it was a beautiful thing to behold. From one moment to the next, he couldn't decide whether he wanted to challenge her to a throw down in hand-to-hand combat or blurt out how goddamn much he wanted her, regardless of whether she was in cahoots with Darkrock or not—or in league with hell, for that matter. She made him feel like an inexperienced adolescent and an over-the-hill loser at the same time.

He gave up and called it a day, heading back to the shop to relieve Kelly. She looked frazzled, and from the state of the tip jar, it had been a big tourist day in town. It always was around the holidays. Oliver emptied the jar and gave her the lot and told her he'd close up.

As he emptied the espresso machine, the bell tinkled on the front door. Oliver groaned. It was five minutes until closing, and he'd hoped to get things cleaned up and shut down so he could get back out and search for Colt. He had a feeling he might find him in one of the old shafts after dark.

He turned with a plastered-on welcoming smile and found Lucy staring back at him. "What are you doing here?"

"Did you find the kid?"

"No. No thanks to you."

"I talked to my brother, the Prince of Hell, and he says the kid's part of a missing pack. There are four of them altogether, all juveniles, and they're not equipped to be on their own in our world."

"Four of them?" Oliver set down his cleaning rag on the counter. "So you're admitting that Lucien is a demon."

"I'd like to keep that from becoming common knowledge, so if you wouldn't mind telling me where you heard it—"

"From a siren. She owns—"

"Oh, I know all about Polly." Lucy came toward the back of the shop, looking relieved. "I thought maybe Darkrock had figured it out."

"If they did, they didn't say anything to me."

"But Polly did." Lucy slid onto one of the stools at the counter and swiveled to face him, one leg crossed over the other, her elbows—in her expensive and very businesslike suit jacket—resting on the edge of the counter. "What brought you to Polly's? Checking up on me?"

"No, I went to see if I could find some kind of safe house for Colt."

"And did you?"

"No. She said she wasn't running an orphanage."

"So how did Lucien come up?"

Oliver put his hands in his pockets and shrugged. "She kind of guessed I was curious about you, I suppose."

"Oh, you're curious about me?"

"You are a bit of a puzzle."

"I'm not a puzzle. You're just threatened by me."

Oliver's jaw dropped. "I'm *threatened* by you?"

"Oh, please. I kicked your ass the first time we met. And then I showed you up in front of your council with my knowledge of shape-shifters."

"You did not show me up. And you just caught me off guard that first night. I'm more than a match for you."

"Oh, really?" Lucy hopped off the stool and took off her jacket, tossing it on the counter. "You wanna go?"

"Do I *wanna go*?" Oliver laughed in disbelief. "What the hell are you—" His breath cut off with a grunt as Lucy punched him lightly in the gut. "Goddammit, Lucy."

"Come on, let's see what you've got."

"I'm not going to fight you."

Now she was rolling up her sleeves.

"Lucy—"

She ducked in toward him, her fist in a sharp extended-knuckle position, with a jab aimed at his right clavicle.

Oliver stepped back with his right foot to avoid it and swung upward in a block with his left arm, but Lucy's move had been a feint, and she hooked her foot around his front leg and yanked him off balance as she dropped low for a sweep. Oliver ducked and rolled instead, darting up to tackle her at the waist and take her down as she turned. He narrowly missed having his windpipe punched.

Lucy rolled with him, using his weight to her advantage, and came up with one knee against his sternum as he landed on his back, her right arm poised for a strike. Instead of grabbing for it or blocking the punch, Oliver lowered his arms to the floor.

Lucy paused. "What are you doing?"

"Refusing to fight you. If you feel like punching me in the face to prove your point, go ahead." It was like dealing with a weird school yard bully who insisted on picking a fight, and Oliver wasn't having any of it. He voiced the thought that accompanied the image. "You're like one of those kids in grade school who keeps punching girls in the arm because he likes them."

"It's pretty weird to compare yourself to a defenseless schoolgirl." Lucy scowled. "And I do not like you."

"Oh, you do so. You just can't admit it without a fight first. And I don't feel like fighting you." He stretched his arms wide. "So have at it."

"What did you give Polly?"

"What?" She'd thrown him again, only mentally this time. "I didn't give Polly anything. What are you talking about? What does she even have to do with anything?"

"She's a siren. She never gives away anything for free. I just want to know what you gave her for the information."

Oliver was dumbfounded. Did all of this actually have something to do with the fact that he'd gone to the siren? "I didn't give her anything. I mean, she asked for a kiss—"

"You gave her a kiss?" Lucy's pale eyes had darkened.

Was she actually jealous? His head was spinning. "Yes, I gave her a kiss. It seemed like the polite thing to do."

"You very politely handed over a piece of your soul."

"Oh, come on."

Lucy moved her knee off his chest. "I'm not kidding."

Oliver sat up. "What would she do with a piece of my soul?"

"I don't know. Maybe nothing. She likes to keep her little 'trinkets' in case she needs them later. But that's a pretty costly piece of information you bought."

"So that's why you've been trying to beat me up? To get information out of me about what transpired between Polly and me? I already told you what I learned from her."

"She guessed that you wanted to know more about me, so she told you more about Lucien."

Oliver shrugged. "Which really doesn't tell me anything about you—except she did mention that you guard the gates of hell. I guess that's why you've been hunting this thing. It escaped from hell, like Colt."

Lucy straightened and stood. "Yes."

Oliver stared up at her. "I feel like that's supposed to be significant, that you guard the gates of hell, but I really don't get it."

"My brother rules hell because he has infernal blood."

He studied her for a moment. "And you…"

"Have infernal blood."

Oliver got to his feet. "You're telling me you're a demon?"

"A demi-demon, if you want to get technical."

"Okay."

"Okay?"

"Am I supposed to run screaming or something?"

Lucy threw her hands in the air. "Well, a normal person would."

"Well, thank God I've never been accused of being normal."

Before Lucy could respond, the little bell on the door handle jingled. He'd forgotten to lock up.

Kelly peered around the door and smiled tentatively at them. "I left my purse. I'll just run in back and get it."

"No problem. I was just about to close up." Oliver discreetly wiped the dust off the seat of his pants while Kelly dashed into the back. Good thing she hadn't shown up a few minutes earlier. That would have been awkward.

She returned with the purse strapped over her shoulder. "You guys looked busy when I came by, so I went to Rags & Riches for a little bit. Have a good night."

Oliver groaned as she closed the door behind her. At least they hadn't been naked wrestling. As much as he'd have preferred that, to be honest.

Lucy was still staring at him warily, as if she expected him to throw her out. Oliver walked to the door and locked it and pulled the shades.

Lucy's eyes were suspicious as he walked back toward her. "What are you doing?"

"Making sure we aren't interrupted. I thought I might give you a little piece of my soul."

Chapter 15

Lucy didn't stop him as he stepped in for the kiss. *Dammit*. He was right. She'd been picking a fight like some stupid, awkward adolescent. She did like him, and she wasn't at all accustomed to the feeling. For that matter, she couldn't remember ever having sex with the same man twice. Sex was for releasing tension, getting an itch scratched, and that was it.

She melted into Oliver as he slid his arms around her, ignoring the part of her brain that was reciting a litany of why giving in to her attraction for Oliver was dangerous, could compromise her integrity in doing her job, why she didn't deserve to be desired because she was bitchy and cold and picked childish fights. And had infernal blood—but not, as her dream-id hell beast had pointed out, enough infernal blood to be worthy of hell's throne.

She told her brain to suck it and indulged in the taste and texture of Oliver's mouth and the feel of his skin as she slipped her arms over his shoulders and curled her fingers into the hair at the back of his neck.

His hands had moved from caressing her to studiously, methodically undoing the buttons on her shirt, which he tugged from her waistband to get to the last of them. She shivered as he reached the bottom button and laid open the shirt, his hands inside the shirttails lightly stroking her sides.

To Lucy's disappointment, Oliver paused and released her mouth. "What are these?" His thumbs brushed over the healing marks of Rhea's artwork peeking out over the top of her waistband.

"Oh." Lucy hadn't expected anyone to see them. "Inkless tattoos." She sucked in her breath as Oliver unzipped the pants for a better view. "They were… ceremonial. They're not permanent."

"They're beautiful." He dropped to his haunches and kissed the top of one hip bone, letting his mouth linger and intensifying the shiver still rippling through her.

"My sister-in-law's sister…"

Oliver paused and looked up. "What?"

"Nothing. Never mind."

He returned his attention to the tattoos, kissing his way down from them to the band of her underwear. His mouth hovered over the fabric, damp heat from his breath drawing damp heat from between her thighs, and she gasped as he closed his mouth over the crotch of the panties, pressing his tongue between the cleft and against her clit.

Lucy closed her eyes, falling under his spell again, ready to throw caution to the wind, ready to break all her rules. Her irritating, rational brain was like a trapped animal rattling its cage in futility. *Don't do it. (Shut up.) You can't trust him. (Who cares?) You're pathetic.* She continued to ignore the voice as Oliver slipped her underwear down. *You're on your period.* Her higher brain seized on that one.

Eyes snapping open, she took a stumbling step backward.

Oliver was on his knees, looking puzzled. "What's the matter?"

"I'm on my period."

He blinked up at her with a sly smile. "I'm not seeing the part where that's a problem." Lucy's eyes widened, and Oliver laughed. "Honestly. I don't mind."

But she was already pulling things up and zipping things and putting herself back into place, feeling awkward. "I do."

Oliver straightened. "Okay. No worries." He watched her button her shirt. "I'm sorry. I didn't mean to upset you."

"You didn't upset me."

"You seem upset."

"I am not upset!" Lucy sighed and combed her fingers through the swoop of hair in front of her eyes. "Sorry. I am upset. I'm upset with myself."

Oliver studied her quizzically, as if she were a new species he'd encountered unexpectedly in the wild. "What for? You haven't done anything wrong."

"For wanting you." The words came out too loud and harshly, as if it were a condemnation of him instead of herself, and Lucy was horrified to feel tears burning behind her eyes. Worse, she could tell from his expression that he could see it. She turned away from him, blinking rapidly, and grabbed her coat from the counter.

When she turned back, he had his hands in his pockets, watching her with a frown. "I don't really understand what's going on here."

"Nothing's going on. I just made a mistake."

"By wanting me."

She shoved back her bangs in frustration. "No—it's not about you. It's about me. I have responsibilities— to Smok International, to your council. To the people of this town and this state."

"To yourself?"

She ignored that. "It's partly my fault that this hell beast is even in our dimension. It's here because a necromancer held the gates open to absorb hell's energy and prevent my brother from descending until the necromancer had gotten as much power as he wanted. And that necromancer used a shade—an unanchored spirit of the recent dead—to control me and lure Lucien into his trap. So for those few minutes before the necromancer was defeated, the gates swung both ways. And I've been tracking down every demon that escaped ever since. This is one of the last, and it's the worst. And while I'm indulging my sexual urges, someone else could be dying."

Oliver looked down at his feet, his forehead creased in thought. "I see. So I'm distracting you." He nodded thoughtfully and glanced up again. "Though I have to say that, from my end, at least, it's a little more than just sexual urges."

For some reason, the idea that it was more than sex made her cheeks warm with embarrassment in a way that sex itself did not.

"I think about you all the time. Half the time, it's because I'm furious with you." His mouth curved in a slight smile. "But you've gotten under my skin, Lucy Smok. And that doesn't happen to me very often. And if I've gotten under yours, even half that much, maybe you owe it to yourself to examine why you think you don't deserve that." He held up his hand before she could refute the statement. "Because that's what I see all over your face. That you think desire—whether it's for sexual pleasure or even just companionship—is selfish. And I wish I could confront whoever taught you that and give them a damn piece of my mind."

Lucy was speechless. She pulled on her jacket slowly, trying to formulate a response, any response.

"So that's it? You're leaving again?"

"I have a hell beast to kill. But I will. Examine it."

"It?"

"Why I don't deserve to desire or be desired."

Oliver frowned. "No…why you *think* you don't deserve to."

"Same thing."

His head shook definitively. "Nope. Not even close." He stepped in toward her once more before she could move past him, a question in his eyes as he brought his hand to the side of her neck and stroked his thumb along her jaw. "Am I wrong in thinking you feel what I feel? Just tell me if I am, and I'll keep my distance. I don't want to be that guy. Tell me you want me to back off, and I will. No hard feelings. I'll respect your boundaries."

Lucy closed her eyes for a moment, his scent and his touch making her heart beat faster and her breath quicken, everything inside her crying out for him—except for that holdout, that one corner of her brain saying she was stupid to let go and fall. She could regain her professional footing here, put up her wall. Feel safe. Feel nothing.

"You're not," she said.

His expression was puzzled when she opened her eyes. "I'm not?"

"That guy. And you're not wrong."

With both hands framing her face, he lowered his head and brought his lips to hers, and she was ready to lose herself in him, to tumble into the unknown territory of trust and emotional surrender and unfettered desire. But the kiss was brief and tender, almost chaste. No, definitely not *chaste*, but it was different from the frantic, overwhelming kisses they'd shared. It was a promise that there was more to come. He would be there. There was no rush.

But now he was all business, moving aside to let her pass. She'd almost forgotten she was leaving. She buttoned her coat, trying to adjust her internal compass as he walked her to the door.

"Have you considered my suggestion about teaming up?" he asked as they reached the front. "This thing has eluded capture twice—"

"Three times."

"Three?"

"It attacked me the morning I met you, right after I left Jerome. I stopped for gas in Clarkdale, and it was waiting for me."

"You never told me that."

"I wasn't working for you then."

"You're not working for me now. You're working for the council. And I think the cat's pretty much out of the bag that my experience makes me at least tactically qualified to help hunt."

She turned back at the door and studied him. Was it experience or current job skills?

He seemed amused by the way she was sizing him

up. "I *am* the one who recommended Smok Consulting to the council after all."

Lucy raised an eyebrow. "I thought you voted against it."

"I did. But since they were determined to bring in an outsider, I wanted to make sure it wasn't Darkrock." Maybe he was just trying to convince her that he wasn't on active duty, but he sounded sincere.

She tried to hide her surprise. "Do you promise to let me take the lead?"

Oliver smiled. "In every possible way. So, do you have a plan for where to hunt tonight?"

"Going back to the mine shaft."

"You think it's sticking close to it? Hiding out in there during the day?"

"I don't think it hides at all. I think it takes advantage of its human form to blend in. And I think it wants to fight with me, so it doesn't really matter where I go, it's going to be there."

"Then why the mine?"

"Because I can back it into a corner if I play my cards right."

She brought the crossbow again, despite Lucien's assertion that an arrow would be no more effective than a bullet. The creature had shown that it felt pain, so if nothing else, she could make it suffer, and hopefully slow it down long enough for Oliver to get off some shots of his own. He brought the tranquilizer gun loaded with darts containing a dose of ketamine designed for big game like ogres and trolls. And they took Oliver's truck just in case they needed to haul away a carcass— or an unconscious beast.

Lucy tried to ignore the little voice in her head that still didn't quite trust Oliver as they drove to the site. She was being ridiculous. No one could have two such distinctly different personalities. Still, on the remote chance that he really was the hell beast—or working with Darkrock—she held back a few details of her plan.

She left the sight off the crossbow this time in favor of thermal-imaging goggles—and Oliver, oddly enough for someone who was no longer a Darkrock operative, had a pair of his own. Her plan was to hit the beast from a distance with a single arrow followed by a barrage of rounds from her Nighthawk Browning to incapacitate it. She might get lucky this time, and it might go down. But if it didn't, Oliver would be standing guard at the entrance to the mine with the trank gun.

Oliver argued with her, wanting to head into the shaft with her, but Lucy "pulled rank" on him, reminding him that the council had hired her because of her expertise. She knew what she was doing. It would have been even better, of course, if she were half as confident as she sounded.

She chose the same entrance as before, going in as far as the tracks they'd left the last time—scuffed by their fight but still distinguishable. The cart rail tracks turned off here toward another section, while the path to the right was less defined. Lucy scanned the ground, her crossbow at the ready. There were tracks here, all right. Two sets. One large…and one small. The hellhound was here, and the beast was following it.

She paused and lowered the crossbow as she looked deeper into the tunnel. If she hit the hellhound, the Soul Reaper would shatter its corporeal form. The process was agonizing, but she'd hardened herself to it, knowing she was doing a necessary job. And the creatures she sent back to hell were fine, of course, once their matter reconstituted in their own plane. A little temporary agony was the price they paid for taking advantage of the breach to enter a realm they didn't belong in.

It was still her job to return the hellhound to where it was supposed to be. But she wasn't sure she could take aim at a juvenile wolf, much less a boy. She also wasn't sure she ought to. *Goddammit.* Oliver's sensitivity crap was rubbing off on her. And who knew how much harm his treating the hellhound like a human boy had done it? She'd checked out the storage unit after he left this afternoon. He'd brought the boy comic books and a little handheld video game system. He'd shown him caring and affection. How was a creature bred in hell for the purpose of hunting lost souls supposed to process that kind of information?

A piece of gravel bounced on the path behind her as though a boot had kicked it, and Lucy whirled, ready to let an arrow fly, only to see Oliver making his way down the tunnel.

"Jesus, Oliver. I could have killed you. I told you to wait at the entrance."

"I got to thinking that it would make more sense to hit the thing with the tranquilizer first. Isn't slowing it down the whole point?"

"Keeping it from escaping again is the whole point."

"But if we hit it with a trank dart, it won't be escaping."

"And if we don't hit it with anything and it gets past us, we've left a killer on the loose. Again. This damn thing has been toying with me. I can't afford to let it outsmart me anymore."

"If it comes at either one of us, we have each other's backs. Don't worry. We've got this. It's not going anywhere."

It felt like he was deliberately sabotaging her. Which would make sense only if he was working with Darkrock to take it in alive—or he *was* the hell beast. Lucy studied him through the night-vision goggles. She'd noticed a fading scar on his left shoulder earlier that her conscious mind had eagerly ignored. She'd hit the beast in its left shoulder the other night. But he didn't feel like a hell beast.

"Lucy." Oliver nodded toward the path ahead of them. Something was moving in the dark.

Lucy trained her crossbow on a flash of bright fur and a hulking shape, but Oliver knocked her arm aside with a shout as she fired, sending her arrow wide and high as her target headed deeper into the tunnel.

"Dammit, Oliver!"

"You were going to hit Colt."

"The hell I was. I had the beast in my sights, and you ruined the shot."

"It wasn't the wolf. It was the kid."

"Oliver, I know what I saw."

"I'm telling you, Colt was there."

"We can argue about what you think you saw later. We're losing it." Lucy took off in the direction the thing had gone. She spotted it around a corner and got off a shot this time. It hit the beast's flank but didn't go deep, and the creature shook it off and kept running.

"You hit him." Oliver grabbed her by the arm and spun her about. "You could have killed him!"

"I hit the damn hell beast!"

Oliver's face was a mask of fury. "You're so damn

sure that everything not fully human is evil that you're telling yourself stories about what you're hunting. At least have the decency to admit that you don't care what you hit."

Oliver was out of his mind. It was four times the size of the little wolf that had run from them this morning. She knew the beast when she saw it.

She shook him off. "Stay out of my way. If you mess with my shot one more time, I can't guarantee you won't take the next one."

"Now you're threatening me?"

"I'm telling you to stay the hell out of my way." At the end of the tunnel, the creature had turned to face them. Lucy raised her crossbow, and Oliver lifted the dart gun, but he was aiming it at her. "Jesus Christ, Oliver. Are you fucking crazy? Put that thing down or use it on the wolf!"

"I'm not going to stand here and watch you kill him."

"It's not a *him*, it's a thing."

"It's Colt. He's a goddamn kid."

"It is *not Colt*."

They'd lost their advantage by bickering, and it was coming for them, fast. Lucy tossed the crossbow aside and drew her gun, but Oliver had moved in front of her.

"Get the hell out of my way, or I'll shoot it right through you," she warned. But he'd cost her the shot, and the hell beast leaped on him, knocking him against the side wall of the shaft before turning to face Lucy with a grinning snarl. Lucy shot it. Twice. Three times. The bullets didn't faze it. It knocked the gun from her hand before she could shoot again, and Lucy felt the infernal blood surge in her veins as it struck her. The goggles were knocked off as they rolled in combat, the wolf snapping at her limbs and Lucy whipping it aside with a long-taloned wing.

At the periphery of her wyvern-enhanced vision, she was aware of something moving toward them, Oliver finally ready to use the gun, but something else moved from the other side, the juvenile wolf leaping at the larger creature in Lucy's defense. Oliver fired the dart gun at the same moment, hitting the smaller wolf in the flank, as the hell beast turned and threw the hellhound off with a slash of its razor-sharp claws and flung Oliver back.

The young wolf yelped and tumbled into the darkness, but the hell beast's attention was on it now, and it stalked toward it. While Lucy scrambled for her gun, Oliver fired once more from where he'd fallen, this time managing to hit the hell beast. It turned with a snarl and tore the weapon from Oliver's hand and backhanded him against the wall with a curled, clawed fist. The impact of Oliver's head against a metal railing was ominously loud in the enclosed space.

The beast's eyes locked on Lucy's as she got to her feet with the gun in her hand. It wasn't collapsing, wasn't slowing exactly, but something had given it pause. In an instant, it had taken on the form of a man—of Oliver. "I knew you had my toy," he snarled, recoiling with a roar as she fired. He stared down at the blood on his shirt where the bullet had struck and yanked the dart out of his chest beside it. "He's mine, and I *will* taste his blood. Mark my words." Just as swiftly as it had shifted into human form, it vanished.

Chapter 16

Her enhanced vision fading with the adrenaline surge, Lucy felt around in the dirt for her goggles. Oliver was slumped against the passage wall with his own goggles askew, looking dazed, and the young wolf lay motionless beside him.

Lucy crouched and felt for the wolf's pulse at its throat. It was weak, but it was there. She could see the movement of its narrow chest now, rising and falling shallowly.

"Oliver." Lucy shook him. "We need to get out of here. Colt needs help."

Oliver breathed in suddenly as if surfacing from underwater and opened his eyes wide. "What happened? Where's Colt?"

"He's right next to you."

He turned and checked the wolf as she had. "I think I hit him with a dart." He rubbed his chest absently and grimaced. "But I think the wolf got in a good blow, too, before he went down."

Lucy moved her hand over the softly panting body

and felt something wet and sticky matting in the fur at the side of his rib cage.

She nodded. "It doesn't look like he's losing a lot of blood, but it definitely swiped him pretty deep."

Oliver got to his feet, straightening his goggles, and lifted the wolf in his arms. "We'll take him to my place. I've got supplies there."

"Yeah, I remember."

Lucy gathered up the rest of the weapons and followed Oliver back out through the mine shaft to the surface. Cold rain was drizzling over Cleopatra Hill when they emerged, and the dust on their clothes had turned to mud by the time they reached the truck.

"I'll drive," she insisted. "You took a pretty good blow to the head." She glanced at him as he laid the wolf on the seat and climbed in. "I'm honestly not sure how you're conscious right now."

"I have a very strong constitution." It was nonsense. He had something far more than a strong constitution. Only something inhuman could have gotten up and walked away from a blow like that. As something inhuman herself on occasion, she ought to know. For the time being, Lucy kept it to herself. She was still trying to figure out how the hell beast had looked like Oliver. And how it had disappeared.

"It's strange," said Oliver, echoing her thoughts as she drove toward his place. "I could have sworn you were going after Colt. I mean, I *saw* Colt. I didn't see anything else until the wolf jumped me."

"I didn't see Colt until he came to my rescue. And I honestly don't believe he was there, except hiding in the side tunnel."

"You're saying I imagined I was seeing him the whole time."

"And maybe I imagined I was seeing a large wolf creature. Because we were both seeing what it wanted us to see." Lucy glanced at him. "I also saw you."

"What do you mean, you saw me? What did I do?" He grimaced. "Besides get in your way."

"I mean the hell beast, when it got mad, after we'd finally slowed it down. It looked like you when it spoke to me."

"How is that possible?"

"It's not a therianthrope—a human/animal shifter. It's something far worse. Like malevolent energy personified." Lucy's eyes went to Colt. "And it wants him."

Oliver stroked the wolf's fur. "Colt told me he was hiding from something that was after him, something dangerous. But why would that thing want him specifically?"

"Because Colt is something young and vulnerable. It probably followed the pack of juveniles out of hell. And it may have already gotten the other three."

"Well, it's not getting this one, goddammit."

By the time they reached Delectably Bookish, Oliver seemed to have fully recovered from the effects of the blow to his head, but Colt's condition hadn't changed. After cleaning and bandaging the wolf's wounds, Oliver put him in one of the guest beds to sleep off the drug.

Lucy watched him from the hallway as he closed the door. "You know he's not a human child. You can't keep him."

Oliver glared, arms folded as he stared her down. "You're not going to put one of those bullets in him and send him back to hell."

"No, I'm not. But he has to go back. Somehow."

"He may not be a human child, but he's a scared—and now injured—kid. Let's just worry about protecting him from that thing for now. We can argue about where he belongs after we've figured out how to deal with the…malevolent energy."

"I'm worried about protecting *us* from that thing. I have no idea how to kill it."

Oliver headed into his room. "We'll figure something out. Right now I just want to get out of these muddy clothes and scrounge up something to eat. I'm absolutely starving." He stripped off his shirt and opened his dresser drawer to grab his pajamas, and Lucy admired his ass as he stepped out of the pants to pull on the blue-and-black flannel bottoms.

He caught her looking and threw a sly grin over his shoulder. "So you're staying, right?" He tossed the top of the pajamas to her, but Lucy's answering smile faltered as he turned to face her fully. Oliver tilted his head at her look. "What? What's the matter?"

Where his chest had been mostly scar-free just hours ago, it was now sporting four jagged craters of healing tissue.

Oliver followed her glance. "Oh. Yeah. Shit."

Chapter 17

He'd forgotten about the newest wounds.

Oliver rested his hands on his lower abs as he studied the marks. "I'm betting you want a good explanation for how I got these."

"Do you have a good explanation?"

He glanced up with an apologetic look. "No."

"Oliver."

"Where do *you* think I got them?"

"Are you serious?" Lucy's pale eyes had that dark, suspicious cast to them. "It looks like every bullet I've fired at that monster has somehow gone straight into you—and then immediately healed."

"That's because they have."

"I don't understand."

"I don't really understand it, either. All I know is that ever since I came to Jerome and started looking out for its underground citizens, when one of them gets attacked…it shows up on me."

"You're telling me that when I shoot or stab that hell beast—I'm actually shooting and stabbing you?"

"Or when you or anyone else harms any other inhuman creature in the area, yes. Evidently, within at least a five-mile radius, given the attack in Clarkdale. It doesn't hurt, though, don't worry. I mean, it *does*, it hurts like hell when it happens, but it doesn't cause me any harm. And it heals up in just hours. As you can see."

Lucy was still clutching the pajama top like she was trying to decide whether to run. "Why did you lie to me about the scars I saw on you the other day?"

Oliver sighed. "Because I didn't know how to explain it." He crossed the room and uncurled her fingers around the shirt. "Your hands are freezing. Why don't you warm up in the shower and join me in the kitchen when you're dressed? I'll try to tell you what I know about it. But fair warning, it really isn't much." He kissed her—and at least she didn't recoil—and left her to give her time to absorb what he'd told her while he whipped up a jumbo omelet with chorizo and green chilies for them to share.

Lucy appeared at the doorway to the kitchen dressed in his pajama top just as he was dishing up the omelet. He left some in the pan for Colt in case he woke up later.

"Perfect timing." He smiled and set the plates on the table. "Do you want anything to drink? It's a little late for coffee, but I've got orange juice if you want the full midnight breakfast experience."

"Juice is fine." Lucy sat and dug into her omelet, obviously having worked up as much of an appetite as he had. And she wasn't even burning his peculiar metabolism. "So?" She wasted no time as he joined her. "Why are you taking on other inhuman creatures' injuries? And what does that make you?"

"I honestly don't know what it makes me. I don't have any other extra-human abilities. That I know of," he added carefully, since that wasn't entirely true. "It never happened before I moved to Jerome, and I don't know why it's happening now. It's been going on for about three years. The first time it happened was right after I moved here and became aware of the underground community. I had a run-in with a pickpocket, a young were-coyote who lifted my wallet. He didn't realize I was onto him, so I followed him for a while to see where he'd go. It turned out he was stealing for his dealer, apparently wholly human, who was supplying him with meth. I confronted the dealer and told him he didn't have any business exploiting these kids and that if I caught him in Jerome again, I'd kick his ass."

Lucy concentrated on her omelet with a slight smirk. "Sounds familiar."

"Yeah, well, I'm nothing if not consistent." He smiled down at his food. "The pickpocket asked if I was their protector, and I said sure, I'd protect them if I could. I didn't have anything against shifters and sub-vamps and whatnot, and as long as they weren't hurting anybody, I'd defend them from anyone who wanted to hurt them. It seemed like they needed someone to look out for them. They weren't underage, but they were still really just kids, and they obviously didn't have a lot of human life skills. So the next night, I'm downstairs reading, and it feels like someone has knifed me in the gut. I look under my shirt and see the wound closing up. By morning it was almost undetectable. I found out later the dealer apparently came back and stabbed the pickpocket as a message to the rest of them. And the kid just got up and walked away."

"And you have no idea what gave you this power."

Oliver shrugged, eating his eggs. He had a suspicion, but it wasn't one he was prepared to voice, because it would only lead to more doubts he didn't want to bring up. She already suspected him of working with Darkrock, and in a way he *was* working with Darkrock, and the less said about it the better.

"What about your parents?"

"My parents?"

"Were they fully human? Did they have any abilities?"

Oliver sat back in his chair, pushing his food around the plate for a moment. "I didn't know my parents."

"Oh… I'm sorry, Oliver."

"Don't be sorry. I had terrific foster parents. I just never got to meet my birth mother. She was institutionalized— she died in a mental hospital when I was six. And she never identified the father—*my* father—on the birth certificate. All I know is that he was from the UK. From Wales. He'd gone back home before I was born, and her family wasn't able to take care of me. They're Navajo, but I don't know anything else about them." Oliver waved his hand to dismiss any misplaced sympathy she looked like she was about to express. "Anyway, it's never really affected me, since the only people I knew were the ones who raised me. But if my birth mom had any special abilities, certainly no one ever told me about them."

He hadn't talked this much about himself in years— since Vanessa—and having the focus on himself was making him uncomfortable. He glanced up to find Lucy smiling at him oddly.

"I guess we've all got our family skeletons. My father forced my mother to sign a nondisclosure agreement that said she would never tell us who she was when he granted her a divorce—then he hired her as the family doctor." Lucy took a sip of juice. "And he bargained my brother's soul to save his own while we were still in the womb. So, you know, knowing where you come from isn't always a bonus."

"Yikes. I guess not. But you had Lucien."

"True. We fought a lot trying to one-up each other for our father's approval growing up, but Lucien is the one person in the world I know I can be completely myself with, who really gets me, in all my ugliness. Even if he is a self-centered pain in the ass."

Oliver coughed on a bite of omelet that had gone down wrong. "Back up a sec. Ugliness? I can't imagine how anyone could find you anything other than stunningly beautiful."

Lucy looked down at her plate, her dark brows drawn together. "Thanks, but I wasn't talking about my looks."

"Neither was I." Oliver laughed at the expression of annoyed disbelief on her face as she glanced up. "I mean, obviously, *also* about your looks. But from everything I've seen, you're exceptional inside and out."

"You haven't seen everything."

"I'd like to."

Lucy put her napkin on the table and pushed back her chair. "Okay, this just got way too serious. I should probably get dressed and head home."

"You don't have to go. It's late, and you're all dressed for bed. Besides, I might need help with Colt when he wakes up."

"Oliver."

"Lucy." He smiled at her exasperated look. "We'll just sleep. That's it." He gave her a teasing grin. "You kind of owe me after disappearing last time."

"Oh, do I? I didn't know that was required."

He nodded, managing a mock serious expression. "It's in the rule book. If a man manages to give you two orgasms, you have to spend the night."

"I see." Her eyes were amused. That was a good sign. "Just so you understand, we *are* just going to sleep. I don't like messes."

"Or menses."

"Very funny."

Oliver grinned. "You're the boss." It was about time he finally won a round.

After cleaning up in the kitchen and checking on Colt once more, they climbed under Oliver's sheets as if it were the most natural thing in the world. He'd kind of expected Lucy to lie stiffly to one side, avoiding him. When he kissed her, she didn't pull away. And he'd come to the conclusion that, as Polly had said, if you did it right, kissing was everything. It certainly was when it came to kissing Lucy.

He drew back and studied her a moment, trying to figure out how he could be so comfortable with someone he'd only met a few days ago. And someone who wasn't Vanessa.

Lucy's brow wrinkled. "What?"

"I was just looking at your eyes. They're so…"

She rolled the pale blue eyes in question. "Yeah, I know. They're stunning. You've never seen any so pale, especially with the dark color of my hair. I've heard it a thousand times."

"No, I meant…they're just so serious. Melancholy, even."

"Melancholy?"

"I've never seen that kind of gravity in the eyes of anyone who hasn't been through war."

The pale blue eyes blinked in surprise, a bit of brightness in them, moisture, that hadn't been there a moment before. The question was, with whom was she at war? He had a feeling it was herself.

He'd gotten too serious again. Oliver smiled and propped his head in his hand, playing with the buttons on Lucy's pajama top.

She raised an eyebrow, crossing her arms behind her head. "I thought we were going to sleep."

"We are." He unbuttoned the top one. "Eventually." Oliver smoothed her hair behind her ear and kissed her temple. Her short cut was growing on him, even though he'd loved running his fingers through her hair while she was naked beneath him. "What made you cut your hair? It looks fantastic, by the way. Just took a little getting used to."

"Why does something have to have 'made' me cut my hair?"

"It doesn't. You just seem like a person who very carefully considers her appearance."

"And I carefully considered that I needed a haircut."

There was more to it than that, but he wasn't going to push it. Not when he could be doing other things.

He kissed her lightly on the lips. "I'm impressed by how long that lipstick stays on. Doesn't seem to come off on anything, either."

"It's Blood Moon lip stain, specially blended for me by an aesthetician at Smok Biotech. I can get you some if you're that into it."

Oliver laughed. "I'm only into kissing what's under it, but thanks for the generous offer."

"You seem really curious about my beauty routine tonight. Is there something else you wanted to ask me?"

"Not at all. Just appreciating having the time to… appreciate you."

"I thought maybe you were wondering about something you saw tonight."

He paused in kissing her neck. "What would I have seen?"

"If you didn't, then nothing."

"Okay, now you have me curious."

Lucy pushed him onto his back and climbed over him. "There's nothing to be curious about. I just…get a little ugly when I'm fighting mad."

So that was what she'd been talking about earlier. Something must happen to her appearance whenever she tapped into the infernal blood. But he'd been so out of it from the blow to his head that he hadn't noticed. And she thought he'd find her less attractive because of it.

He opened his mouth to tell her that nothing could make her unattractive to him, but a sudden pressure squeezed his chest, knocking the breath out of him. Before he could make a sound or signal in some way to let her know, Lucy's phone rang.

She glanced at it on the bedside table and bit her lip. "I'm sorry. I have to take this. It's Lucien. He's topside."

He managed to sit up as she climbed off him, still trying to figure out what was going on. The pressure was getting worse. God, was he having a heart attack?

Lucy frowned at her phone as she listened. "What do you mean you have to go to Polly's? Where are you?"

Oliver clutched his chest. He was having trouble breathing.

"You see? This is why I don't like owing people any-thing. All right, all right. I'm on my way." Lucy clicked off the call. "I have to help Lucien with something. I'm really sorry." She paused as she slid off the bed and stared at him. "Oliver? Are you okay?"

"I don't know. I don't think so. I feel very strange."

Lucy considered for a moment. "You gave her a kiss."

"You're bothered about that right now?"

"Polly's Grotto is under attack. Certain trinkets she's received—like the kiss you gave her—are designed to keep her protected. Those who've gifted her with them feel compelled to come to her aid. She calls them her gammon—part of her siren 'gam,' like a dolphin pod. Lucien and his wife belong to that group. And from the look of you right now, I'm guessing you do, too. That's what she's doing with that little piece of your soul." She grabbed his hand to pull him from the bed. "Come on. You'll feel better when you answer the call."

"Answer the call? I can't leave Colt here alone. He'll be scared when he wakes up in a strange place."

"With the dose of ketamine he got, he won't wake up for hours. But if you resist Polly's call, I think you're going to get very sick."

Oliver sat on the edge of the bed with his head in his hands. Just the mention of Polly's name was starting to feel like an imperative. God, how stupid had he been? Lucy was right. He had to go. The thought of doing so made him feel instantly better.

He went to the dresser to grab some clothes while Lucy put on the suit she'd been wearing earlier. "Did Lucien say anything else about what's happening? Who would attack Polly?"

"He called it a 'raid,' but he doesn't know anything else. He's still on his way there."

"A raid?" Oliver frowned as he buttoned his pants. "Darkrock." They'd followed him the other night, and he'd led them right to a treasure trove of inhuman creatures.

Chapter 18

Lucy had been thinking the same, and their suspicions turned out to be right on the money. A small fleet of black vans and Humvees was parked in front of Polly's when they arrived. The Grotto was normally protected by its own dimensional displacement, which meant Darkrock must have possessed some kind of magic to counter it. Only people with enhanced blood were able to find the place easily. It currently sat in a little corner of Sedona on the banks of Oak Creek—access to a living body of water was essential for the siren's well-being.

Lucy wondered why Darkrock hadn't already rounded up Polly's clientele and carted them off in the vans to Darkrock's headquarters. After all, it had taken Lucy and Oliver more than thirty minutes to get there. But it became obvious as soon as they entered the club. The doors to the outside disappeared.

Polly, in layers of red velvet and sporting a mane of flaming ruby hair to match, was surrounded by a group of her loyal gammon—Lucien and Theia among them.

Even Rhea, apparently, had given Polly a drop of blood at some point in the past. She was there beside her sister, while the Viking, Leo, stood off to the side looking ready to start ripping souls out of the assembled operatives. Like Lucy, he was only there to help someone he cared about. And Darkrock had brought a small army. Which of course was their specialty. But their weapons would do them no good within the dimensional displacement field of the Grotto.

Oliver's entrance caused a small stir among both groups.

"Hey, there he is. Chief Benally." One of the operatives, a short, stocky ginger built like a fireplug and sporting a flattop with shaved sides, came forward and slapped Oliver on the back.

Oliver nodded tersely. "Artie."

Polly's eyes glittered with menace in the candlelight being thrown by a sort of rippling disco ball at the center of the club. "Son of Gwyn. You know these assholes?"

Who was Son of Gwyn? Lucy glanced around, surprised when Oliver moved away from her toward Polly. The gammon parted for him, as if they shared one mind.

"I know them," said Oliver. "They're my former comrades. I didn't send them. But I believe I must have led them here the other morning." He turned to stand as a sentry in front of her, arms crossed to display his pecs and biceps to excellent effect in the white T-shirt he'd thrown on. "They won't come any closer."

"You keep interesting company these days, Chief," said the one Oliver had called Artie. "Quite a change from our Red Squad days."

Oliver ignored the implied insult. "What have these

people done to warrant the deployment of a full platoon of Darkrock troops?"

"That's not a question you used to ask."

"It's a question I should have asked." He addressed the other operatives. "One you should all be asking yourselves."

"They follow my orders here," Artie reminded him.

"And you follow Darkrock's. Blindly."

Artie rolled his eyes. "Oh, my God. When did you become such a cuck?"

Lucy couldn't contain the sharp outburst of laughter the word always evoked.

Artie turned in her direction and looked her up and down contemptuously. "Oh, right. That's when." He turned back to Oliver. "Vanessa would be ashamed to be seen with you right now, man."

Oliver's arms unfolded slowly, as if he was about to take a fighting stance, his eyes smoldering. "Don't talk about Vanessa."

"What really happened the night you got her and the rest of the team killed? Were you standing there with your thumbs up your ass trying to decide whether a bunch of murdering bloodsuckers deserved a little consideration while they drained her dry?"

The siren put a hand on Oliver's shoulder. "Never mind your concerns. You can settle whatever score you like with them on your own time."

Oliver nodded reluctantly and stepped back into formation. "Looks like we're at an impasse here, boys. Maybe you should move along. Hunt your prey elsewhere."

One of the other operatives made a sweeping gesture with his gun toward the group. "Looks to me like the predators are all in this room. What the hell is that freak?" He gestured toward the were-tiger beside Polly, the same one that had welcomed Lucy the last time she was here. The tiger growled low in his throat.

Polly stroked his fur. "Now, now, Giorgio."

"I'm in command here, Finch," Artie barked. "I'll handle it."

Polly sighed audibly and sat on the bench seat of the booth next to her, the velvet layers of her gown spreading out around her like a sea of flame. "I find this all very boring. And *male*." She said the word as if it represented the height of banality. "What would be a really lovely twist to this little drama would be to watch all of you boys do each other. All that sweating and grunting and groaning and clutching each other as you gave in to your primal desires." She emphasized the active words with approximations of their sounds, and pumped her fists with a lewd insinuation to punctuate the sentence. "Just really *giving* it to each other. A strutting, hyper-masculine man orgy for our entertainment."

"Pols." Lucien shook his head at her. "Let's not get carried away."

Lucy folded her arms and tilted her head with interest. If that was really something Polly could compel them to do, Lucy was here for it.

Artie spat on the floor, his fragile masculinity obviously threatened. "We're immune to your mind games, bitch. Darkrock wouldn't send us in here without adequate protection."

Polly laughed. "Well, feel free to use all the protection you want. Safer sex is always advisable."

"Very fucking funny."

"So is your Freudian little tongue, you adorably angry little bundle of roid rage."

Close enough for Lucy to hear, Finch leaned toward his team leader. "Stop provoking her, man. She's just trying to get a rise out of us."

Polly evidently heard it as well, judging by the ripple of delighted laughter that flowed out of her.

"Maybe you should quit while you're ahead," said Oliver, watching his former comrades with amusement.

"We'll quit when we have what we came for," Artie snapped.

"And what would that be?"

"These freaks." He indicated the obviously inhuman creatures with a wave of his AK-47. "I'd particularly like to see Darkrock cut open the brain of that one." For some reason, these guys were fixated on Giorgio, the tiger. Probably because he wore only fur and they were forced to acknowledge his furry, uncut junk.

Giorgio, however, had apparently had enough. He sprang forward with a snarl, and Artie opened fire— and discovered his weapon didn't work. Oh, the humanity. Giorgio knocked him to the floor.

Polly examined her nails, demonstrating her eternal ennui. "Your little toys don't work in here, boys. Did I forget to mention?"

Artie scrambled to his feet with as much dignity as he could muster, giving Giorgio a wide berth.

"You see, you may be immune to my influence—to a degree—but my Grotto is utterly immune to yours. You can certainly challenge my gammon to hand-to-hand combat if you like, but I wouldn't recommend it." She looked up and nodded at Lucien. "Lucien, sweetheart, would you take off that skin, please?"

Theia and Rhea stood back automatically.

Lucien, whose human appearance in the physical world was only an illusion facilitated by Theia's presence, rolled his shoulders and cracked his neck. With the sound of the joints cracking, his skin literally fell away, and he emerged from the shell he'd occupied as a full-size brilliant blue wyvern—reptilian eyes, horns, wings, tail and all—as far from human as one could get. With a roaring hiss, he took two steps forward on his lizard-like back legs, the shortened forearms ending in vicious claws, and his webbed wings raised above his head in a threatening posture, while his barbed tail switched in warning.

Lucy stole a glance at Oliver to see if he was making the connection between Lucien's appearance and her infernal blood. He seemed unconcerned, perhaps under Polly's thrall in some way that connected all of the gammon to each other with a collective consciousness.

The Darkrock troops wisely took a step back toward the front wall of the club, their AK-47s trained on Lucien despite the demonstration they'd just seen of the futility of the gesture.

Polly smiled at their alarmed expressions. "Who wants to challenge the Prince of Hell? Anyone? Or perhaps you'd feel more comfortable going up against the lovely twins? I believe the last time someone challenged them, he ended up being dragged straight to the bottomless pit, where he's spending eternity sulking. You boys look like sulkers. Maybe we should just skip the formalities."

"What the hell do you want?" Artie shot back, his voice shrill with frustration.

"Ah, now it's what *I* want. A moment ago, you were

making demands. You see, the thing about my little Grotto is that I decide who enters and who leaves. And if I choose, I can open a back door straight into hell, where lovely Lucien here will be happy to escort you to your eternal rest."

Theia took an apologetic step forward. "It doesn't really work like that," she murmured.

"Nevertheless..." Polly glared at her. "I call the shots here. The Grotto is neutral territory, and any aggression toward my patrons will be met with the severest reprisals. So now that we understand each other, just let me know when you're ready for me to show you the door. Literally. It's still there, but I've kept you from seeing it." She rolled her eyes. "Immune to my influence, my ass." With a wave of her hand, the doors reappeared.

Without waiting for orders from their team leader, the rest of the Darkrock troops beat a hasty retreat.

Artie tried to save face. "This isn't over, Benally."

"Of course it's over," said Polly. "You won't remember where the Grotto is by morning. I wouldn't be surprised if you drive around all night trying to find your way back to the highway."

The atmosphere in the club shifted from tense to relaxed, with people going back to their drinks and conversations, and the electronic dance music that had been just barely at the level of hearing now pumping and thumping as if nothing had happened. Lucien appeared human once more, and Leo had joined him and the twins, the four of them joking about something like they were old friends. Maybe they were. Lucy had never been one for friendships, and she hadn't really kept track of what was happening with Lucien's social life during his brief stays in the mortal plane.

She supposed she should tell Lucien the latest about the hell beast—and find out if he had any corroborating information. Oliver was occupied with Polly for the moment.

Lucy approached the group. "Hey, baby brother. Nice display earlier."

Lucien grinned. "Yeah, sometimes being a monster comes in handy."

"Speaking of monsters, I had another run-in with the creature I've been tracking. I think you're right about it not being one of your fugitives."

"Well, of course I'm right. I think I know what kind of creatures I have in my domain."

"This time I was with Oliver, and we both saw something different, like it was manipulating our perception. I think it must be a coincidence after all that it showed up at the same time as the breach. Or maybe the breach drew it out of wherever it had been dormant."

"Why do you say that?"

"Because it wants those hellhounds in a bad way. And I think it may have already gotten some of them."

"Damn. I was afraid something might have happened to them."

She was about to tell him about Colt, but the idea of sending the boy—creature—back was too fraught with personal conflict, and she wasn't ready to have that conversation yet.

"So, this Oliver you mentioned." Lucien glanced toward Polly's infamous booth, where Oliver still stood as if he were on guard. "That's him with Polly? The ex-Marine?"

"Yeah, he's my client."

"Looks like he's a little more than a client."

Lucy realized how it must have appeared that they'd shown up together and had obviously been together when he called her and got her out of bed. For once, she didn't have a smart comeback. Which was even more damning.

"Lucien, leave her alone." Theia took Lucy's arm. "I wanted to tell her about a dream I had." She drew Lucy aside.

"A dream?" Lucy was skeptical of dream premonitions, but she couldn't entirely dismiss them after having Theia dream-walk into hers.

"You were in the middle of a burning building, but the flames didn't touch you. And there was a man made of flame holding your heart in his mouth."

"A man made of flame?"

"Interpretation is always tricky. I wasn't sure if it was a herald of something or a warning, you know? Good news or bad—it's hard to tell. And sometimes it's nothing. Anyway, I thought I'd pass it along. Often the meaning of the symbol is clearer to the subject of the dream. So...make of it what you will."

"Uh, thanks."

"I know what I'd make of it." Rhea bounced over to them, draping an arm on her sister's shoulder. "A man made of flame? As in a hot guy?" She gestured with an exaggerated roll of her eyes toward Oliver. "And I bet it's not your literal heart in his mouth. Heart can be a euphemism for lots of things, like heart as in your core, your center. As in your—"

"Okay, MoonPie," Theia interrupted and turned Rhea around, shoving her back toward Leo. "Go find a Valkyrie to play with or something."

"Hey." Rhea put her hands on her hips as Leo hooked

his arms around her shoulders and rested his chin on her head. "I told you that in confidence."

"That was your first mistake."

Lucy raised an eyebrow, not sure what that was about, but she was beginning to feel like the odd man out. After a nod to Lucien in a nonverbal goodbye, she made her way to Polly's booth, where the siren was monopolizing Oliver's attention with a stern lecture.

"I'm not at all impressed with your friends, Son of Gwyn."

"I assure you, they're not my friends."

"The short one who kept barking orders and insulting people—he came here by himself earlier today, pretending to be a patron. I see now that he was taking inventory. I'll have to beef up my wards that keep out nosy parkers like him. Thankfully, I can always count on my gammon to deal with any riffraff."

"About that," Lucy interrupted.

Polly glanced up at her with a sly smile. "Lucy, dear. Did you find what you were looking for Sunday afternoon?" She gave Oliver an appreciative look. "Oh… I guess you did. Well done."

Oliver's brow wrinkled. "You were here Sunday afternoon?"

Lucy ignored the question, addressing Polly. "You had no business tricking Oliver into joining your little gam. He'd never been here before. He hadn't been warned about you."

Polly picked up her drink and held it out for someone to fill, and in seconds, a waiter appeared at her side to do it. "You needn't worry about Oliver, dear. He's special. I haven't conscripted him, merely linked with him." She fingered the solitary pearl in a silver filigree cage that hung from a delicate chain at her throat. Lucy had the distinct impression she was looking at the physical manifestation of Oliver's kiss.

"Linked?" Oliver and Lucy repeated the word together.

"Oliver's magic is unique." She smiled at him. "You're a natural protector. I'm rarely in danger of physical harm because my gammon are so loyal. But a little extra protection never hurts." She sipped her drink. "I mean, it might hurt *you*, and for that I apologize, but it *is* your nature. What's one more little undergrounder under your protection?" Polly winked.

"You're telling me that those chest pains I was having, that pressure and shortness of breath that I thought was a heart attack…that was your pain?"

"Oh, no, sweetie. I think I've misled you again. A link to me isn't simply a link to *me*. It's a link to all that I am. You're linked with the entire Grotto."

Lucy took Oliver's arm as his face clouded with anger. "We should probably get back to Colt, don't you think?"

After a deep breath that seemed like he was swallowing his rage, Oliver nodded. "My apologies for leading those idiots here. Let's hope there are no similar incidents in the future."

Lucy steered him out before Polly could toy with him anymore—or with her. She'd narrowly missed Oliver finding out about Finn and her out-of-control hormones.

As they drove back to Jerome, it turned out the miss was narrower than she'd hoped.

"What were you doing at the Grotto Sunday afternoon? Was that where you were when I called you about the Henderson interview?"

"I was just getting some information from Polly."

"I thought you were all about not giving anything to the siren."

"Well, it wasn't information, exactly." Lucy felt her cheeks growing hot. "I was just looking for someone, and she pointed me in the right direction. No token required." She hoped he wouldn't ask for whom. She felt his gaze on her for a few moments longer, but he didn't press her.

Delectably Bookish was dark and quiet, the way they'd left it. Oliver went into the guest room to check in on Colt but came back out into the hallway abruptly.

"What's the matter?" Lucy glanced at the door. "Is he awake?"

"He's gone. And Darkrock took him."

Chapter 19

"How do you know it was Darkrock?" Even knowing Colt wouldn't be there, Lucy looked around Oliver into the room. "Maybe he just woke up and ran off."

"Because they left this." Oliver held out his hand, a small black pebble resting in his palm. "It's their calling card. They staged that entire goddamn thing at Polly's Grotto just to get to him."

"Are you sure? How would they even know about him?"

"They must have been keeping a closer eye on me than I thought. Jesus. I've been such a colossal idiot."

Lucy rubbed the back of her neck. "If you're right about how they found you, this is my fault. I think I must have a mole at Smok Biotech." Thanks to Lucy's suspicious nature, Darkrock now had knowledge of an entire paranormal underground it could seek to exploit—and had taken a young boy to be tortured. She noticed Oliver wasn't exactly rushing to absolve her. "I'm sorry. I know that's inadequate. I had no idea my research department was vulnerable to Darkrock operatives." And she intended to do something about it the minute she had a free moment.

Oliver was watching her speak, but she had a feeling he wasn't listening to her. "Maybe we can use Smok's influence to get Colt back."

"Smok's influence?"

"You said Darkrock had tried to arrange a partnership in the past."

Lucy drew her hand away from the back of her neck, curling her fingers into a fist at her side. Maybe it was the other way around. Maybe Darkrock was using Lucy's vulnerability to Oliver and his to Colt to force a partnership.

"No way am I joining forces with those assholes."

"You don't have to join forces with them, just make it seem like you're willing to. Make them an offer, anything to get them to hold off on whatever plans they have for Colt. Maybe tell them *you* had plans for him. Or, hell, tell them the truth, that you want to send him back to hell. It'll probably be more effective if you can keep me out of it, anyway. Let them think we've had a falling-out because you disapprove of my sympathy for inhuman creatures."

Something was off between them, and it wasn't just that Colt was gone. It was as if something had wedged its way between them since they left Polly's. Or maybe at Polly's. Maybe his connection to Polly had done something to sever theirs. He was bound to the Grotto through a piece of his soul. Or maybe it was Lucy. She'd screwed up with Colt at the storage facility, and now she'd screwed up by leaving him here. And as open and vulnerable as Oliver had been with her, she'd insisted on playing things close to her vest. Were they actually having a falling-out? And, dammit, when had she fallen so far *in*?

Oliver voiced her worry. "And it wouldn't exactly be untrue, would it? You don't approve."

"It's not that simple, Oliver."

"At least they haven't hurt him yet." He still wasn't listening to her. "I'd feel it if they had. Please do what you can. What you think is right. In the meantime, I'm going to see if I can find out where they're holding him."

"What are you going to do, try to bust him out by yourself? They'll probably have him in an armed facility."

Oliver's gaze focused fully on her at last. "You know where it is, don't you? You know where they're holding him."

"What? Why would I know?"

"You've dealt with them before. Smok must have information on their sites in the area."

"That doesn't mean I automatically know where they took Colt. I have no idea where their holding facilities are. I'm not just walking around with all of my company's resources in my brain like I'm hooked up to some kind of neural net."

"But you can find out. In minutes, I'm guessing."

"Oliver—"

"Is there some reason you don't want to give me that information?"

"*Oliver*. I'm on your side here. It just isn't that simple."

"It is simple. You could make one phone call right now and get a map of every site they own in the Southwest."

Lucy swore and took her phone from her pocket. "All *right*. I'll see what I can find out. But you're acting like this is some kind of conspiracy against you—like I can just magically find Colt for you and I'm refusing—and I have no idea why."

After walking away from him for a few minutes to talk to her assistant and give her Oliver's email to send him everything on Darkrock's properties, Lucy put the phone away and turned back to him. "My assistant is on it. She'll send you anything she can find. But this isn't like swinging a magic pendulum over an enchanted map. They have dozens of operations, and I'm sure there are plenty of black sites Smok has no way of knowing about."

"It's a start. Thank you."

Whatever had come between them was still there, like an invisible field of mistrust. Maybe seeing what Lucien was and extrapolating it to Lucy had hit him on the drive home.

And maybe Lucy had lost her damn mind and let her hormones convince her there was something between them in the first place. She'd never bothered with more than the occasional hookup, and there was a reason for that. Sex was a release valve, something that was useful every so often so she could go back to concentrating on what was really important. Relationships were unnecessary complications that distracted her from her work. But Oliver had been right. It was more than just sexual between them. And that had been her big mistake.

Lucy slipped her phone back into her pocket. "I'd better get going. My assistant reminded me of several clients I've been neglecting."

Oliver's expression was inscrutable. "It's three in the morning. I thought you were going to sleep here."

"I told you, I don't sleep."

* * *

Lucy was keeping something from him. Over the past twelve hours, he'd forgotten who she was, letting desire—and the fact that he'd felt it again for the first time since he'd lost Vanessa—cloud his mind.

Oliver fiddled with his ring as he sat in the kitchen drinking coffee in an attempt to get a little clarity. What Artie had said at the Grotto had gotten under his skin. Vanessa would be ashamed of him. Not because he had compassion for people who weren't fully human but because he'd lost sight of his personal integrity. Lucy Smok and Smok International were inseparable, and he'd allowed himself to forget that.

He still couldn't even be sure that Darkrock finding him hadn't been part of her plan. They could all be playing him. Except he didn't really think that of her. What the hell was his problem?

The ring gleamed at him again as he turned it. *Semper Fi*, the motto of the Marines, was engraved on the inside. It had been Vanessa's and his promise to each other: they would always be faithful, always stand by each other, always have each other's backs. And the knowledge that he hadn't had her back on that last mission ate away at him like a slow-acting corrosive agent. They had argued about the mission beforehand. Argued a lot beforehand, in fact.

Vanessa had talked about getting out, and Oliver was dead set against it. Despite his misgivings about Darkrock's overall mission, he'd thought they were providing a useful service. They were getting lowlifes off the streets—both human and otherwise. And fewer predators on the street was a good thing, even if Darkrock wasn't entirely ethical in how they went about it. Van-

essa had talked about going into business together, a
private enterprise where they offered their services on
a consulting basis, setting their own terms. Darkrock
was too much like the military, too much unquestion-
ing loyalty, with someone else always calling the shots.

The night they'd gone to the meth-and-blood lab,
Vanessa had given him an ultimatum: Darkrock or
her. He would have chosen her. He had to believe that
deep down, she'd known it. But he was too stubborn to
let her "win" the argument. Even though he'd already
been privately questioning his loyalty to Darkrock, he
wasn't going to let her push him into making a decision. They'd argued on the way there. She'd announced
that she was pregnant, and Oliver had accused her of
doing it on purpose.

And ten minutes later, a vampire lord had smiled at
him with Vanessa's blood on his lips and told him how
delicious it was to get two for the price of one. That was
when Oliver had burned the place to the ground. Vanessa was lost, and he couldn't let the bastard drink from
his child who would never be born. And the possibility
that the bloodsuckers might keep Vanessa's body alive
to incubate not only her own fresh blood but also their
child as a blood slave was horrifying.

Even then, it hadn't been a conscious decision. He'd
told Artie he'd used incendiary tear gas to ignite the
fire. But it had been Oliver himself. His rage had shot
out of him like chaotic energy, sparks of uncontrollable
grief and fury catching on everything in sight. Without
an accelerant or an incendiary device, Oliver had called
the fire through some primal, unconscious power he

hadn't known he possessed. And tonight, the siren had told him what it was.

The same thing that gave him the power to absorb the injuries of the underground folks in his "territory"— something he'd unwittingly laid claim to that night three years ago with his promise of protection to the young pickpocket—had given him the ability to manifest his rage through external control over the element of fire. Polly had told him who his father was, showing him with a touch of her hand on his. Images had come to him in a flash, a vision of a dark green place by the sea. He'd always known his father had been Welsh. It was the only information he'd gotten from his grandparents— the reason they'd refused to take him in was his "Anglo" paternity. He just hadn't expected his father to be the ruler of the Welsh Otherworld—or a son of the ruler of the Welsh Otherworld, at any rate.

Son of Gwyn, Polly had called him when they first met. Gwyn ap Nudd was the king of the Ellyllon, the Welsh elven race, and Oliver's father was apparently one of Gwyn's numerous offspring. And his father, Oliver had seen in Polly's vision, had been there at his birth and had kissed Oliver's head "with fire," as Polly put it. It was the reason for the reddish highlights in his otherwise dark brown hair from his mother's side. His mother, consequently, had gone mad. Or maybe they'd just believed she was mad if she'd made any claim to have been impregnated by an elven prince. The vision hadn't told him that, but it seemed like a reasonable assumption.

Oliver set down his cold coffee and pushed back his chair. This was too much to deal with right now. Not unsurprisingly, his head felt like it was on fire with all this knowledge. He'd spent the past five years cultivating a practice of daily meditation to keep from burning anything else down, not knowing how he'd done it in the first place, and if he didn't stop thinking about it, he'd end up setting his own house ablaze.

He could kill two birds with one stone. Sitting on the floor of the room where Colt had last been, he cleared his mind and let go of his anger and his guilt and tried to let his mind fill with unconscious knowledge. Lucy's assistant had sent him the list of Darkrock's properties, and he meditated on those, letting the locations float by in his mind—Bagdad, Skull Valley, Bullhead City, Quartzite—not assigning any significance or judgment to them, as if they were meaningless.

But they weren't meaningless. He opened his eyes. Blackstone Ranch in the desert south of Golden Valley near Bullhead City on the Nevada border was the site of the compound where Darkrock had trained Oliver's unit. The compound, three hours west of Jerome off I-40, had supposedly been decommissioned afterward.

He took the pebble out of his pocket. Darkrock had left him a small black stone. They'd wanted Oliver to know. Colt's abduction served more than one purpose. They wanted Oliver back, and Colt was their leverage.

Lucy had changed clothes in her car once more before leaving Oliver's place. Her go bag had never gotten more use. It was time to get this job done. Something Theia had said had gotten her thinking. Not about the flaming man eating her heart—because what the hell?—but in the dream they'd shared. She'd mentioned that Leo Ström had a wolf aspect. And while Rhea had worked on Lucy's dream tattoos, Leo himself had brought up Fenrir, the giant wolf destined to swallow the sun—or the world; she could never remember which—during Ragnarök. She doubted this thing was Fenrir, but it was definitely something otherworldly.

She just hoped she wasn't the only one who wasn't sleeping tonight. She'd solicited Leo's help before to track the beast. As the chieftain of the Wild Hunt, he had a direct line to a well of knowledge about the murderers, sexual predators and "oath breakers" in the region. Who better to help her catch a malevolent, murderous energy that presented itself as a wolf than the wolf aspect of the chieftain of the Wild Hunt?

Lucy texted Leo's number, hoping she wouldn't be waking him up. A minute later, he replied. He was, in fact, on the Hunt tonight. It was the usual season. Lucy had forgotten. Odin's Hunt normally rode during the period between the late harvest and Yuletide, though Leo, as a mortal chieftain, had the power to call up the Hunt at will.

In moments, she heard the blast of the hunting horn and found herself sitting in the midst of a freak winter storm at the base of Cleopatra Hill. Roiling clouds and thunder and lightning ushered in a hailstorm that pelted the soft top of her little Alfa Romeo Spider, and the thundering of hooves soon distinguished from the atmospheric thunder as Leo and his entourage emerged from the clouds.

She stepped out of her car when Leo slowed, while the rest of the Hunt thundered past them into the hills.

"How do you manage to ride a phantom horse if

you're not a phantom?" she asked as he dismounted and tipped his cowboy hat at her. In keeping with the setting, his Hunt had taken its inspiration from the Western "Ghost Riders in the Sky."

"Everyone contains a phantom self. Most people just keep theirs locked up at night in their dreams. My *hugr*, my thought-self, is awake when others sleep, even though it no longer leaves my body as it did when I was immortal."

"So...your thought-self inside your mortal frame is what's keeping you on the phantom horse?"

Leo grinned. "If that makes sense to you, then, yes. I don't even understand it." He patted the horse-that-wasn't-a-horse and rubbed its nose. "Your message said you'd thought of something I had that might help you track the beast."

Lucy nodded. "I'm not sure if this is an indelicate request, so please don't be offended if I'm way off base here, but Theia mentioned that you had a wolf aspect, as well."

Leo removed his hat and ran his fingers through his permanently tousled light ginger hair. "You think my wolf has something to do with this monster you're hunting?"

"No, sorry. I didn't make myself clear. I was hoping I could...borrow your wolf."

"You want to borrow my *fylgja*?"

"If your *fylgja* is your wolf-self, and if you're not using it—and if this isn't totally rude of me to ask—yes."

"It's not rude. I've just never been asked to lend out part of myself." Leo shrugged. "I don't see why not. But how is it going to help you?"

"It's your harbinger, if I understand correctly. A representation of your essential spirit that's intimately connected to you and your fate that presents itself to others."

"That's a rough approximation, sure."

"So since you can sense malevolent energy, your wolf can sense it."

Leo nodded slowly. "I think I see what you're getting at. As the wolf, it will be a more primal tracker, and it can home in on the wolf aspect of this evil, a sort of sympathetic magic."

"Exactly. I'm not sure it will work, but I'm willing to try anything at this point."

"But Lucien tells me you still don't know how to kill the beast."

"No," Lucy admitted. "But now that I'm convinced that it isn't a strictly physical being and more of a projection of malevolent intent, I'm hoping that projecting my own intent when I fire on it will do the trick."

"I suppose it's worth a try." Leo closed his eyes and gave his broad shoulders a little shimmy, and the wolf appeared beside him. It looked more like a scruffy hunting dog with wolf ancestry, but hopefully it would do. "Just don't get it killed," said Leo. "If my *fylgja* dies, I die. And Rhea would haunt you to the depths of Náströnd if you were responsible for my death." He grinned, but it was a warning that sobered Lucy a bit. She was asking a lot of him.

"Thanks, Leo. I promise to take care of it as if it were my own."

As the dog trotted over to her, Lucy opened the door

of her car, and it promptly hopped in. "Do I need to do anything special to communicate with it?"

"He'll understand you. Just talk to him like he's me." Leo hopped back into the saddle and galloped into the air before she could thank him again.

Sliding into the car beside the dog, which had obligingly settled into the passenger seat, Lucy studied it for a moment. "I assume you got all that. But in case you didn't, I need your help to find the wolf I've been hunting. I don't think it's really a wolf, but I'm hoping the wolf energy it's putting out is something you can tap into."

The dog panted at her. What the hell was she doing? Was this dog even listening to her? She was starting to feel a little nuts. But she'd suggested this, and Leo had been extremely generous in lending her his *fylgja*. The least she could do was commit to her own idea.

"Okay, let's hit the road, I guess. I'm heading back up to the mine shaft where I've fought this thing before. Hopefully, you'll let me know if I'm off track." It didn't seem to object, so she went ahead with the plan.

At the end of the dirt road, she parked and got out and opened the door for the dog. It hopped out while she grabbed the crossbow and quiver and put on her thermal-imaging goggles. When she turned around, it was trotting toward the path to the open mine shafts. So far, so good.

The dog's hackles rose as they neared the opening she'd used before, and it growled low in its throat. Lucy took out her Nighthawk Browning. She'd loaded it with specially modified bullets this time, containing ketamine instead of Soul Reaper serum, with twice the dosage as the darts Oliver had used. If she could get enough bullets in the thing, maybe she could finally knock it out and shoot some Soul Reaper arrows straight into its heart.

Leo's *fylgja* ran ahead of her into the shaft, and Lucy called out after it. She'd promised Leo she wouldn't get him killed, and now he was already charging ahead to face the monster.

She switched on the goggles and hurried inside. The dog was halfway down the tracks. "Leo—Leo's *fylgja*—whatever—wait!"

Thankfully, it slowed and waited for her to catch up. She stepped up beside it, petting its scruff. Maybe she should have asked Leo for a collar and leash. Yikes, no. *That* would have been rude. If she was going to trust Leo to help her, she had to trust the dog's instincts, as well.

"So you've brought your own little hound."

Lucy whirled at the sound of the rough voice behind her. Oliver stood between her and the exit. Beside her, the *fylgja*'s growl kept her grounded. This wasn't Oliver.

She managed to maintain a cool demeanor. "I thought maybe you two could relate."

"Do you think I'm afraid of the master of the Wild Hunt? I *am* the Wild Hunt."

This thing seemed to have an ego bigger than Lucien's. Maybe if she got it talking about itself, she'd get some more information about it and distract it from the shot she was simultaneously getting ready to take.

"How exactly are you the Wild Hunt and Death and the Pit and a ravenous devouring maw all at the same time?"

The Oliver-beast grinned lasciviously. "You forgot Sex. I'm also Sex."

But that part had been in her dream, not something the actual beast had said.

"Did you think I didn't join you in your sleep, lovely Lucy? I'm everywhere you are."

The dog moved closer to her with another throaty growl.

"What do you mean?"

"You breathed life into me."

A chill crawled over her skin. "When the hell did I breathe life into you?"

"Don't you remember my birth? You and my father were there on the hill before the great cross."

"The hill before the… The Chapel of the Holy Cross?" She was having trouble not breaking down into a full body shake as it began to dawn on her.

"Now she starts to remember. You could feel me there, couldn't you? My father held open hell's mouth and let the seed of his hatred spill over the ground through Lucien's infernal blood. Through you." He'd been stepping slowly closer to her, and Lucy was locked in a paralysis of bone-chilling fear.

Carter Hamilton had been absorbing hell's energy while the gates were open—and Lucy had been possessed by a shade under Carter's control.

"You remember now, don't you? Mommy." The Oliver-beast was right in front of her, and he slipped his arm around her waist and thrust his pelvis against her with a rude gesture.

"I am *not* your mother. And ew." She tried to take a step back, but her legs weren't working.

"You were the vessel. My father let the energy of hell flow into the dirt and up into you, open and willing for him."

"No."

"That's why I take this form. The form of your desire."

"No."

His other arm went around her, pinning her gun arm to her side. "How else could Father have used you to lure your own twin brother to him on that hill? Your own blood, once half of yourself. How else could he have used your hand to take the charm that was keeping your own father alive from around his neck and let him slip into oblivion? You were born to break Madeleine Marchant's curse, and Father was ready to help you do it. Just let me in and we can devour everything together."

"I don't want to devour anything." She could barely get the words out. Her jaw felt frozen. Her brain felt frozen. She couldn't think. What had she come here for? She'd had a plan. "Leo," she murmured. "What do I do?"

The beast laughed, his breath warm against her cheek, and he ran his tongue over her skin from her temple down to the hollow of her throat. "You think a dog is going to help you? Look down. He ran away like a coward."

Lucy glanced down, turning her head. *Goddammit*. The *fylgja* had abandoned her. If she lived through this, she and Leo Ström were going to have some fucking words.

The Oliver-beast kissed her throat. "Let me in, dear heart. I'll give you more pleasure than you've ever known. More than you ever dreamed. I was made for you. I am the embodiment of your desires."

"Get. Off. Of. Me." With a monumental effort, she managed to squeeze her finger against the trigger of the gun and fire a tranquilizer bullet into Oliver's leg. The beast's leg. Well, damn. Oliver's leg. Because he was going to feel it.

Oliver-beast shuddered with the impact, and his eyes went dark. "That wasn't very nice. I'm offering to give you supernatural orgasms, and you shoot me in the thigh?" He grabbed the gun from her hand and tossed it aside. "Maybe I shouldn't have wasted my time with you. I could be sucking the marrow out of tasty little hellhound pup bones." He licked his lips. "You have no idea how delicious that is. If you're good, I'll save you some."

"You're not getting anywhere near Colt." Whatever else Darkrock's minions had done, they'd gotten the hellhound safely out of the hell beast's grasp for the time being.

The Oliver-beast laughed. "I have news for you, Mommy dearest. I know precisely where your little puppy dog is, and he is far from safe. Your fool of a fireman is retrieving him for me right now."

Fireman? Jesus. Fire *man*. Man of flame. She was an idiot. And so was Oliver, apparently. They'd both played right into this thing's hands. If it actually had hands.

The Oliver-beast stroked her arms, nipping at her neck. "I'm saving him for later, though. Because you taste like warm p—" He made an odd grunting noise against her at the same moment that a shot rang out, and his knees buckled, forcing Lucy to grab hold of him to keep them both from hitting the ground. Behind the Oliver-beast, Leo stood holding Lucy's gun. He'd shot the beast in the ass.

"Fucking…dog," the beast murmured, and shoved Lucy away, turning on Leo. He grabbed for the gun, and Leo fired again, this time into his neck. Oliver-beast's hand went to the blood streaming from the wound. Leo had hit a major artery, and the drug was going rapidly to the beast's brain. He slumped onto his knees with a gurgling roar and shifted into wolf form before vanishing with a strangled little snarl.

Chapter 20

"Leo, thank God. I thought your *fylgja* bailed on me."

"It's Gunnar."

"I'm sorry… Gunnar?"

"I'm Leo's *hamr*, a projection of his physical self. The *fylgja* warned us there was trouble, and Leo sent me, imbued with his luck-self, the *hamingja*. We thought you could use some backup."

"Ah. Thanks, Gunnar. You saved my ass."

The dog trotted up behind him, eyeing Lucy with reproach as if to chastise her for having doubted him.

"And you, too," she acknowledged. Unfortunately, they hadn't killed the thing. But she knew more about it now. More than she'd ever wanted to know. Now she just needed to figure out where Oliver had gone and make sure the beast hadn't managed to rematerialize there to take Colt.

"I hate to ask for another favor, but can either of you help me find someone who isn't a murderer or an oath breaker?"

Gunnar smiled. "With our extra luck from the *hamingja*? I can help you find anyone."

"Fantastic." She was really going to owe Leo one after this. And Rhea, for that matter—if she didn't kill Lucy first.

Oliver's instincts hadn't been wrong. The Blackstone Ranch compound lit up the night like a sparkling power plant in the flat expanse of the farming valley southeast of Bullhead City. And like a power plant, it was well guarded. And they were expecting him.

Finch and another agent approached him as he walked up to the gate. "Benally." Finch eyed him with apparent newfound uneasiness after what had gone down at the Grotto.

Oliver handed him the pebble. "You have something of mine. I want it back."

"Artie didn't think you'd show up here without that Smok bitch."

"Watch your mouth."

"Sorry. Don't mean anything by it." He was definitely rattled by Oliver's connection to the siren. "I'm supposed to escort you to him. To Artie, I mean, not the kid." Finch nodded to the guard at the gate, and the gate buzzed loudly, sliding open on heavy wheels. "I gotta say, I don't know what's so special about that kid. He hasn't done anything but sleep."

So at least he wasn't awake and terrified or being physically or psychologically tortured. That was something. "There isn't anything special about him. He's just a kid. Darkrock's intel is fucked up."

"Tell it to Artie. This is his mission."

They led him inside the compound to a brightly lit

corridor, industrial bulbs buzzing within metal cages in keeping with the power plant theme, to where Artie and his security retinue were waiting outside a locked door.

"Here comes the chief." Artie sneered.

Oliver stepped in front of him. "One of these days, Artie, you're going to call me that, and I'm going to split your skull before you finish saying the word. So if you like to gamble, just keep saying it."

"Relax, man. It's a nickname. It's meant with affection."

"It's racist, and I've asked you a dozen times to knock it the hell off with that. I'm also having a hard time seeing how there should be any affection between us at this point."

"All right. Jesus Fucking Christ. Goddamn snowflake." Artie's hand rested on the butt of his gun in his holster as if he expected Oliver to attack him at any moment. "I take it you get why we brought you here."

"For a trade."

"Hey, he's a bright boy. Give him a medal."

"I want to see Colt first."

Artie nodded to the guard at the door, who unlocked it and pushed the door open. Inside, a bright bulb hung from the ceiling, illuminating Colt's sleeping form on a foldout cot. They'd put him in an oversize uniform—he'd been unclothed under the covers at home, since he'd still been in wolf form. The fact that he was in human form now meant he must be closer to consciousness. And according to Finch, they hadn't seen him as a wolf when they abducted him. With any luck, they didn't know what they had.

"See?" Artie stood between Oliver and the open doorway. "No harm done."

Oliver folded his arms. "You didn't have to bring him into this. He's an innocent kid."

"Is he your kid?"

Oliver's jaw tightened. "No, he's not my kid. He's a street kid. I'm trying to find him a safe place to stay."

"Kinda looks like he could be your kid. Plus, there's the fact that he ain't human. And you…" Artie shook his head. "We're not too sure what you are."

A few hours ago, Oliver would have scoffed at that. Despite his odd ability to take wounds that weren't his and heal them in record time and his inexplicable control over fire, he hadn't doubted his own humanity. Now… what did being half Welsh elven royalty make him?

"Finch said you were willing to trade. I'm here. What are you going to do with him?"

"We don't need him, so as soon as he wakes up, he can go."

"How's he going to go anywhere? We're out in the middle of nowhere."

"That's his problem."

Oliver didn't doubt that Colt could travel back to Jerome—or wherever he wanted to—on his own. But they weren't just in the middle of nowhere; the hell beast was still looking for Colt.

"Let me take him back to Jerome. You can follow me, and I promise to turn myself over to you as soon as he's safe."

"No deal. You're not going anywhere." Artie nodded to the guard, who pulled the door shut and locked it once more. "Take him to the interrogation room, Finch. Blake wants to talk to him."

Oliver stood his ground as Finch took hold of his arm.

"I'm warning you. If I don't have proof that Colt has been allowed to leave, there's going to be blood spilled."

Artie rolled his eyes. "All right, Chie—tough guy. We'll get you the footage from the camera on the gate when he leaves. Now move."

Gunnar turned out to be better than metaphysical GPS. It was nice having luck on her side for once. Lucy had shown him the list her assistant had sent of the Darkrock sites, and he'd perused them for a moment, before pointing to the Bullhead City site.

"This looks like a good bet," he said. "It's out near Golden Valley and there's nothing else around for miles, so they have good visibility for keeping it secure. Which of course doesn't exactly work in our favor, since they'll see us coming."

"I don't care if they see us coming. I just want to get there before the hell beast thing wakes up and re-materializes."

"Gus will alert us if it does."

"Gus?" Lucy glanced at Gunnar as they got into her car.

He nodded to the dog lying down patiently on the back seat. "That's what I call him. Easier than saying 'the *fylgja*' or 'the harbinger' all the time."

"Makes sense. Okay, Gus, we're counting on you."

The drive west from Jerome was a roller-coaster ride through dozens of switchbacks. If the road up the mountain from Clarkdale was slow, this was a virtual crawl. Golden Valley was a three-hour drive once they'd gotten to flat ground.

As they neared the lights of the compound, eerily illuminated against the predawn sky, Gus began to growl quietly from the back seat.

Lucy steeled herself. "The hell beast?"

Gunnar glanced back at Gus. "I think it's the hellhound. We must be on the right track. Gus isn't sure what to make of him. Smells funny."

"How do you know what Gus thinks?"

Gunnar laughed. "Lucy, he's me. We're all Leo."

"This is just weird."

"That's what Rhea always says."

Armed security guards lined the gate in front of the compound, and Oliver's truck was parked just outside. Lucy parked next to it. So she'd been right about what he'd do. And so had the Oliver-beast. And Darkrock. Everybody was batting a thousand tonight.

She approached the guards at the gate. "I want to see Oliver Benally. Now."

The pair closest to her glanced at each other, and one of them addressed her. "Who the hell arc you?"

"Lucy Smok."

The other guard called it in on his two-way radio. "Lucy Smok is out here demanding to see Ollie Benally."

The gate buzzed and started rolling open. Apparently, that was her answer. She started inside with Gunnar and Gus at her side, but the guards stopped them.

"Not them. Just you."

Great. So she was leaving her extra luck outside as well as her hell beast alarm. Her own luck and intuition would have to do.

"Thanks, guys. I can take it from here. And thank Leo for me."

Gunnar smiled. "Already done. Good luck."

Lucy grinned. "Nice one."

A guard on the inside of the compound stopped Lucy as she reached the entrance. "No weapons."

"It's only loaded with trank bullets."

"No weapons," he repeated, holding out his hand.

With a sigh, she turned over the Nighthawk Browning. "I want this back." He continued to hold out his hand.

Lucy rolled her eyes and slipped the knife from her boot and the larger tactical knife from inside her belt holster at the small of her back. "That's it. I swear. I left my crossbow in the car."

He didn't crack a smile, but he let her in. "This way."

Lucy followed him down the overly bright corridor to what looked like an interrogation waiting room. "What is this?"

"You're supposed to wait here."

"I want to see Oliver Benally."

He shrugged and took his place to stand guard at the door. After several minutes, a dazed-looking, half-awake Colt was escorted into the room. His eyes widened when he saw Lucy, and he pulled away from his escort and ran to stand behind her.

Lucy drew him close to let him know she would protect him. "Where's Oliver?"

Colt's escort held the door open. "You and the boy are free to go. Agent Benally is remaining voluntarily as an employee of Darkrock."

"I want to talk to him."

"Send him a letter."

Getting Colt away from them—and getting him somewhere safe from the beast—had been Oliver's singular goal. Short of taking on the entire compound single-handedly and unarmed, there was nothing she could do here. Lucy let the escort lead them out to her car, making sure he returned all her weapons.

Still out of it, Colt fell asleep on the way back to Jerome, and despite the fact that it was morning by the time they returned to Oliver's place, after drinking enough water to operate a fire hose, Colt climbed into the guest bed and went back to sleep. Lucy had figured Oliver's place would be more comfortable for Colt than her own, but she was going to need a better solution. They were sitting ducks here. What she needed were some magical wards. There were witches on retainer at Smok Consulting, but it was better to keep something like this off the books, and if the Carlisle sisters were Lucy's family now, as Rhea had said, Lucy had one of the most powerful witches in Sedona in her family.

She didn't really know Ione Carlisle at all, but there was no more talented witch in Arizona than the high priestess of the Sedona branch of the Covent, the world's largest organized coven.

After calling Leo to thank him for his help last night, Lucy dialed Ione's number. Halfway through explaining the nature of her request, she realized what a tricky subject this was going to be for Ione. The beast Lucy needed to ward against was a creation of none other than Carter Hamilton, the last person Ione ever wanted to hear about. His campaign to steal whatever power he could get his hands on had begun with Ione, who had unwittingly dated him while he was stalking her sister Phoebe in order to steal Rafe Diamante's "quetzal" power—Rafe was an avatar of Quetzalcoatl, who could command the dead. At the same time, Carter had been murdering local sex workers to use the shades of his victims as "step-ins" to control other women during sexual transactions his clients paid for.

"There's something I should tell you about the thing I've been hunting," she said to Ione. "But I think it would be better to talk about it in person. I'm kind of babysitting the subject in need of protection here in Jerome. Could I possibly impose on you to drive all the way out here?"

Ione was gracious. "I don't have anything on my calendar this morning. Anyway, it's stronger magic if the work is performed on-site by the witch providing the wards, so it only makes sense for me to come to you."

When Ione arrived, she wasn't alone. Phoebe had come along for the ride. As the lawyer who'd put Carter in prison, she'd also been a victim of his ongoing campaign for revenge when he cultivated the Carlisles' long-lost half sister Laurel as an apprentice to try to steal Phoebe's soul. This was going to be awkward.

Phoebe and Ione were as much a contrast in style as the twins. Where Ione's style was button-up conservative—even more so than Lucy, who was going for professional but chic—and her dark chestnut hair, highlighted in gradually lighter tones of auburn to dark gold from top to bottom, was professionally straightened, Phoebe looked like something out of a vintage pinup calendar—Bettie Page bangs, bouncy curled ponytail, tight sweater, cigarette pants and all.

Phoebe glanced around the café after Lucy let them in—double-checking to make sure the Closed sign was still up and the door was locked. "This is fantastic. What are you doing in Jerome? You don't own this place, do you?"

Ione frowned at her. "I'm sure that's none of our business, Phoebe."

"It is," said Lucy. "But it's fine. There's no reason for secrecy. I'm kind of watching the place for the owner, Oliver Connery. He's my client."

Phoebe turned back from perusing a stack of arcane books. "A client, huh? That's not how Rhea described him. I think the term she used was 'that insanely hot silver fox that Lucy bagged.'"

"Phoebe." Ione was still playing the disapproving mom. A role she'd apparently taken on after the Carlisle sisters' parents were killed when she was only nineteen. Lucy found Ione more relatable, even if—or maybe because—her manner was a little cool. Early responsibility was something Lucy knew well, even if she hadn't had to raise any siblings. Unless you counted Lucien's years of playing the irresponsible screw off. "You'll have to forgive Phoebe," said Ione. "She's just giving you the Carlisle treatment. Take it from me, it never ends, and it's maddening."

"The Carlisle treatment?" Lucy raised an eyebrow.

Phoebe laughed. "Affectionate ribbing about our marvelous taste in men. And it's not really the Carlisle treatment. The twin terrors started it. It just rubbed off on me. Love the hair, by the way."

"Thanks." Lucy fingered the back of it reflexively. "But Oliver really is a client. And I wouldn't call him a silver fox, exactly." The words were accompanied by a burgeoning heat in her cheeks, which ruined the whole protest. "I mean, he's not even forty. He's just…" She was digging herself in deeper. "Oh, crap."

Ione smiled politely. "Welcome to the family, Lucy. It only gets worse from here. Now, what kind of wards were you looking to put up? Is it a general protection spell you're looking for, or is there a specific threat you want to address?"

She hated to ruin Ione's day when she was being so generous. "I think you're both going to want to sit down."

Phoebe and Ione exchanged looks as they sat on one of the plush couches.

"The creature Oliver's group hired me to hunt is something I've never encountered before."

"Right," said Phoebe. "Some hell beast Lucien let out."

Ione was more diplomatic. "Theia mentioned to me that there had been a brief period during Lucien's transformation that allowed some unorthodox creatures to enter our world from the underworld."

"That's true. But it turns out this isn't one of them. At least, Lucien has no record of it in hell."

"Thank goodness." Phoebe breathed a sigh of relief. "I was afraid this was going to be another Carter Hanson Hamilton nightmare where he was using power from hell somehow, still letting things out."

When Lucy cleared her throat, Ione groaned. "Oh, no. Don't say it."

"Sorry. But if the beast itself is to be believed, Carter created it."

Phoebe jumped up and paced in frustration. "Goddammit. Why the hell can't he just die already?"

"Well, technically, he did," said Lucy. "Being dragged to hell will do that to you. But, sadly, there's no way to wipe out someone's soul from the universe itself, or I'd be happy to help do it."

Phoebe clenched her fists. "We should have had Leo take him to Náströnd and throw him into that corpse lake to let the dead feast on his bones along with that

damn Nazi's. You know how Carter met that guy, right?
In prison. They met through Carter's Aryan Nations
pals. That bag of Nazi dicks. I'm surprised he didn't
end up as a special adviser to the White House."

"The thing is," said Lucy, wanting to get to the point,
"I apparently…helped."

Phoebe stopped pacing. "Helped what?"

"Create this thing. It claims to have been…sort
of…birthed…by me as Carter channeled the energy
he was stealing from hell through the earth and into
me—something he was able to do because of the step-
in that was possessing me." Lucy sighed. "Because I'm
weak and empty, apparently."

Phoebe sat carefully on the couch. "Being accessible
to step-ins does not mean a person is weak and empty."

Lucy blanched. She'd forgotten that hosting step-
ins was what Phoebe did. "I didn't mean to suggest—"

"No, of course you didn't." Phoebe smiled thinly.
"Most people don't appreciate the strength it actually
takes to host someone else's essence for an extended
period of time without going completely insane. You
simply weren't prepared for it, and Carter took advantage of that. But he wouldn't have been able to use you
if you were weak. It's quite the opposite."

"I see."

"I don't think you do, really. Theia told me you were
able to regain control long enough to do your dragon
shift thing and save her from falling off a cliff that
night. The fact that you were able to do that without
any training while a seasoned, powerful necromancer
was actively directing a shade to control you is nothing short of amazing."

"I don't think it's amazing that I stood there like a

zombie while Carter filled me up with hell energy and hatred to bring this nasty thing into being."

"No, sweetie, that's not amazing, it's horrifying. And I'm so sorry he did that to you."

Lucy ran her fingers through the hair hanging over one eye. "I thought you guys would be furious with me." Maybe Ione was, though. She hadn't said anything yet. Lucy glanced at her nervously.

Ione's hands were clasped in her lap. She was the kind of person who tried to keep everything in. "We are most certainly not furious with you, Lucy. We're furious *for* you. So I take it that's the reason for the wards you need, to keep this thing from coming for you."

"No, I'm still coming for it. I just haven't figured out how to destroy it yet. But I need to keep it from getting to Colt, the little boy who's asleep upstairs."

Phoebe glanced at her curiously. "Oliver has a son?"

"No, Colt…well, to be perfectly honest, Colt is one of those things Lucien let out. He's under Oliver's protection."

Ione frowned. "An escaped creature from hell hardly qualifies as a boy. I'm surprised you'd approve of harboring something like that."

"Not half as surprised as I am." Lucy shrugged. "But he hasn't done anything to harm anyone, and he even risked his life to save me when the beast was attacking me, and it was four times his size. I know we can't keep him here. He has to go back where he belongs. But I'll be damned if I'm going to kill a little boy to right the dimensional balance—or stand by while a malevolent energy I helped into the world kills him for sport. Until Oliver gets back, Colt is staying right here."

"And where is Oliver?" Ione asked.

"In the belly of the beast. So to speak."

Chapter 21

Artie and Finch had been sent to "debrief" him. Oliver refused to engage until he had proof that Colt had been freed unharmed. After several unsuccessful attempts to coerce him physically, Artie gave in and brought in a laptop, pulling up the footage from the surveillance camera showing Colt walking out the front gate—hand in hand with Lucy.

What had Lucy been doing here? He had no way of knowing whether she'd taken his advice and proposed a cooperative effort as a ruse—or was actually in league with them. But for all appearances, Darkrock had fulfilled its end of the bargain with Oliver.

"Satisfied?" Artie closed the laptop and set it on the steel desk behind him.

Oliver licked blood from the corner of his split lip. "For now. Are you going to keep these cuffs on me and keep punching me like a coward?"

Artie ignored the dig. "If I have your word that you'll cooperate, I think we can take the cuffs off, sure." He nodded to Finch, who stepped forward with the key.

"You already had my word. I was just waiting for you to stand by yours."

"Fair enough. Finch." While Finch unlocked the cuffs, Artie waited with arms folded to accentuate his overdeveloped pecs and his legs planted in a wide, imposing stance, clearly not intimidated by Oliver at all. "So let's hear it."

Oliver rolled his shoulders and wiped his mouth with the back of his fist. "Hear what?"

Artie's broad arms unfolded. "Don't fuck with me, man."

"I'm not fucking with you. You asked me about forty questions before honoring the deal. Which one do you want me to answer?"

"All right. If you insist on being belligerent, let's start with the firebombing of the blood lab. There was no explosion, despite the official story given to the press. No incendiary devices or accelerants were found. Was it or was it not accomplished through telekinetic means?"

"I don't know about 'telekinetic,' but I don't have a natural explanation for what happened."

"You admit that you were the cause of whatever unnatural phenomenon occurred there."

Oliver sighed. "As far as I know, yes."

"And how long have you had this ability?"

"I don't know. It had never manifested before that night."

Artie looked doubtful. "There's another question that's been on my mind, personally. Did you start the blaze before or after your team was compromised?"

Oliver steadied his breathing. "I'm not sure I'm hearing you correctly. It sounds like you're accusing me of betraying my own people. Of *murdering* my own people."

"Nobody said the word *murder*." Artie's face was stone hard. "I'm asking when this mysterious blaze started. You said yourself you didn't know how it happened. I'd just like to know if it happened after your teammates were killed…or before."

"My *wife* was on that team."

"Yeah. Oh, I get that, man. So maybe you wanna answer the question carefully. Because a lot of us cared about the guys on that team. A lot of us cared about Vanessa."

He had to swallow this rage before he let Artie provoke him into doing something he'd regret. Which was probably what Artie was hoping for. Not that it made what he was insinuating any less despicable.

"You want all the ugly little details, Artie? Fine. When Vanessa and I broke down the back door, Baker's and Keene's bodies were being held upright while a couple of vampire lords drank from where their heads used to be like they were their own personal fountains. Another one grabbed Vanessa and cut her throat before either of us could even process what we were seeing. So if you want to get technical, yeah, Vanessa was still 'alive' when I started burning things. I doubt her spine was fully severed by the human bone blade the vamp was holding and licking, because her limbs were convulsing when he started drinking the blood straight out of her mouth."

"Jesus Christ."

"Fuck, man." Finch looked green.

Artie actually took a moment to compose himself before he went on. "So you just…went nuclear." He nodded as he processed the idea. "Guess I can't blame you for that. But Darkrock's going to want to get to the bottom of how this ability of yours manifests."

Oliver shrugged. "Guess you've gotta do what you've gotta do."

"As for the other thing…"

Oliver wasn't giving them anything. Whatever they knew, they were going to have to tip their hand first. He sure as hell wasn't going to tip his. "What other thing?"

"Come on. Are we really going to do this again?"

"Why don't you just be clear? I'm not a mind reader."

Finch laughed. "Well, that's one thing he can't do."

Artie glared at him. "Shut up, Finch." A little something, almost imperceptible, flashed in Finch's eyes. He'd been with Darkrock longer than Artie had. Oliver imagined he didn't appreciate having a pompous jarhead promoted over him. "There's a rumor that you've been protecting subhumans in Jerome. That you're some kind of sin eater."

"Sin eater?" Oliver laughed. "How does that work, exactly?"

"We've interviewed a few of these subhuman locals. They say any violence done against them is somehow countered by you. They get punched, but the bruise disappears. Somebody stabs them or shoots them, the wound closes up without leaving a scar."

"That's very imaginative, but I have a feeling they're exaggerating my pledge to protect them. It's just magical thinking. Using the idea that they can't be harmed as a sort of ward against anyone who threatens them."

"Well, we'll see about that."

Oliver frowned. "What do you mean?"

Artie switched on a screen behind him, showing another room like the one they were in. Watched over by a pair of Darkrock troops, a young were-badger was seated in a metal chair like Oliver's. Oliver recognized him—Pete, he thought his name was. He hung around the Mine Café sometimes, looking for scraps.

"Is this one under your protection?" Artie asked.

Oliver kept his mouth shut.

Artie spoke into the intercom on the wall. "Let's try one."

One of the agents punched Pete in the face. Nothing happened. Oliver could have told them it wouldn't. Only drawing blood seemed to trigger the protective magic.

"Why don't you try a sustained effort?" Artie said into the intercom. "Let's make it good this time."

Despite his outrage, Oliver tried not to react as the agent punched the were-badger, beating him relentlessly until Pete was semiconscious. Only when Pete's face was dripping with blood did it start to affect Oliver. He sucked in his breath, partly in anger and partly because of the pain.

Finch peered closely at him. "Damn, Artie. I think it's actually working." He touched the left side of Oliver's face, where pain was starting to throb in his cheek and his jaw as if bones had been broken. "Those are new bruises."

Artie smiled. "Hard to tell with all the others."

Through the video feed, Pete's bruises were fading.

Artie hit the button again. "Let's have another demonstration."

This time, the agent unsheathed his knife and stabbed Pete in the gut. The initial pain was clearly felt by Pete, despite his disoriented state, but the agent lifted Pete's shirt to reveal that although the blood was still there, the wound had already closed.

Artie nodded to Oliver. "Lift up your shirt."

Oliver didn't move, not because he was trying to

defy Artie, necessarily, but because the pain from the stab to the gut had taken his breath away.

"Finch, do the honors," said Artie.

Finch pulled up the hem of Oliver's shirt to reveal the stab wound. It would be a few minutes before it began to heal.

Artie, looking pleased with himself, directed the agent with Pete to perform one more test. The agent took out his gun.

Oliver jumped to his feet. "All right, dammit. You've made your point. You don't have to keep putting him through this."

"Putting him through it, Ollie? Or putting you through it?"

"Maybe just skip the middleman, then, and do it to me yourself, if you have the guts."

Glaring, Artie barked an order to shoot.

The agent fired into Pete's knee, and Oliver buckled with a shout, falling back into the chair, swearing profusely. With a nod from Artie, Finch took out his knife and cut the bottom half of the jeans away from the leg that should have been affected. There was no blood— Oliver rarely bled from these wounds—but it was clear the kneecap had been shattered.

"I gotta say…" Artie shook his head. "I'd love to find out what would happen if we blasted away half that thing's skull or hacked off its head, but I think this demonstration has been sufficient to prove the claims." He opened up a case next to the laptop to reveal a med kit with syringes and an array of filled pharmaceutical vials.

Oliver bit back the pain still throbbing in his knee. "What the hell is that for?"

"Per your own admission, you don't know what the

basis of your fire-based telekinesis is. Do you want to change your story about that?"

"Since it's not a story, no. I'm telling you the God's honest truth."

"And despite your earlier lies, I'm willing to give you the benefit of the doubt about this. So what we're going to do is see if we can find the biological triggers." Artie uncapped a syringe and picked up one of the vials. "This is a little something we borrowed from Smok Biotech's labs." He unsealed the vial and filled the syringe. "I don't understand the science gobbledygook, but the idea is to provide an incentive for your body to do its thing. This stuff is kind of like a flu vaccine, as I understand it. Introduces a little something to your bloodstream that your body has to fight off. Darkrock's research team is hoping it will fight it off with a little pyrotechnic demonstration."

Artie held up the syringe. "Now. Are you going to be a good little freak or do we have to cuff you again?"

Oliver sighed and held out his arm for the injection. There wasn't much point in fighting it. And maybe this drug wouldn't do a thing. Though he'd technically been honest with them about not knowing how his ability had come about, he knew his uncontrolled rage had been the catalyst, and he wasn't about to let them know that.

So far he'd been able to control his anger. Depending on what this drug did to him, he hoped he'd be able to continue to maintain an even keel.

Artie tossed the used syringe and bottle in the trash. "Since we don't know exactly what you can do, we've made sure there's nothing combustible in this room except some boxes of paper." He grinned. "And Finch and I are going to take our combustible bodies outta here.

Have fun." They took their equipment with them and left Oliver in the chair. No doubt they'd be watching over their video feed.

While he steeled himself for the drug's effects, Oliver closed his eyes and repeated his mantra in his head—*Semper Fi*—because it was easy to remember, and it worked on so many conscious and unconscious levels.

He cleared his mind, focusing on nothing but the sound of the words in his head. Let any other thoughts flow in and out without responding to them, without being affected by them. Thoughts were mere impulses in the brain, snatches of memory that floated about in his head like wisps of smoke and dissipated. Meaningless. He was empty. Unencumbered by physical needs or desires. There was nothing but the silence and the words.

Semper Fi. He wasn't feeling any effects from the drug yet. Oliver opened his eyes. He ought to be feeling something by now. Maybe it wasn't formulated for his kind of trigger if it wasn't biological in nature. Or maybe the drug was nonsense, a placebo designed to get Oliver so worked up that he'd display his ability unwittingly.

Semper Fi. Always faithful. Oliver played with the ring on his finger. Had he been faithful? Never during their five years of marriage had he strayed in thought or in deed. But was that the meaning of faithfulness? Checking off sins he'd resisted and winning brownie points? Did it matter that he'd been faithful then if he wasn't being faithful now?

And what would Vanessa think of him now? She'd probably think he was a joke, imagining he had some duty to protect things that weren't human. Just as Lucy thought he was a joke deep down. And Lucy… Vanessa would think he was even more of a joke for imagining someone as sophisticated and wealthy—and young— as Lucy would be interested in him.

Semper Fi. He was having trouble concentrating on what he'd come here for. Some kind of Darkrock debriefing. Right. They'd called him in from the field to report on the progress he'd made in... What was his mission? Damn, that drug really must be messing with his head. How could he forget his mission? Maybe that was the test. The experimental drug was something that affected his short-term memory, and they were testing him to see if he could remain faithful to the mission despite the lack of immediate context.

Other than a little bit of brain fog, he was feeling pretty good.

Semper Fi. What was his ring doing on his right hand? Oliver chuckled at himself and switched it back to the proper finger. Vanessa would kick his ass if she thought he was playing around on her.

The door opened, and Oliver glanced up to see Artie Cooper and Tyler Finch.

Artie smiled. "How's it goin', Chief?"

"Hilarious, Artie. Very original." He slapped his palms against his legs and got to his feet, adjusting the weight on his right leg as his knee gave him a twinge. "So, did I pass?"

"With flying colors," said Artie. "Fit as a fiddle. You're cleared for active duty."

Oliver grinned. "Fantastic. What's our target?"

Chapter 22

Ione's wards were extremely effective against the hell beast. Lucy could tell by the escalating reports of sightings nearby. It was circling Jerome, unable to get within a half-mile radius of Delectably Bookish. What Lucy hadn't counted on was that something else might come for Colt. Or rather, someone else.

Just before dawn, she was instantly alerted by a sound on the stairs. In a light sleep in Oliver's room, she'd kept her conventionally loaded gun by her side. Lucy leaped from the bed, bare feet silent on the hardwood floor, and crept to the door, weapon in hand. Scanning the landing, she was relieved to see Oliver at the top of the stairs. Darkrock had released him after all. But before he turned and saw her standing there, more noise came from below. Three armed men were mounting the stairs behind him. That didn't bode well.

"Oliver?" Lucy lowered her gun but kept it ready at her side. "What's going on?"

He whirled and aimed his Beretta at her, his eyes scanning her—with a brief pause on her bare legs below the flannel nightshirt—as if he didn't recognize her. "Lucy Smok." Evidently, he did. But there was something a little off about him. "They told me you'd be hiding out here, but I guess I had to see for myself."

"Hiding out? What are you talking about?"

One of the other operatives moved toward the closed door to the guest room where Colt was sleeping.

Lucy stepped in front of him and blocked the door. "Unh-uh. You'll have to go through me." With her gun trained on the operative, she glanced at Oliver. "Are you going to do something about this? What are these guys doing here?"

"Following my orders." Oliver hadn't lowered his pistol. "Step aside, or we *will* go through you."

The other two operatives raised a pair of AK-47s in her direction. Darkrock was nothing if not predictably overarmed.

"Give me one good reason."

"Because you're harboring a monster in there, and it's my job to collect it. I would have thought it was your job, too, as the acting head of Smok International."

There was more than a little something off about him. There was something off about this whole thing.

"He's not a monster, and you damn well know it. If you're working with Darkrock, you should be going after the hell beast, not a harmless kid. And why let him go just to come straight here after him? Is this a test for you or something?"

Oliver's finger moved closer to the trigger of his Beretta. "I'm not going to have a discussion with you about my mission, and I'm not going to tell you again. Drop the weapon and step aside."

Instead, she fired her weapon at the operative to

her right. Not to hit him—well, maybe just graze him a little, give him something to think about. It would be the warning Colt needed. They were fast, the other operative striking her arm and going for her gun and the one she'd grazed firing off a round that just missed her as she ducked for a counterstrike against the first operative. The bullet whizzed over her head and hit the wall. After elbow punching the one in front of her in the sternum and knocking the other gunman off his feet with a roundhouse to his shins, Lucy looked up into the barrel of Oliver's gun.

He pressed the Beretta against her forehead while one of the others disarmed her. "Step. Aside."

With her enhanced hearing, she caught the snick of the latch on the window in the guest room. Colt had taken heed.

Lucy shrugged and moved out of Oliver's way. "You could have said please."

Oliver kicked the door in—his own door, which wasn't locked—and his eyes swept the room. Lucy leaned against the busted door frame with her arms folded, giving Oliver a smug smile when his gaze finally came back to her.

"Where is he?"

"Beats me."

Oliver checked the window. Finding it ajar, he opened it to look down into the alley but evidently saw nothing. A faint acrid scent drifted into the room through the window, like a brush fire burning in the distance, and something yipped, and another something answered, like coyotes calling to each other.

He turned back to Lucy, studying her with a closed expression. If he was playing a role for Darkrock to save his own skin, he was hiding it well. He also looked painfully attractive in his Darkrock gear—black combat fatigues and heavy boots, black long-sleeved cotton T that hugged him perfectly. It made him look younger, tougher. He also had a few bruises on his face that appeared to be his own, as though someone had worked him over. And it wasn't the only thing that was different about him. The gray in his hair was significantly less—and his ring was on his left hand.

Oliver holstered his handgun. "This isn't over, Smok. We've got eyes on you."

Lucy followed him to the top of the landing. "What the hell is that supposed to mean?"

"Figure it out." He gestured to his men and headed back down the stairs.

Lucy watched them clomp through the artfully arranged stacks of books, Oliver treating the decor with the same disinterested contempt as his men, and stared after them as the door to the street swung shut behind them with a sharp rattle of the little bell.

The air outside was icy. Lucy shivered and rubbed her arms after locking the door. What had happened at that compound?

"Figure it out." Was that a message of some kind that he was trying to give her without alerting the Darkrock team, or was he just being a dick? Whatever he'd meant, she damn well *was* going to figure it out. All of it—what he was up to, what Darkrock was up to. But she was also going to have to figure out where Colt had gone.

Dammit. After all the trouble Ione had gone to in setting the wards to keep the hell beast out, Colt was out there on his own, defenseless, with both Darkrock and the hell beast hunting him, and Lucy felt responsible for both. As she went back to the bedroom to get dressed, that little echoing yip from the hills haunted her. She had no doubt the first had been Colt's cry. But who had answered?

Before she could head out the door to go in search of Colt, someone rang the bell. As Oliver had made a point of that first day, the shop didn't open until noon. It was probably a delivery. Lucy pulled aside the shade to look and was surprised to see Phoebe Carlisle-Diamante standing outside.

"Phoebe?" She unlocked the door and opened it. "What's wrong? Has something happened?" The Carlisle sisters weren't known for being early risers.

"You might say that. Can I come in?"

Lucy shrugged and held the door open. "Would you like some coffee?"

Phoebe glanced around at the place as if she hadn't seen it before. Or as if she had, actually, and was a little choked up, like someone coming home after a long absence. "No, thanks." She met Lucy's eyes, and Lucy had the distinct impression that her eye color had changed. Didn't Phoebe have the sort of blue eyes that were described as violet? Right now they looked more hazel, almost brown. "I want to tell you, first of all, that this is all on the up-and-up. I have the evocator's consent."

"The evocator?" Lucy's eyes narrowed. It was the term for what Phoebe did, letting shades speak through her. "You're not Phoebe."

Phoebe shook her head and pulled awkwardly at the habitual ponytail, as though its height on the back of her head bothered her. "My name is Vanessa Benally. I'm Oliver's wife."

Chapter 23

Lucy sank onto the nearest chair. "I see. How can I help you, Vanessa?"

"I know you have a physical relationship with Oliver. You don't need to feel awkward about it. It's only natural that he'd find somebody eventually."

"I wouldn't call it a relationship—"

"But you care about him."

Lucy bristled. She didn't do emotional attachments. She hardly knew Oliver. "I'm not sure what difference it makes whether I do or I don't. Whatever you have to say to me, just say it."

Phoebe smiled—a little thin, slightly sad smile that was nothing like Phoebe's. "I am saying it. I've been here for years trying to get Oliver's attention. He talks to Jerome's regular haunts all the time, even though he can't see them. But as much as he's attuned to their vibrations and to the folks he likes to call undergrounders, he's never noticed me. Or maybe he doesn't want to notice me. The point is, when I saw Phoebe here yesterday, I followed her home because I knew she could sense me.

I had to find a way to speak to you." She tugged down the edges of her faux jaguar winter coat as if adjusting a military uniform. "Darkrock is up to their old tricks. They used to treat us all like guinea pigs, telling us they were giving us vitamin shots or inoculations against vampirism. They've used something on Oliver, some kind of mind control drug to make him compliant."

It certainly explained his odd behavior this morning. "So he thinks he's still working for them."

"Yes. And I know it goes against everything he is now. He doesn't want this." She chewed her lip. "There's more, but I need to tell Oliver directly."

"This drug." Lucy rubbed the buzzed hair at the back of her neck. "You don't happen to know what it was called, do you?"

Phoebe's eyes clouded for a moment, literally changing from the muddy hazel to violet right in front of Lucy. "She sees something, a symbol on the bottles, but she can't articulate it."

"Phoebe?"

"Yeah, sorry. Didn't mean to interrupt."

"The symbol…was it a wyvern? A small dragon in silhouette?"

Phoebe thought for a moment, her demeanor changing once more, along with her eye color. "A dragon. Yes. The labels had a dragon on them."

It was Smok's trademark. A sneaking suspicion had begun to nag at Lucy as Vanessa spoke about the mind control drug. Smok Biotech had one in development, one that enabled the person administering it to literally inject a suggestion into the subject's mind. A suggestion like "you're on a mission for Darkrock." The subject wouldn't question it, because it would come with its own little story line to assuage any cognitive dissonance. And it could even include enhancements to make the story work—like getting rid of his prominent gray so he would believe he was younger.

Another detail she'd noticed about Oliver this morning took on greater significance. "He was wearing his ring on his left hand."

Phoebe's expression was puzzled. "His ring?"

"Vanessa's ring. Your ring. His wedding ring. He wears it on his right hand. But he was here with some Darkrock operatives this morning, and the ring was on his left hand." Lucy's gaze fixed on Phoebe's color-changed eyes. "I think Darkrock has convinced him that you're still alive. And still married."

Phoebe's expression shifted into a dark frown. "Then he thinks he's the person he was then. They can make him do anything." She rose and headed for the door. "I have to go. I have to keep an eye on him."

Lucy stood, ready to run after her, but Phoebe stopped at the door and hunched over, gripping the door handle, as if someone had punched her or she was going to be sick.

"Balls. I hate it when they do that. They get all excited and drag my body along for the ride as they're leaping out." She turned to look at Lucy, her face a little green. "Sorry. She's gone." Phoebe glanced hopefully toward the back of the shop. "Did you say you had coffee?"

"I did." Lucy put the coffee on and sat back on one of the stools at the counter as Phoebe hopped onto the other. "Do you remember everything we talked about?"

"Yep. Every word. When I let someone step in, I insist on having full conscious control, even if I let them take over my voluntary movements."

"That must be strange."

Phoebe shrugged. "I've gotten used to it. They've been coming to see me since I was little, so it's pretty much second nature. When they're polite and cooperative, it's mostly a breeze."

"Daisy sure wasn't a breeze." The shade that had possessed Lucy at Carter's command had made her feel dizzy and sick, and her departure had given Lucy a migraine.

"Yeah, it's not pleasant being entered without your consent. Ever. So, how are the wards holding up? Any visits from that thing?"

"No, no sign of it. But unfortunately, I had a visit from Oliver and his new Darkrock teammates. I'm not sure he even knew me. He called me by my name, but he was behaving as if I were someone he'd read about and never actually met."

"Maybe he did. Read about you, I mean. As part of his indoctrination with that mind control drug."

Lucy nodded. "Yeah. And the great thing about that? I think it's my company's drug. That dragon symbol Vanessa saw is Smok's. It's the wyvern."

"How would they have gotten it?"

"It's not on the market. It's one of our private label experimental pharmaceuticals. So the only way they could have gotten any was if someone at Smok Biotech was working for them on the inside." Lucy got up to pour the coffee. "So it looks like I've got a mole."

"That sucks."

Lucy set a cup in front of Phoebe and sipped her own. "Yeah, it does."

"So, where's the kid? The…what is he?"

"Colt is a hellhound."

"An actual, honest-to-God *hellhound*?"

"Looks that way. And thanks to Oliver and Darkrock—Colt is gone."

"You mean they took him?"

"No, but they intended to. He ran away." Lucy sipped her coffee and shook her head. "So now I've got to somehow find the kid and try to keep him safe while simultaneously hunting the hell beast and figuring out how to get to the bottom of who's working against me in my own company. Not to mention trying to figure out what to do about Oliver."

"Can I make a suggestion?" Phoebe offered her a gentle smile. "Maybe don't try to do everything yourself."

"Sure. I'll just fucking outsource some of that." Lucy's patience was starting to wear thin. She didn't "people" well. She'd gotten into a bad habit of thinking out loud to try to problem solve, and she hadn't been looking for advice from Phoebe.

"Why not?" Phoebe was eternally upbeat. "You know, I have my P.I. license now. Maybe I could do some sleuthing at Smok Biotech for you."

Lucy laughed. "I think you underestimate your local infamy, Phoebe. Everyone there knows exactly who you are."

"Well, I wasn't talking about going undercover, but now that you mention it, I do have one sister who's very good at flying under the radar, and she's right there in Flagstaff near the lab."

"Is Theia still topside? I don't see how she'd get anything out of anyone, even with her access. They know her, too."

"Not Theia. Laurel."

"Laurel…"

"She's one of our half sisters."

"No, I know. I'd just forgotten about her." Lucy considered it. "You know, that's not actually the worst idea I've ever heard."

Phoebe laughed. "Thanks."

"She has past ties to Carter, and if anyone at the lab is sympathetic to him—which I have a strong suspicion is how someone from Darkrock managed to get embedded there—that might be her in."

"Do you want me to have her call you?"

Lucy shook her head, the wheels already turning as she plotted the best course of action. "No. Have her call HR at Smok Biotech. I'll set up an interview with someone I trust and have them hire her as part-time holiday clerical help somewhere in the company where she could do some unobtrusive snooping. Do you think she'd be willing to do it?"

"I have a feeling she'll be eager to do anything that vitiates Carter's influence. She still feels terrible about her part in everything he did to us. And rightly so." If Lucy recalled correctly, Laurel had even once tried to kill Phoebe. Lucy wouldn't have been so forgiving. "But she's a good kid. And I know she can probably use the extra holiday cash, too. I think it'll be perfect. Meanwhile, I'll see if I can get Vanessa to talk to me again. She might be able to tell us more about what's going on with Oliver."

"Thanks, that would be… I'd appreciate that." Lucy smiled awkwardly. She wasn't used to having people offer their help without wanting something in return, and she wasn't really sure how normal people responded to such a thing. "You don't really have to do any of this."

"Nonsense." Phoebe reached across the counter and squeezed her arm, making Lucy twitch in her effort not to physically recoil. She was *so* not a touchy-feely person. "That's what sisters are for." Phoebe grinned. "Or sisters-in-law-once-removed, anyway."

With the mole situation being handled, Lucy could focus on what she did best: hunting things. She needed every bit of information she could get on the hell beast's habits, so she spent the day methodically conducting the eyewitness interviews she hadn't gotten to yet, including a drive around the little community—or a walk, which was easier for much of it—to visit each of the locations of the sightings. Like the previous eyewitnesses, these either backtracked, claiming they must have seen a coyote or a mountain lion, or were unwilling to speak to her at all. She'd written off the significance of the Hogback Cemetery, but it was time to leave no stone unturned. And the cemetery happened to be full of stones.

The cemetery trail, with its rusted wrought iron enclosures around the crumbling headstones among the brush, provided little opportunity for anything to hide in, but Lucy thought she caught a glimpse of a kid who looked a great deal like Colt panhandling in the parking lot. When she tried to get close to him, he bolted, and there was no recognition in his eyes. Lucy had the feeling she'd just seen another of the missing hellhounds. And maybe Colt had found his friends, but there was no way to know for sure. The only way to guarantee his safety was to get rid of the hell beast once and for all.

The sun was low in the sky as she drove back up Cleopatra Hill, and as dusk fell, a sort of prickling sensation at the back of her neck made her look in the rearview mirror repeatedly. There was no one behind her, but she couldn't shake the feeling that the hell beast was near. She was beginning to suspect the hell beast was always near, as if it used Lucy herself as a focal point. Which meant Lucy could end up leading the thing straight to the hellhound if she found it.

Even so, she drove to the storage unit just to check to see if Colt had returned to someplace familiar, but there was no sign of him. Darkness was falling by the time she got back to the top of the hill. If the hell beast was focused on her, then she needed to draw it out on her terms. No more ambling about in caves letting it box her in where it limited her ability to use her own assets. She needed to be out in the open to take advantage of her strengths.

Lucy drove to the first site Oliver had shown her and walked down to the tailings pond. A half-moon lent a cool glow to the night, and the field of stars overhead was phenomenal.

She drew her gun and turned slowly to take in a panorama of the hillside. She'd left the crossbow in the car. If neither the arrowheads nor the bullets were going to kill it, she might as well stick with what she was best at to slow it down.

"All right, you goddamn piece of shit," she yelled at the sky. "Show yourself. Or are you afraid to fight me?"

"You're the one who's afraid."

Lucy whirled at the sound of Oliver's voice behind her. He was wearing his Darkrock commando gear, armed as he'd been earlier when they stormed the place. Was it Oliver, or was it the beast?

"What am I afraid of?"

"Of power." He moved toward her, slowly, steadily closer. "Of what we could do together." He was standing in front of her.

"And what would that be?"

Oliver reached out and touched her cheek. "Devouring the world." The last word was delivered on a sexy little growl, and he lowered his mouth to hers. Lucy, her gun still ready at her side, let their lips touch, let his tongue slide between her teeth. And fired a round directly into his gut.

The Oliver-beast roared and reared back, blood swiftly soaking the dark shirt. She'd hurt him this time. Lucy aimed again, and the beast transformed with the swiftness of thought and charged her, knocking her to the ground. She managed to hang on to the gun, but her arm was pinned, and there was no way to hit him with another round even if she fired.

His wolfish eyes glared down into hers, inches from her face, foul breath nearly choking her. "The only thing stopping me from devouring you myself is the tasty treat you keep from me. But I'm growing tired of this game. I can find it on my own."

"Why do you want it so bad?"

This seemed to give it pause. "Because the things of earth are protected here. But *they* are not of earth. They are of hell, and I long to taste its sweet infernal essence."

The things of earth—inhuman creatures that weren't hell fugitives—were protected here because of Oliver. But the claw marks from the swipe Colt had taken from the beast hadn't shown up on Oliver. Was it because Colt wasn't of this earth? But the "hell beast," as she'd grown so used to calling it, was. And Oliver, inadvertently, was protecting it from every bullet Lucy fired into it, every arrow she struck it with.

"If the things of earth are protected… I'm protected. Isn't that how it should work?"

The creature's laugh sent chills up her spine, like the screeching cackle of a reanimated corpse, and it morphed back into Oliver's form. "You, Mommy? You're not of this earth. You're a demon whore."

His transformation back into human form had given her just the moment's advantage she needed. Lucy fired several times in succession into his side and scrambled out from under him when he recoiled from the impact. As he returned to wolf form and leaped at her once more, she released her wings and grabbed it by the throat, digging her talons into the thick, furred flesh as she launched herself into the air, hanging on with all her might.

She spun with it, jamming the talons on her thumbs into the fleshy underside of the creature's chin, preventing it from using its powerful jaws on her, but it had recovered its brute strength, and it sank its claws into her shoulders and scored her arms, digging furrows into them.

Lucy screamed, her own voice unnaturally enhanced into a bloodcurdling wyvern shriek, but there was no way she was letting this fucker go. Not now. Let it shred her arms to the bone if it wanted to. It wasn't getting away.

And then something slammed into the back of her leg, like a bolt of fire. A second later, something struck the hell beast. The red fletching of a tranquilizer dart was sticking out of the beast's thigh. Which meant Lucy was sporting one, too. And it meant Oliver and his commandos were below them, waiting for the drug to take effect so she and the beast would fall to the ground and they could take them both in.

Things were already getting a little fuzzy. Lucy hissed in anger and let go of the hell beast, flapping her wings to knock it away from her, and took off toward the wooded hills.

Chapter 24

Finch scanned the horizon with his binoculars. "Damn, I think we lost it." He headed back down from the top of the ridge to where Oliver and Artie stood over the body.

"We'll get it later." Artie kicked at the massive werewolf lying unconscious at their feet. "We got this thing. Whatever the hell it is."

Oliver took another look through the binoculars while Finch and Artie loaded the dead weight of the beast into the cage in the back of the van. There was something oddly familiar about that bat-winged thing the beast had been fighting with. He'd thought…but it couldn't be. The thing had definitely been female, though.

As Finch came around to the front of the van, he glanced at Oliver. "You sure you're okay?"

Oliver had felt like he was being strangled, something stabbing into the underside of his jaw as the creatures had struggled in the air, and his gut and side were still aching. Must be the transference magic they'd warned him about. The creature could project its injuries outside itself to make someone else take the brunt of them. Though why it only affected him, he wasn't sure. At least the tranquilizer hadn't had much effect on him.

Oliver untucked his shirt and lifted it up to examine the mottled bruises and rapidly scarring flesh. Darkrock had given them all inoculations to prevent any such magic from doing them permanent harm, and it encouraged rapid healing. Thank God. Otherwise, he'd be a shredded mess. He'd taken four "transference" bullets, evidently, in addition to the injuries to his throat.

"Yeah." He tucked his shirt back in. "Yeah, I'm good."

Something wet was touching the side of her face. Lucy jolted awake, going for her gun, only to find a white wolf curled by her side.

"Colt?" She sat up, her head thick and groggy, and glanced around in the early morning light. How the hell had she ended up asleep outside in the snow? She raised her palm into the air. The snow was still falling. The hellhound whimpered softly beside her, its tail wagging and thumping the ground. She remembered now—flying off as the tranquilizer kicked in, going as far as she could until unconsciousness took her and she plummeted to the ground among the firs and brush of Mingus Mountain north of Jerome.

Lucy scratched the wolf's ears, and it panted happily. "Thanks, kid. I think you may have kept me from freezing to death." Her wyvern blood made her core temperature higher than normal, but it wouldn't have prevented hypothermia. Colt had saved her life.

The snow was coming down harder now. The white patches around them would soon be a respectable winter covering.

"We'd better get somewhere warmer than this, though, huh?" Lucy got to her feet, ignoring her throbbing head, and headed for the nearby forest road. Colt jumped up and trotted along beside her as if he'd always been at her side. She supposed it wasn't that odd, really, now that she thought about it. Why shouldn't the sister of the Prince of Hell have a hellhound?

They were both solidly wet by the time they hiked the three miles down the mountainside to where her car was parked. She'd never appreciated the heated seats more. Colt seemed content to stay in wolf form, curling up on the seat beside her as she drove back to Delectably Bookish. She'd noticed a fireplace upstairs in Oliver's sitting room. It seemed like a good day for a fire. Colt lay on the rug while she piled up the logs from the firewood holder by the hearth and threw on some kindling. Before she could light it, however, the distant tinkle of the bell on the door downstairs alerted both her and Colt to the entrance of an intruder.

Colt bolted upright, growling, as she straightened, his hackles raised. Had she remembered to lock the door? Maybe it was a customer. She really ought to put up a sign saying the place was closed for the holidays until she figured out what to do about Oliver.

Lucy unsnapped her holster and moved to the doorway in front of Colt. Whoever it was had started up the stairs. Before she could stop him, Colt had darted past her to the landing, but instead of attacking, she found him greeting Oliver on the top step.

Oliver patted the wolf, looking friendly, but there was no reason to believe he'd suddenly remembered himself.

With her gun drawn, she waited for Oliver to acknowledge her.

"I thought you might come back here." There was no smile in his eyes. "Though I didn't expect to find you both. Makes things easier." He slipped a collar around Colt's neck and held on to it with his left hand, keeping the wolf at his side.

"You're not taking him anywhere."

"I have my orders."

As Lucy opened her mouth to tell him where to stick his orders, her phone rang. She took it out of her pocket, intending to silence it, but the caller ID displayed Phoebe's number. With her gun still pointed at Oliver, she answered the phone. "Find out anything?"

"I did, but there's something more pressing."

"What's that?"

"Vanessa wants to talk to Oliver."

"Okay." Not even questioning how Vanessa could know Oliver was here, Lucy started to hold the phone out to him, but an odd sensation rushed through her as if a little static jolt had zapped her from the phone.

And then she "heard" Vanessa inside her head. *Let me speak to him.*

It wasn't exactly what she'd meant by "okay," but it seemed she'd agreed to let Vanessa step in to her.

Lucy shrugged. *Have at it.*

It was an odd sensation feeling herself move toward Oliver without actively willing it. It reminded her of the possession by Daisy, but this was more conscious. She felt she could stop Vanessa at any moment if she chose to.

"Hey, Ollie," she heard herself say. Oliver's eyes narrowed, but he didn't respond. Vanessa continued. "This

will be hard for you to understand, baby. I know they
told you we were still on the mission, that we'd meet
up after I got back from doing recon. But I'm not coming back."

· Oliver bristled. "What the hell are you talking about?"

"It's me, baby. It's Vee. I'm so sorry."

Oliver's right hand had gone to his sidearm. "Stop it."

"Do you remember our last mission? The blood lab?"

"I've never been on a mission with you. You're not
Vanessa. You're some kind of demon. I saw your wings
and your claws. So you goddamn leave my wife out of
this."

"Okay, baby. Calm down. Let me put it this way.
Just hear me out. Do you remember your last mission
with Vanessa?"

"I don't know what you're trying to prove here."

"Just tell me what you remember. Did you go to that
house with Vanessa?"

Oliver frowned, his fingers curled around the butt of
his sidearm. "The blood lab? You mean the meth head
vamps? Yeah, we…we took the back while Baker and
Keene took the front. So what?"

"What happened when you went in?"

"Same thing that always happens. We busted down
the door, Vanessa went first, and…" The blood drained
from Oliver's face. "No. This is some bullshit demon-
craft head game."

"It's not, baby. It happened. It's real."

A wave of horror washed over Lucy at the images in
Vanessa's mind. She wanted to grab her throat to stop
the blood, even though she knew her own throat hadn't
been slit, but Vanessa was dominant, and her arms
stayed at her sides. The image of a younger, darker-

haired Oliver was superimposed in front of her, his eyes reflecting the pain and horror Lucy was experiencing through Vanessa's memories.

"It wasn't your fault," said Vanessa. "You did what you had to do. I ain't mad, baby. You spared me from what that thing was going to do to me. And our child. You're a goddamn hero, and I love you so fucking much."

Tears poured down Oliver's face as his hand moved away from his sidearm. "No. No. Fuck, no. Please. This can't be true."

Lucy found herself crossing the landing to him swiftly, her arms wrapping around his neck at Vanessa's willing, the gun dangling in her hand. She could feel Vanessa's love and heartache at the loss of Oliver—the loss of the baby she would never know—and it was impossible to bear.

Her own feelings for Oliver were tangled up in Vanessa's, with all the pain and love and all that history between them, and when he kissed her, there were three of them in the kiss. She wanted to stop him hurting, and she couldn't tell whether the thought was Vanessa's or her own. Oliver's love and passion for Vanessa was also apparent in the kiss, and a kind of desolation settled over Lucy as she moved back into her own mind, leaving Vanessa to him.

She had never been loved like that. Would never be loved like that.

"Well, isn't this sweet?"

Lucy and Vanessa released Oliver as one, stepping back to see Artie on the stairs, with Finch and Ramirez behind him. The names came to Lucy instantly with Vanessa's recognition. Along with something else. The knowledge of their part in how Vanessa's last mission had gone wrong.

Artie nodded to Finch as they came up onto the landing. "Get the hound."

Before Lucy could thrust her own will to the fore to take action, Finch had hooked a leash onto Colt's collar and was steering the panicked, yelping wolf down the stairs. Something about the collar seemed to keep him from shifting. Darkrock had planned for everything.

Artie aimed his sidearm at Lucy. "Drop your weapon." As Lucy glared at him and refused the order, he called over his shoulder, "Shoot that fucking thing if she doesn't comply."

Finch had a gun pointed at Colt. With a sigh of resignation, Lucy tossed the gun onto the carpet runner.

Artie looked her over, shaking his head. "Just what the hell are you, sweetie? I'm sure the world will be very interested in knowing that the CFO of Smok International is some kind of demon freak." He jerked the gun toward the stairs. "Come on. Let's go."

Lucy glanced at Oliver, but he looked lost. Darkrock still had a hold on him.

Firecracker, Vanessa whispered in her head. *When you find the right moment, when you think he's broken their hold, use it. Firecracker.* And just like that, Lucy could no longer sense her. Vanessa had gone. She had no idea what the hell "firecracker" meant. Lucy sighed and went down the stairs.

"What are they going to do with him?" Lucy sat beside Oliver in the front seat of the Humvee that followed the van they'd loaded Colt into.

"That's on a need-to-know basis."

"Are you going to let them experiment on him?"

Oliver glanced at her and looked quickly away, eyes focused on the road. "I don't know exactly what you did to me back there, but don't think for a minute that I'm buying any of it."

Lucy sighed and leaned back against the seat. "Believe what you want to, Oliver. I didn't do anything back there, and I think you know that as well as I do."

"You talk to me like you think you know me. You don't know a damn thing about me."

Lucy shrugged. "I suppose that's true. I know what you look like when you come, but that's about it."

The Humvee lurched forward as Oliver's foot slammed the gas pedal to the floor inadvertently.

He eased up, deliberately not looking at her. "And how exactly would you know that?"

"You don't remember the last few years, let alone the last few days." Lucy shook her head. "I don't know what to tell you."

"You expect me to believe I have some kind of relationship with you."

A sharp little "Ha!" burst out of her. "No, Oliver. We don't have any kind of relationship. You can be assured of that."

"But you're saying we've had sex."

"A few times."

He was silent for the next several minutes, the Humvee following the twists and turns of the road through the mountain to Prescott Valley in the west in a rhythmic, almost-wavelike motion—forward, slow turn, back toward the mountain, slow turn, forward toward the next curve of red rock. It was calming. Almost hypnotic.

"Okay, let's say what you're claiming is true."

Lucy jumped slightly. Her eyes had been half-closed. "Sure."

"Did I know about your…aberration?"

"My aberration?" Lucy turned an icy gaze on him. "You mean the fact that I share infernal blood with my twin brother, the current ruler of hell? Yeah, you knew about that."

He made a scoffing sound. "Why would I willingly have a sexual relationship with something inhuman?"

"I'm not inhuman. Darkrock has you convinced that there's some kind of purity test that can be applied to people, and anyone who's a little different is impure, not worth the dignity of being treated like a human being." It struck her that Oliver might have said the same to her when they first met. And she'd willingly perpetuated the belief she was now accusing Darkrock of harboring. That shifters and sirens—and demi-demons—weren't people.

"Look, I'm just doing a job."

God, she'd said that, too. Lucy studied his profile, little worry lines creasing his forehead. Vanessa had almost snapped him out of it. He wanted to know the truth, but Smok's pharmacogenetics were the best in the world. It wasn't going to be easy to undo a biologically induced false reality.

"You know that bookstore café Darkrock keeps having you raid? That's yours."

Oliver darted an incredulous glance at her. "Delectably Bookish? You're out of your mind."

A subconscious impression she'd retained from Vanessa's step-in came to her. The bookstore café B and B had been Vanessa's dream. She'd hoped they could retire and raise a family in a place like that.

"You bought it for Vanessa. To honor her memory."

He glanced at her again, this time not so incredulous. "How do you know that?"

"Vanessa's shade told me. She was touched when she saw it. That's where you've been living for the past three years. You changed your name to Oliver Connery—"

A hearty laugh interrupted her. "Now, that I can almost believe. That's kind of a private joke of mine. I used to do a Sean Connery impression for Vee—Vanessa."

"In your spare time, you're a volunteer firefighter." Despite the circumstances, she gave him a little sidelong smile. "The uniform looks very nice on you, by the way. I may have a little bit of a fireman fetish."

"Oh, really?" An answering smile flickered at the corner of his mouth.

"And you sit on an unofficial town council that monitors the paranormal activity in the town of Jerome."

Oliver's eyebrow lifted, but he didn't offer a comment.

"That's how we met. Your council called me in to deal with that thing you guys took down last night."

That interested him. "The werewolf?"

"I call it the hell beast. I thought it had escaped hell. That turns out not to have been the case."

"What do you know about it?" His voice had taken on a sort of falsely disinterested tone, something he'd been trained to affect. He was in full commando mode.

If she told him what she really knew, it would be like telling Darkrock. He wasn't ready to believe what she was telling him about himself. He would report on everything she said to him.

"I asked Lucien—my brother. He has no record of it in hell's inventory."

"You brother is *actually* the ruler of hell."

She probably shouldn't have mentioned that. But she figured whoever was leaking information and biotech from the firm had probably leaked that already, as well.

"It's kind of a family tradition."

"So you already knew about this thing before this 'council' called you in. The council I supposedly sit on."

"No. I mean, I was tracking something that was killing people up north of here, so when I got the call, I figured it was probably the same thing. But I didn't know what it was at the time." She watched him, wondering how much more he was able to hear right now. "Are you aware that when the hell beast is wounded—you share the wound?"

"Darkrock thought that might happen. It has the ability to project transference magic to keep itself from being fatally injured." It was an interesting theory on Darkrock's part.

"That isn't why."

"Oh? I suppose you're going to tell me why."

"If you want me to."

"It's been a really entertaining story so far. Makes the drive seem shorter."

"The morning I met you—the morning before your council called me in on the job—I was tracking the thing, like I said. I ended up in Jerome, unaware of the paranormal population, and I went after a reptilian shifter—a single mom working as a waitress in a Jerome coffeehouse. You jumped me when I tried to take her out. Said you were Jerome's self-appointed protector of all things 'extra-human.'"

Oliver laughed. "This story just keeps getting better."

"You told me later that you'd promised a young

shifter that you'd watch out for his kind after some drug dealer tried to take advantage of him. Somehow you've inadvertently managed to take on any injuries to paranormal creatures in the vicinity ever since. And you have no idea how or why."

"That sounds like a load of crap."

"Yeah, that's what I thought when you told me, to be perfectly honest. I figure you know exactly how. You just didn't feel like telling me. Maybe you don't really trust me."

"Should I trust you?"

There was something about the way he said it that seemed like more of a sincere plea, as if he needed to be able to trust her, to trust someone.

"Yes. You should. I may not know everything about what you're involved in or what's going on, but I would never lie to you." And that, she realized, was a pretty rare thing for her. She considered lying to be a business necessity much of the time. Though she preferred to call it "creative omission."

They'd reached the valley, and they picked up speed on the highway, heading for Bullhead City.

"One of the creatures you protect is that wolf they've got in the back of the van."

Oliver's jaw tightened. "I'm protecting society, as a matter of fact, by getting things like that off the street."

"And things like me."

Oliver met her eyes for the moment, obviously conflicted. "Yeah. And things like you."

Chapter 25

The sense of familiarity he'd had the night before as he watched the winged creature—Lucy—fly away was even stronger now. It was uncanny how her scent seemed as familiar to him—and as essential—as Vanessa's.

Oliver tossed his gear aside as he undressed for decon. It was some bullshit she was projecting, some hell thing—infernal blood, she'd called it. She'd managed to make him believe for a few minutes that he'd really seen Vanessa die. And what kind of sick imagination would have put that method of death in his head? Trying to play to his emotions, she'd made him see Vanessa pleading with her eyes for him to put her out of her misery after her vocal cords had been severed by a vampire lord's knife. And that extra little detail about Vanessa being pregnant—that was the giveaway that this whole thing was bullshit. Vanessa would have told him if she'd been pregnant. He'd never have let her go on the mission if that were true.

Except that he could remember a conversation with

Vanessa now in vivid detail where she had. He'd accused her of lying and tried to pull rank on her to keep her from doing the job. She'd read him the riot act for that dumb stunt.

No.

Oliver hit the button on the decontamination shower and stepped under the scalding spray. That wasn't real. It was all a lie. And as soon as he met up with Vee later this morning, he could stop letting that demon mess with his head.

As the water streamed over his abs, he noticed the bruises from the transference injuries had already faded, the scars looking like they were from weeks or months ago. Quite a trick that thing was able to pull off. They'd have to neutralize that somehow if they were going to do any exploratory surgery on the beast, because those bullet wounds had felt all too real. He didn't relish having to experience every cut of the scalpel. It probably wouldn't have the ability to project its injuries on to him if it were unconscious, but Oliver knew better than to hope Darkrock would want it sedated. They were big fans of the vivisection.

"Stop stroking your dick and get moving." Artie tossed a towel at him as he came around the wall from the dressing room, and Oliver managed to step out from under the spray and grab it before it got soaked. Artie grinned. "I'm sure we're all very impressed, but they're waiting for you in Block D for testing."

Oliver wrapped the towel around his waist as Artie stepped under the shower. "Your mom was very impressed last night."

"I think you're confusing my mom with that four-hundred-pound werewolf you shagged in the back of the van while it was out cold, but it's a common mistake."

"Jesus, dude."

Artie shrugged. "What can I say?" He indicated the thick hair on his chest as he rubbed the soap over it. "The whole family's hairy."

Oliver rolled his eyes as he went around the partition to get a clean uniform out of his locker. "Hey, any word from Vanessa? Shouldn't she be reporting back from her recon mission today?"

"You know that's classified. Relax. If I'd heard anything negative, I'd have let you know, rules or no rules. I'm sure she's fine."

He couldn't shake the images Lucy Smok had infected him with as he got dressed and headed down to Block D. He wasn't going to be able to get them out of his head until he saw Vanessa in front of him.

They'd put Lucy and the wolf—the small one—in two adjacent cells with the same magic-dampening technology as the cell they'd put the bigger wolf in. He couldn't see what damage these two could possibly do even with their abilities intact, but it wasn't his area of expertise. Oliver kept his eyes straight ahead as he passed the bulletproof glass front walls of the cells and reported to the technician on duty.

"Hey." He nodded to the tech. "Artie says you need me to take some tests."

"Actually, we need you to oversee some tests."

"Oversee?"

"They want you to observe the intake procedures for the new acquisitions."

"Why would they need me to observe them?"

The tech shrugged. "Beats me. Just passing along

the orders." He switched on the screen in front of him to reveal side-by-side feeds of the cells where Lucy and the hellhound were being kept. The wolf was now in human form, huddled naked in the corner, and the glass between the cells allowed the two to see each other, as well. Security guards were stationed inside each cell. The tech spoke into the mic on his laptop. "Ready when you are. Let's start with Subject A."

One of the guards in Lucy's cell stepped forward without warning and punched Lucy in the jaw. He got his ass handed to him as a reward, with Lucy moving so swiftly to immobilize him and drop him to the floor with a knee to his throat that it took his partner a moment to recover and pull his sidearm on her, ordering her to back off. She did so, her stance ready to take them both on if she had to. He had a feeling she might be evenly matched despite being unarmed.

The tech glanced at Oliver and marked something down on his notepad. "Nothing so far. Let's try option two."

While the second guard had his weapon still trained on Lucy, the first took out his knife. "Give me your arm," he ordered.

Lucy looked him up and down. "How badly do you want me to break yours?"

He looked a little nervous. "I'm just going to make a small superficial cut."

"Or I can just shoot you," the other offered.

She studied him with a withering look. "What exactly are you hoping to achieve here?"

"That's on a need-to-know basis."

"For fuck's sake." Lucy sighed, holding out her arm. The guard pushed her sleeve up and drew the blade across the top of her forearm, painting a thin line of blood.

"Nothing," the tech reported, making another note.

"We probably should have cuffed that one," Artie observed as he came up behind Oliver and the tech at the desk. "Can you imagine what she's like in the sack?" He grinned as Oliver looked up at him. "But I guess you don't have to imagine, eh, Chief?"

Oliver decided to let the slur go—for the millionth time—and focused on the insinuation. "What's that supposed to mean? If you're trying to suggest that I'd ever cheat on Vanessa—"

"Oh, right, sorry. Vanessa. Of course you wouldn't. I forgot. You're not only a chief, you're a Boy Scout."

"If by 'Boy Scout' you mean 'not an asshole,' then, sure. I'm a Boy Scout." Oliver studied the monitor. "What's the point of this exercise?"

"Just seeing if either of these two has the same magical transference capacity as the ugly one."

"Nothing so far," said the tech. "Shall we move on to Subject B?"

Artie nodded. "Go for it."

Oliver's brows drew together. "Why would either of them have the same skill?" He cringed, a little flare of anger sparking in him, as one of the guards in the boy's cell punched the kid in the gut hard enough to cause internal injuries.

Artie nodded at Oliver. "Lift up your shirt."

"I didn't feel anything. This is absurd. Why would they have it? And why would it affect me if they did?"

"Just humor me. Let's see."

With a tight-jawed sigh, Oliver lifted up his shirt to reveal an unbruised surface.

Artie raised an eyebrow. "Huh."

While the hellhound was doubled over, the guard stabbed him in the side, eliciting a doglike yelp of pain and fear.

Oliver held up the shirt on the same side. "Nothing, goddammit. Now leave the damn thing alone."

"Grow a pair, Benally. Or do you let Vanessa keep them for you in her purse these days?" Artie turned to the technician. "Looks like these two are duds. I think we can call this test done. Captain Blake wants to have a word with the Smok bitch. Have Ramirez and Daniels bring her up to his office. We'll meet them there."

Lucy shook off her escorts as they brought her into their CO's office. When they'd moved on to torturing Colt, she figured they were trying to gauge whether she and the hellhound were under Oliver's protection. They hadn't figured out what she'd only just learned herself from the hell beast—that she and Colt didn't count because they weren't "of the earth."

Oliver stood off to the side with his buddies, but the focus of this room was an older man seated behind the desk who projected an air of authority.

The older man rose and offered Lucy his hand. "Captain David Blake. So nice to meet you, Ms. Smok. I've heard a great deal about you."

Lucy didn't take the offered hand. "Yeah? Well, I've heard nothing about you. Who the hell are you supposed to be?"

He seemed unfazed by her rudeness. "I'm the commanding officer of this facility. Of the entire Southwest division of Darkrock, in fact. We've had our eye on Smok for a long time. I tried to broker a deal with your father a few years ago, but he turned me down."

"Let me save you some time. I'll be turning you down, too."

Blake laughed. "You're not here to be offered a deal, Ms. Smok. The time for that has passed. I've brought you here to meet with me because as interesting as the prospect might be, keeping you in a cage and experimenting on you would be too high risk. Unlike most of our guests, you would no doubt have people looking for you. Someone would be bound to leak the information, and it wouldn't look good for either of us. I think you can agree that having the world know about what you are would be bad for business. Not our business," he amended. "Yours."

"I see. So Darkrock intends to blackmail me into cooperating with its efforts. Is that it?"

"Not exactly. As I said, we're no longer interested in cooperation. We intend to launch our own biotech center, specializing in the same discerning clients who've previously depended on Smok Biotech's monopoly. We already have someone on the inside at Smok who's been gathering information and acquiring intellectual capital. What we want is to be assured that Darkrock's efforts won't face any legal challenges from Smok for trademark violations. And to that end, we intend to document your transformation into an inhuman monster as our assurance. We'll have your dirty little secret on file, and you'll let us operate unfettered."

Lucy laughed. "You're out of your damn mind."

"I figure all you need is the right incentive." Blake picked up a remote from his desk and clicked it to display a large video screen beside them showing Colt in his cell—and the hell beast in the cell beside him, a wall of glass between them. The beast was awake. It paced like a tiger in a cage, salivating, as it watched Colt huddling in the farthest corner. "As you may have noticed earlier, there's a dampening field in operation around these cells preventing its occupants from transformations and any other magical influences they might otherwise be able to project. I'm about to turn that off."

Oliver made a startled motion from where he stood. "Sir...do you think that's wise?"

"We've cleared the level." Blake clicked another button on the remote. "I've left the dampening barrier in place between the two cells for now. But let's see what they do."

The lack of a dampening field was clearly felt immediately by both. Colt rose onto all fours and transformed into his wolf form, hackles raised, while the beast broke into one of its inhuman grins. Lucy held her breath as it charged the glass, but the barrier held. The beast stood upright and drew its claws along the glass as if testing it.

"Now," said Blake, "with a click of a button, I can dissolve the magical barrier between them, and we can let the little wolf take his chances against the larger."

A rush of rage-fueled adrenaline surged through Lucy's veins as she started toward him, but the guards held her back. "You can't do this."

"I most certainly can." Blake smiled. "But I'm betting that right about now you're feeling much more compliant. If you give us what we want, I'll leave the barrier intact and restore the dampening field to the whole cell block."

Lucy shook off the guards. "And what exactly is it you want?"

"We just need you to make a little video stating your identity—and your aberration. Before you demonstrate it."

The beast had made another run at the glass, snarling in frustration when it refused to budge. But now it was looking at the glass to the front.

"All right, dammit. Restore the dampening field and I'll make your fucking video."

"Make the video, and then I'll restore the field. It will give the whole thing a nice artistic sense of urgency."

One of the operatives had taken out a camcorder and pointed it at Lucy. "Whenever you're ready."

The hell beast charged the front wall of its cell, and the glass cracked.

"All right." Lucy glanced around. "But you all need to step back." She faced the camera. "My name is Lucy Electra Smok. I'm the CFO of Smok International. And I have infernal blood." She felt like she was at an AA meeting. "It gives me enhanced senses and strength when I experience a partial transformation into a wyvern."

Blake's brow wrinkled. "Sorry, a what?"

Lucy sighed. "It's a kind of dragon. It's my demon form."

"Okay, let's see it."

She'd never done this on command before. Usually, fury combined with the fight-or-flight response triggered it. But she'd put off taking the suppressing meds. Watching the beast make a larger crack in the glass as it rammed it with its shoulder did the trick.

Lucy closed her eyes and shook her shoulders, feeling the heat of the bony chitin that formed the horns on her head, the talons on her fingers and the wings on her back. The fabric of her T-shirt tore as her wings erupted. She allowed them to expand, and the Darkrock operatives took a few steps farther from her as she stretched them as far as she could within the office.

She opened her eyes, avoiding Oliver's, and glared at Blake with the full fury of her wyvern mien. "Restore the barrier. Now."

She'd evidently startled them all a bit, and Blake had to shake himself. "Of course. Thank you for your cooperation." He clicked the button a split second too late, as the glass front of the beast's cell shattered on the monitor. It was out now, loose, but it sensed the change and knew that it couldn't get inside the other cell. It made a snarling howl of anger as it battered its shoulder against the glass before turning and looking straight into the camera.

"I will tear off all your heads," it hissed in a voice that sent a surge of discomfort through Lucy's bowels—and from the looks of it, through everyone else's. "And I will suck the marrow from your bones while I fuck your corpses."

"You're sure the area's secure," said Ramirez.

Blake glared. "Of course I'm sure. Cooper, Benally—get down there and put that thing under again."

"You're going to need my help," said Lucy as the two men moved to follow the order.

Blake hesitated, but another rage-filled howl from the beast made him swallow visibly. "Go ahead." He indicated the video camera. "We've got everything we need here."

Lucy folded her wings and followed Oliver and Artie

Cooper to the elevator. They had already grabbed a few weapons from the locker beside it.

Oliver glanced at her curiously after checking his ammunition as they stepped inside the elevator. "Is that as far as the transformation goes?"

Artie snorted. "What, you think she's got dragon tits or something?"

Lucy turned her wyvern gaze on Artie. "How would you like to find out about my dragon teeth?" That seemed to shut him up, at least temporarily. "Yes," she answered Oliver finally. "This is the whole deal."

The elevator arrived at Block D. Oliver and Artie raised their weapons, Artie armed with the tranquilizer gun and Oliver holding an AK-47, and the doors slid open. There was no sign of the beast as they scanned the corridor, but Lucy could sense it. It was using its ability to visually confound them.

"It's here," she cautioned. "Don't trust your eyes."

"Maybe we should stay between it and the elevator," Oliver suggested. "If we can't see it, it could get past us and escape."

"Good thinking," said Artie. "Let it come to us."

Three cells down, Colt's wolf form was pacing and growling, watching something.

"It's close," said Lucy. She could feel the skin-crawling sensation of its breath, even though the stench of it was absent.

Artie took a step forward. "How the hell are we supposed to shoot it if we can't see the fucking thing?"

Lucy put out a cautioning hand. "I don't think you should—" Her words were cut short by a guttural sound of surprise and a shuddering recoil from Artie, as though something had punched him hard in the gut.

His black T-shirt was growing darker black at the center as if it had gotten wet, and he began to cough up blood.

The beast materialized in front of them, grinning, its claws dripping with Artie Cooper's blood. Artie managed to get off a shot that went wildly off target before he buckled and fell to his knees.

Oliver fired—and shouted with pain as the bullet ripped through the beast's shoulder. Any shots he took at the beast—and any damage Lucy managed to do—were going to be felt by Oliver.

Lucy leaped at the beast with a kick to the head and knocked it back several feet on the slick tile, giving them the briefest moment to strategize. "Oliver, you have to relinquish your protection," she urged. "That's the only way we're going to be able to kill this thing without killing you."

"What are you talking about? What protection?" He seemed reluctant to use the gun again as the beast picked itself up and rushed toward them, but he fired once more and hit the beast in the chest. The impact knocked them both backward an equal distance.

"The hell beast isn't projecting its injuries. You made a vow to protect all unnatural creatures in the Jerome vicinity. That's why you feel the wounds. You're taking them for everything inhuman."

Oliver winced, trying to line up his aim once more as the beast got to its feet. "Ridiculous. How would I even be able to do that? Besides, it didn't happen with you or the kid."

"Because we're both infernal, not earth-based. This thing is as earth-based as it gets. It was born out of rage and hate." She met the beast's charge, but it dematerialized as she swung at it, reappearing behind her.

Oliver fired again and fell to his knees as the shot hit the beast in the stomach at close range. He was doing some serious damage, even if it was temporary, and it was taking its toll on them both.

The beast backed off for a moment, snarling, but something behind it caught its attention. The white wolf was standing in the corridor growling. Someone had unlocked the doors.

Lucy cried out as the beast bolted toward Colt. It slashed its claws across the smaller wolf's side, spraying blood across the white tile and whiter fur.

"Revoke your protection!" she yelled at Oliver as she barreled after the beast to try to get between it and Colt.

"How?"

"Just say it! 'I revoke my protection!'"

Oliver groaned, the AK-47 falling out of his arms. "I revoke my protection."

As she reached the beast, Colt suddenly leaped for its throat, his eyes glowing with red fire and his teeth unexpectedly razor sharp as he bared them, and the hell beast seemed to stop dead with surprise at its attack. The young wolf had torn out its throat. After the instant of shock, the beast flailed, claws swinging wildly, its eyes almost plaintively on Lucy's as Colt eviscerated it.

Its unwitting "mother" or not, Lucy had no sympathy for the creature. She turned to make sure Oliver wasn't also lying shredded on the tile, but he'd stood up, beginning to recover already.

Oliver stared aghast at Colt. "He was holding back to keep from hurting me. I didn't realize. All this time, Colt was suppressing his own power to kill the damn thing and putting himself in danger. Because of me."

"Colt?" Lucy scrutinized Oliver's face. "You said Colt."

"That's the name I gave him, because he—" Oliver wiped blood on his pants from the hand he'd been gripping his gut with. The left hand. Blood clogged the ring. He stared at it. "Oh... God, how did I forget that?" He raised his eyes to Lucy. "How could I have forgotten you?"

Self-conscious discomfort at her wyvern state gnawed at her as it hadn't while Oliver was under the influence of the drug. Sometimes it took a while for the transformation to subside when she hadn't taken her monthly dose of shift control. And now everyone would see her this way if she didn't acquiesce to Darkrock's scheme. Smok International would be ruined either way.

"We should probably get Colt out of here." She turned toward the blood-covered wolf. She was glad he hadn't returned yet to his human form. The blood and gore smeared across his face would have been even more unsettling.

As Colt trotted toward her, a crack of gunfire went off beside her. At first she thought it was Oliver's weapon, but she spun about to see Artie Cooper holding his handgun as he slumped against the elevator door. And Oliver... Oliver didn't look like himself. His face had filled with a white-hot rage, and his eyes were glowing orange, like flame was igniting inside them.

Lucy turned back to the corridor, trying to make sense of what was going on. Had the hell beast somehow managed to rally after all that? But Colt was lying on his side, blood pouring from his hip and his breathing rapid and shallow.

"No." She moved toward him in a daze and sank to

her knees beside him. "Colt." She was vaguely aware
as she laid her hand on Colt's rising and falling rib cage
that Oliver had dragged the wounded Artie to his feet.

"What the fuck did you do?"

"Just following orders," Artie gritted out. "You've
gone soft, Chief. I had to take care of it. Like I had to
take care of you and Vanessa."

"What are you talking about? What about Vanessa?"

"Your last mission. It was *supposed* to be your last,
anyway. Made a deal with those vamp lords to have you
taken out. Your team was collateral damage."

"You sold us out."

Artie was gasping for air. "Vanessa…submitted her
resignation. Said she wanted out. We knew you'd follow."

"You son of a bitch."

Lucy lifted the wolf in her arms and watched as Artie
choked out his last breath.

Oliver let him slip to the floor. "Darkrock did this."
His voice was unrecognizable. "They did this to me.
To Vanessa." Tears poured down his cheeks, steaming
as they fell. "To Colt."

The word that Vanessa had said echoed in Lucy's
head, and she voiced it aloud. "Firecracker."

Something seemed to snap inside Oliver. As the
rage exploded across his face, the tile beneath their
feet began to melt, and in an instant, flames were licking up the walls.

"Run," he said, his voice like crackling fire, and
Lucy ran for the stairs, charging up to the surface with
Colt in her arms. The building was burning, and ex-
plosions were sounding throughout the compound. Ignoring the shouts of the operatives running past her in

the opposite direction and the sprinklers raining down on her, Lucy burst through the door into the yard and took flight under the cover of night, carrying Colt's body away and leaving Oliver to the inferno of his fury and grief.

Chapter 26

Lucy took Colt to the only person she could think of who might be able to save a hellhound: Fran.

"He doesn't deserve this." Lucy felt hollow as she watched Fran work. "He killed that thing—the monster Carter used me to make. He protected us."

"I've stopped the bleeding, but he lost a lot. And there's something else going on with him. His temperature is spiking. I don't know what to make of it. It's as though he's fundamentally unwell. My guess is it's something infernal. He might not be suited to living in this plane. I think the only thing we can do now is send him home."

Lucy exploded at her. "I am not going to use the Soul Reaper on him!"

"Sweetheart." Fran touched her arm gently. "I wasn't suggesting that you shoot the poor thing. Of course not. But you need to contact Lucien."

"Oh." For some reason, her eyes were stinging. She'd transformed back while Fran was working on Colt. It was probably just a residual effect of the shift in her irises.

"You know it's okay to care about him. To care about anyone."

"Ha!" The sharp, dismissive laugh circumvented a less dignified emotional response. "You make me sound like some cold, inhuman bitch."

"That's not what I meant. I've watched you your whole life swallowing your emotions, believing they made you feminine and weak."

"That's not—"

"And I'm partly to blame for that. I gave in to Edgar. I relinquished my right to be your mother. I abandoned you."

"No, you didn't."

"I did. Don't do that."

Lucy scowled irritably. "Do what?"

"Bury your hurt and anger under the Smok stoicism. Let everybody else off the hook but yourself."

"Well, what do you want me to do? Scream at you? Fly into a rage because I didn't have a real mother because you protected yourself instead of protecting us? What goddamn good is that going to do either of us? Edgar made us both what we are."

"No. He doesn't have the power to make you—or me—anything. Don't give him that. He failed you, and I failed you, but that doesn't define you, sweetheart. You are who you are—brilliant, strong, compassionate—because you have the power to be whatever you want to be. To feel however you want to feel. And to express it." Fran touched her once more, despite knowing that Lucy didn't do touching, and let her hand linger on Lucy's forearm. "It's okay to cry. It doesn't make you weak."

"Dammit." Tears were pouring down Lucy's cheeks. "Maybe it doesn't make me weak, but it sucks. It feels like shit. I hate it. I hate crying." And now she was blubbering.

She let Fran hold her, crying a little harder when she realized it was the first time she could remember her mother hugging her—partly because of the NDA Fran had signed relinquishing her parental claim but also because Lucy had always refused any displays of affection. It was sentimental. And made her have feelings. And she fucking hated feelings. Because feelings hurt. Like the little piece of glass that seemed to be stuck in her heart whenever she thought about Oliver's bond with Vanessa—and that seemed to twist deeper when she wondered whether he'd made it out of the compound alive.

By the time she'd pulled herself together, Theia had answered the text she'd sent her while Fran was stitching Colt up. Yes, she was still topside, and she'd go get Lucien immediately. They could meet at Phoebe's place. The quaint, cozy ranch house seemed to be the hub for the Carlisle clan, despite the fact that Rafe Diamante owned several high-end properties around town.

Fran helped Lucy load the unconscious Colt—still in wolf form—into Fran's Range Rover, since Lucy had flown here. "Bring it back when you can." She gave Lucy a quick little hug, which was really pushing it, but Lucy allowed it.

Theia and Lucien hadn't returned yet when Lucy arrived at Phoebe's. Sometimes time passed at a slightly different rate when they were below. Lucy hoped this wasn't going to be one of those times when an hour below was a day above.

Phoebe helped her bring Colt inside and put him in the guest bed.

Lucy observed him as Phoebe tucked a blanket around the little wolf. "He might shift when he wakes up." *If he wakes up.* "I should go get him something to wear."

"I'll text Laurel and have her pick up something. She's on her way here to report back on her undercover assignment."

Lucy had forgotten all about the mole at Smok Biotech. "I'm not sure it matters what Laurel found out, to tell you the truth. Darkrock command bragged that they had someone inside, and they've blackmailed me into outing myself if I don't let them basically destroy everything the company has worked for and let them take what they want."

"Well, just wait to see what Laurel has to say. You may be surprised."

Lucy raised an eyebrow but didn't ask what that meant. Right now she was too tired and worried to care.

"Around what size is Colt's human form, would you say?"

Lucy shrugged. "He's about four and a half feet tall, maybe seventy-five, eighty pounds?"

Phoebe texted the details to Laurel. "She's on it."

Lucy doubted it would matter. From the way Colt was breathing, it wouldn't be long before it became a moot point.

"Do you want something to drink? I have hot mulled cider brewing for Yule—Leo wanted glögg, which I thought was mulled wine, but when I told him that, he said to leave it alone. He'd do it himself." Phoebe laughed. "Apparently, real glögg is more like eating soggy chunks of drunk fruit and nuts out of a glass."

Lucy followed Phoebe down the hall while she chattered on. "Cider's fine." She hadn't thought to drink or eat anything. Phoebe opened up a steaming slow cooker in the delicious-smelling kitchen to ladle out the drink. "Yule…isn't that closer to Christmas?"

Phoebe made a little obvious glance at the huge Christmas tree in the corner. Come to think of it, there were lights all over the outside of the house that Lucy hadn't been paying attention to when she arrived. "What day do you think this is?"

"Um…" God, what the hell day was it? Sometime in early December, Lucy thought.

"Today's the solstice. We're celebrating Christmas early because Ione has to give a big convocation thing or something at Covent Temple, and Leo prefers to celebrate Yule, so it all works out."

"I'm sorry. I didn't realize I'd be interrupting a family gathering."

Phoebe handed her a mug of cider with a little half slice of orange on the rim and a cinnamon stick in it. "Lucy. You're family. And I really should have invited you. I didn't even think of it. I'm sorry. We didn't think Theia would be able to get here for it, so it was just going to be small. But it's all good." She smiled and clinked her mug against Lucy's. "I've got a huge rib roast in the oven."

So that's what that fantastic smell was. She was actually feeling a little faint with hunger now that she thought about it.

Phoebe watched her for a moment. "There's a tray

full of *saffransbullar* and meat pies on the coffee table. Have a seat and dig in. That's what they're there for."

Lucy sank onto the couch and loaded a little plate with savory and sweet saffron buns. Her wyvern metabolism needed some serious replenishing.

Laurel arrived shortly after, quickly followed by Rhea and Leo, while Phoebe made the introductions. Phoebe dragged them to the kitchen to help with chopping things, and the kitchen seemed to bubble over with laughter and joy. Lucy had always wondered what it would be like to have a sister. Or a joyous family celebration, for that matter. The Smoks' had always been grand, solemn, corporate affairs designed to show off Edgar's money and might.

With her hunger slightly mollified, she set her plate down as Laurel sat in the chair adjacent to the table with a cup of cider. "So Phoebe says you have some news for me."

Laurel nodded, cupping her mug in both hands and breathing in the mulling spices. "First, I wanted to thank you for the job. Things were pretty tight this year, and I wasn't sure how I was going to make my rent next month."

Lucy wasn't sure what to say to that. She'd never even considered the idea of rent—or missing a meal, or having any material need met, really.

"I'm glad it worked out for you," she said awkwardly. She felt like an asshole.

"Oh, I know it wasn't about hiring me, exactly, so I'm just pleased that our needs coincided." Laurel smiled warmly and took an experimental sip of cider. "Ow. Too hot. So here's the thing." She set the cup down on the table. "I don't know if Phoebe mentioned to you that I have one of Madeleine's gifts." The Lilith blood passed down from Madeleine Marchant was the source of the Carlisle sisters' abilities.

"She didn't, but I assumed you must. What's your gift?"

"I see certain near-future events when they intersect with events in front of me. It's kind of hard to explain. It's like a probability projection of the butterfly effect. If A happens, B will happen, causing C to happen and on down to the most likely outcome."

"And you saw something at Smok?"

"I did. I mean, first, literally, I saw your assistant putting an entire terabyte drive in her purse. She wasn't very subtle about it."

Lucy gaped. "Allison? She's the mole? But I vetted and hired her myself."

"No, I don't think she's the mole."

"I don't understand."

"I don't think you have a mole. I think you have a magical virus. Something a certain necromancer put in place before he got dragged to hell." Laurel wrinkled her nose with distaste. "It had his nasty smell all over it."

"A virus." A vein throbbed at Lucy's temple. She really wished she'd had the opportunity to punch Carter in the throat. "He infected my staff?"

Laurel nodded. "All of them. They don't even know they're doing it, and no one notices it when anyone steals something right in front of them. I wear an amulet that prevents necromancy from affecting me. Otherwise, I think it would have just drifted onto me from close contact."

"Why don't I have it?"

"Because of your infernal blood, maybe?" Laurel shrugged. "I disinfected the place with some help from Ione, so I don't think you'll be having any more problems."

"Wow. Well, thank you, Laurel. I never imagined it would be something this widespread. Of course, it doesn't actually matter now. Carter played every hand just perfectly to continue screwing Smok after his departure."

"What do you mean?"

"Stolen data and research were being sent directly to Darkrock, and they used Colt as leverage to get me to let them record my transformation. They've threatened to release the video if I try to sue them for anything they've done. They can just take it all now with impunity. Or I can let them release the video, and I can kiss everything goodbye."

"Colt is the little boy?" Laurel looked over at the bag she'd set at her side and passed it to Lucy. "Oh, here's the clothing, by the way."

"Thanks." Lucy rose. "I'd probably better check on him." She started toward the guest room but remembered what Laurel had said about things being tight. Damn. She really needed to start paying more attention to her privilege. "How much do I owe you?"

Laurel waved her away. "Oh, it was nothing. Don't worry about it. I'm happy to help."

"Laurel." Lucy walked back to the couch. "To me it's nothing, because people have been giving me things all my life without me giving any of it a second thought. To you, it matters. Tell me how much it was."

Laurel blushed. "It really wasn't much. I stopped at the dollar store." Lucy took out her wallet and handed

Laurel a one-hundred-dollar bill, but Laurel balked. "No, no. I mean it. It was like twenty-three bucks."

"I don't have anything smaller. Just consider it a thank-you for everything you've done." Lucy set the bill on the table and took the bag into the guest room.

Colt's condition hadn't changed, except that he seemed even warmer now. She took out the clothes and removed the tags and laid them out on a chair just in case.

As she adjusted the blanket around him, however, the rapid breathing sped up like an engine revving, and the wolf opened its eyes. Three things happened in rapid succession, almost too swiftly for Lucy to register: the wolf recognized her, Colt resumed his human form and a ball of fire seemed to roll off Colt's skin and onto the bed, setting the bedding aflame.

Colt bolted out of bed as if he meant to crash through the window, but Lucy grabbed him around the waist and swung him back toward her. He looked up at her with anxious eyes, shaking his head vehemently. Another little ball of fire dripped off him onto the floor, and Lucy stamped it out, but the fire on the bed was spreading rapidly. She could either keep him here or keep Phoebe's house from burning down.

As yet another ball of fire rolled across the carpet, Lucy shoved Colt through the door toward the bathroom across the hall. "In there! Water!" He'd drunk gallons of water at Oliver's place, and perhaps this was why. She prayed she wasn't sending him to set the whole house ablaze as she threw another blanket on top of the bed to smother the fire and yelled for help.

The smoke alarm had been triggered, and Phoebe

came running with a fire extinguisher and put out the bedding and a streak of smoldering carpet.

She turned to Lucy when it was under control. "What the hell happened?"

"Colt," said Lucy. "I think he was dehydrated." She grabbed the clothes from the chair and pushed through the crowd in the doorway that now included Rhea, Leo, Ione and Ione's husband, Dev Gideon, to reach the bathroom and make sure she'd been right.

Colt had climbed into the porcelain bathtub—smart kid; he'd minimized his flammability—and was drinking from his cupped hands under the running water.

Lucy closed the door. "I'm so sorry, Colt. I didn't realize." She should have had Fran hook up an IV drip to keep him hydrated, but it had never occurred to her what the consequences would be of his not getting sufficient water. And she'd honestly thought he wouldn't make it through the night. "I brought you some clothes." She set them on the toilet seat lid. "Once you've cooled down a bit, you can put these on, and we'll get you some proper water from the kitchen. And something to eat."

Colt nodded and continued drinking. Whatever it was that kept him from speaking—whether it was a choice or a physiological impossibility—he seemed to fully understand human speech.

She stepped out to find the hallway had cleared— except for Leo, who stood waiting in the guest room doorway, arms folded as he leaned one broad shoulder against the door frame. "The little wolf," he said, pushing himself away from the wall. "He's a hellhound."

"Yes."

"You know they're meant to hunt."

Lucy shrugged. "I guess, yeah."

"But he's not one of mine."

"I'm not sure what you mean. One of yours?"

"One of my hounds. They accompany the Wild Hunt. They're spectral, but Colt is flesh and blood. I think he may be part of a hunting pack meant to join another Wild Hunt."

"Another?" Lucy pushed back her hair. "I didn't know there was more than one."

"Oh, yes. They come from many regions of the world, many traditions."

"Lucien said he'd escaped hell with a small pack of juveniles. Maybe you're right. But why is that significant?"

"Because I think these hellhounds would have escaped with a purpose. To hunt—or to seek the hunter." Leo started walking back to the living room as if he was done with the conversation.

"Leo." Lucy walked after him. "Do you know something about this hunter?"

Before he could answer, the front door opened at the end of the hall. Theia and Lucien had arrived. Behind Lucy, a soft growl sounded. She turned to see Colt, dressed in his new clothes, standing with legs planted wide, arms out at his sides, ready to run. His eyes had gone red, and they were fixed on Lucien.

Lucy returned to him and took his hand. "It's okay, Colt. He's not here to hurt you. You're not in trouble."

Lucien seemed to recognize Colt as well, whether simply because of his description or because of some infernal sense, Lucy wasn't sure. "So there you are. You and your brother and sisters have caused quite a bit of chaos, my little friend. I don't suppose you know where they are?"

A narrowing of the red eyes was Colt's only response.

Lucy drew Colt a little closer to her side. "He doesn't have to go right away, does he? I know he can't stay, but he seems to be doing much better than he was."

Phoebe came out of the kitchen with oven mitts on her hands. "He could at least stay and eat something, couldn't he? I mean, you guys just got here."

Rhea stepped past her and grabbed Theia's hand, dragging her toward the breakfast counter that separated the living room from the kitchen. "Of course they're staying. It's Yule. And Leo's making honest-to-God glögg. I bet you don't have that in hell."

Lucien put his hands in his pockets, gazing after his stolen wife. "Well, actually, hell isn't really that different. It's just on another…" He stopped and rolled his eyes. "Oh, for fuck's sake. I'm devilsplaining. Never mind. Let's eat, drink and be merry!"

Chapter 27

The food and drink were as amazing as they smelled, and the company, despite the crowded little house, was far more enjoyable than Lucy had expected. After dinner, the Carlisle sisters shared a tradition of "passing fire"—one person lighting the next person's candle and continuing around the circle as they welcomed the return of the light—and even Colt participated, blowing a little bauble of flame onto the candle in Lucy's hand with a shy smile.

Colt never did warm up to Lucien, but Lucy took the boy aside before the evening wound down and explained to him that he had to go home and that Lucien was her brother and she trusted him. She wasn't sure if Colt finally agreed or simply gave up, but it broke her heart a little to see his head hanging as he walked out between Lucien and Theia.

As she headed home, she remembered her car was in Jerome, and she had to get the Range Rover back to Fran. She parked the SUV in the lot at her place and called Allison in the morning to have a car sent to drop her off in Jerome and have the Range Rover picked up and returned. She hesitated a moment when Allison answered, remembering that she—and everyone else at Smok Biotech—had been sabotaging Lucy for months. But it wasn't Allison's fault, and if Laurel was right, it was all sorted now. Whether it mattered or not. If Darkrock had uploaded that footage to the cloud, she was screwed—even if everyone in the compound was dead.

Lucy stared at the tiles while she stood under the shower. Was Oliver dead? How could he not be? He'd been in the midst of the flames fifty feet below the ground, and unlike Lucy, he couldn't transform into a dragon and fly away.

She felt empty again, the way she'd always felt before Oliver. The difference now was that she knew she was empty. All she'd lived for was her work. And now she might not even have that. Oh, some semblance of Smok International would survive, but the usual consulting jobs—exorcising demons and chasing down wayward therianthropic millionaires who'd forgotten to take their meds—didn't hold the same appeal they once had. Biogenetics was the real excitement. That was where the future was. And Smok Biotech was finished.

The water had run cold. Lucy shut it off and stepped out to get dressed. She wasn't really feeling the Prada suits today. A pair of khakis and a black cotton turtleneck would do. She slicked back her hair with a little glosser and applied her signature stain to her lips. She was going to have to report back to the council today that the creature was dead…and that Oliver was, too. Might as well grab a suit jacket and wear the boots that gave her a little height. People seemed to respect her expertise more when she was taller.

Even in the daytime, colored lights and strings of white seemed to drape everything as her driver took her through Sedona, the red rock formations above them sprinkled with snow making it look like a holiday postcard. How had she not even noticed it was almost Christmas? What, even, was the point of Christmas? She might as well be spending it in hell. Goddamn Lucien. He always got the better end of the deal.

She'd emailed Nora that she had news to deliver, and they'd agreed to meet at the Civic Center building at noon. Nora and Wes rose to greet her as she entered the meeting room.

"I've tried calling Oliver to let him know about the meeting, but his phone seems to be out of service, so it's just the two of us today." Nora smiled tentatively as they sat. "I hope it's good news you have to share with us? No new sightings have been reported recently, so that's a good sign."

"It is," said Lucy. "I'm happy to report that the problem has been handled. You shouldn't have any more trouble."

"Oh, that's marvelous! And just in time for Christmas."

Wes was a little more reserved. "Was it a werewolf, like we thought?"

"It was a…" Lucy paused. "I'd call it a malevolent shape-shifting entity. That's really the closest I can come to describing it."

Nora shuddered. "Well, thank goodness it's gone. Oliver's nose is bound to be out of joint when he finds out he was wrong."

"About Oliver—"

"What about Oliver?" The words were delivered in an amused baritone from behind her.

Lucy turned to see Oliver standing in the doorway looking remarkably none the worse for wear—not even a singed eyebrow to show he'd been in a fire. She started to her feet, relief so complete rushing through her that her knees went weak, and she dropped back onto the chair.

"Oliver..." She'd lost the capacity for professionalism. Or human speech.

"I had a little trouble with my phone. Sorry I'm late." He came into the room and sat across from her. "So, did I hear right? You were talking about our shape-shifting menace in the past tense?"

"I..."

"Yes." Nora beamed. "Ms. Smok explained that she's taken care of it."

"Oh, *she's* taken care of it."

"I didn't say..."

"Well, that *is* terrific news. I have to admit that I wasn't sold on the idea of bringing in an outsider to handle town business, but I think we were totally out of our league here. Bringing in Ms. Smok was the right call." Oliver's smile had a devious twinkle to it. "So, Nora, I trust you've handled the payment details?"

Nora pulled a check from her purse and held it out to Lucy. "Absolutely. The fee we agreed on, plus a little extra as a thank-you."

Lucy took the check, still feeling like she was several seconds behind everyone, and the others rose.

Oliver offered his hand to help her up, evidently aware that she was feeling shaky on her feet. "Can I treat you to a coffee and a muffin over at Delectably Bookish, or are you off to your next appointment?"

"I'm...no, I'm good."

Oliver raised an eyebrow. "No, I can't treat you?"

"I mean, yes to the coffee and muffin. No appointments."

Nora and Wes had left the room.

Oliver closed the door. "Sorry to surprise you like that."

"I thought you were dead."

"I gathered. You look like you might even have been a little upset at the idea." He'd stepped closer to her, so close, but not touching. Lucy was having trouble forming words. Oliver leaned down so that his mouth was next to hers. "Were you? A little?"

"Oh, shut up." Lucy grabbed him by the collar and breached the distance between their mouths. Slipping his arms around her, Oliver pressed her close, deepening the kiss until Lucy pulled away breathlessly, realizing how horribly unprofessional this was. And that Oliver was still in love with his dead wife, who might even show up at any moment and want to take over.

"We should probably get going. You mentioned coffee and muffins."

Oliver put his hands in his pockets and studied her for a moment. "You are a damn hard nut to crack."

Lucy turned and pushed open the door. "I'm not any kind of a nut."

Oliver snorted. "I beg to differ."

At the shop, he paused as he unlocked the door. "Before we go in, I should warn you that we're not alone."

She'd managed to regain her composure on the walk over, and she glanced at him curiously. "Oh, is Kelly working?"

"No, she has the week off for the holidays, but I have a couple of houseguests."

Lucy's skin prickled with apprehension. Had some of his Darkrock compatriots managed to survive along with him?

Oliver opened the door and stepped back to let her go first, and Lucy glanced around. "I don't see anyone."

"They're upstairs." Before the words were out of his mouth, three juvenile white wolves with red-tipped ears came racing down the stairs with wagging tails, bouncing around Oliver in greeting.

Lucy watched with amazement. "You found the other hellhounds."

"Actually, they found me. When I used my power to call fire, it apparently called them, as well."

"Why would the hellhounds come to you?"

"It turns out, at least according to a certain siren, that the father I never met was a son of the king of Annwn."

Lucy blinked. "Of where?"

"The fairy realm of Welsh mythology. Which is apparently not so mythical."

"So you're…"

"Half Fae. And it seems these little wolves belong to the Cŵn Annwn, the Hounds of the Otherworld. And they consider me their pack leader."

"You're the hunter."

"The hunter?"

"Leo Ström told me Colt was looking for the leader of the Wild Hunt. Or *a* Wild Hunt. Leo is my sister-in-law's sister's…" Lucy paused. "Oh, hell. There's too many layers. Suffice it to say, he happens to be the leader of Odin's Hunt—you can thank him for the extra-snowy winters we've been having—and he said there were many Wild Hunts, and that Colt must belong to one."

Oliver's expression grew sober. "Where *is* Colt? Is he okay?"

"He's fine, but I..."

"Lucy?" His brows drew together with displeasure. "What did you do?"

"They can't live in this world, Oliver. I had to send him back."

For an instant, the flames returned to his eyes. "You what?"

"I didn't hurt him. I told you, he's fine. But Lucien and Theia came to collect him. He's gone home." Lucy folded her arms, tucking one hand tightly at her side, uncomfortable under his continued glare, though the flames had receded. "My mother's a doctor—she's the one who took the bullet out of his hip and stitched him up. She said he seemed 'fundamentally unwell,' as though something essential to his continued survival was lacking in our world. I imagine the same is true for these three." She shrugged helplessly. "I'm sorry."

The wolves had settled around him, sitting on their haunches and watching Lucy intently.

"You don't know anything about them," Oliver said at last.

"No, I don't. You're right."

"I'm right about something?" Oliver threw his arms in the air. "Let me mark this day on my calendar." Light glinted off the ring on his left hand.

Lucy uncrossed her arms. "I think I'd better take a pass on the coffee and muffins."

"Lucy—"

"See you, Oliver." She turned and walked out to her car without glancing back, and he didn't follow her. Whatever had happened between them, whatever she'd thought might happen in the future, he was already taken. Better to make a clean break. She had enough experience with broken bones to know that it was the best chance at healing. This was why she didn't do relationships. Because all you had to do was disappoint someone once and they would disappear from your life.

And maybe she wasn't thinking about her almost-relationship with Oliver at all. Maybe she was thinking about how she'd spent the first twenty-five years of her life walking on eggshells around her father, always being so careful never to disappoint him the way her mother had. But the fact remained that not getting involved meant not having to feel like she felt right now. Because somehow, she *had* fallen for Oliver.

When she got back to the villa, Lucy left instructions with Allison to clear her calendar for the next few days and not to put any calls through to her or bother her unless it was an emergency. It was Christmastime, she realized, so she gave Allison the rest of the week off, as well.

She was tired. Tired of being on alert all the time, tired of trying to suppress her wyvern nature, tired of trying to navigate a world where people kept insisting on dragging her into their emotional nonsense. She stripped out of her clothes and turned off her phone and took the remaining dose of the dreaming compound she'd gotten from the lab—along with her shift control meds—before climbing into bed. Time to sleep. Finally. Maybe hibernate. Fuck the world.

Chapter 28

A persistent rapping dragged her out of a deep and—despite the drug—blissfully dreamless sleep. Who the hell could be at her door? Lucy pulled on her robe and slipped her gun into the pocket. She couldn't even remember what her last job was. Were there still any hell fugitives left to collect? Not that they would knock.

The pounding was growing louder.

"Goddammit. What the fuck do you want?" Lucy yanked the door open to find Oliver standing on her doorstep. She said it more quietly. "What the fuck do you want?"

"Can I come in for a moment?"

"Why?"

Oliver sighed and looked up at the falling snow—there were already several inches of it on the ground, unusual for Sedona—before meeting her eyes once more. "Does everything have to be a contest of wills?"

"Yes." Lucy moved away from the door without closing it. That was all the invitation he was going to get.

Oliver stepped inside and closed the door. "I talked

to your brother's sister-in-law's—I talked to your friend Leo. Polly hooked me up with him. And don't worry, I didn't give her any more tokens of my gratitude. You were right about the hounds. They aren't meant to stay in this realm long-term. Leo put me in touch with the rest of the Carlisle clan." He smiled and shook his head. "They're an interesting bunch. Rafe Diamante and Dev Gideon arranged for me to communicate with the other side, as it were. Dev apparently shares his physical form with a Sumerian dragon demon that simultaneously exists within the underworld. Were you aware of that?"

Lucy shrugged. "Yes."

Oliver tilted his head like one of his hounds. "Your family and extended family are chock-full of extra-humans, and yet you spend your time hunting them down."

"I hunt the ones that don't belong here. Can you just get to the point?"

"The point is, I spoke with someone in Annwn and got the boys back to where they belong, including Colt. They weren't supposed to be in Lucien's domain. Some necromancer temporarily thinned the walls between some of the underworlds in an attempt to escape hell."

"Oh, for God's sake." Carter Hamilton was like some kind of killer maniac from an '80s slasher movie that just kept coming. Someone should buy him a goalie mask. And then punch him in the junk.

Oliver smiled. "The Carlisle women all had the same reaction. At any rate, the thinning has been repaired and the Cŵn Annwn are safe and sound. Including Colt. He's been reunited with them."

"I'm glad." And she was. Those little downcast eyes had been haunting her. Lucy rubbed her arms. She hadn't bothered to turn on the heat, and her wyvern hormones had finally tapered off now that she'd taken her meds.

"You look cold."

"Yeah. I had the heat off while I was sleeping."

"I could help warm you up."

"Oliver."

"Can you just tell me why you're so mad at me? I know I overreacted about Colt—"

"I'm not mad at you. I just… There's a certain time of the month when my infernal blood is more active, and it makes me lose perspective around…certain things. And I think I allowed myself to get a little carried away. So I'm the one who should apologize."

"I see. So you're not attracted to me now."

"I didn't say that." *Shut up, Lucy.*

"Okay, so you just don't like me now."

Lucy let a little half smile slip out. "I never liked you. I told you that."

"Oh, right. I forgot. Well, would you like to punch me again? We could start with that."

She wanted to laugh, but the sound that came out was more like a whimper. "Oliver, I…" She closed her eyes so she wouldn't have to see his expression. "You still love Vanessa. She's never left your side. I don't want to come between that. I can't compete with a ghost."

"Lucy." He'd crossed the distance between them, and she opened her eyes to find him just inches away. "I will always love Vanessa. But she's gone. She's been gone for half a decade. Phoebe let me say goodbye to her."

"She told me she had more she needed to tell you."

Oliver's eyes flickered with emotion. "She did. She wanted me to know what happened that day—the day she died."

"I saw it." Lucy shuddered. She didn't need to hear that story again.

"Not that part, but before. She was part of a secret task force. So secret, I didn't even know about it. Because it was about me. Darkrock had dug up my father's identity, and they knew about my magical blood. They hadn't seen me demonstrate it, and they wanted to find out what it was I might be able to do so they could find a way to use it for their own ends. Vanessa was chosen to administer the catalyst and to give me a trigger word while I was under a hypnosis spell."

"You mean—"

"Probably don't say it just now." He smiled wryly. "Just in case. But yes. The word she told you to say to me. She wasn't supposed to try it that night. But when we went into that nest and she saw what had happened to the rest of our team—and knew what was about to happen to her—she breathed that word to me in the instant before her throat was slit. Darkrock had no idea that she'd triggered my magical ability. And neither did I. I just acted on instinct, out of pain, and I..."

He paused for a moment, lost in his thoughts. "At any rate, it was the reason she wanted out of Darkrock so badly. She couldn't live with the knowledge that she was being used to manipulate me. That's what she wanted to tell me. To tell me she was sorry. Which, it turns out, was all *I* still needed to say to her. But Vanessa's business is finished here. She's crossed over. And getting the chance to say goodbye to her freed me from the oppressive cloud of her specter that I'd allowed to hang over me." He touched Lucy's fingers, and she didn't pull away immediately. "There's nothing to compete with. And I know you have some issues with relationships..."

Lucy let out a sharp little laugh, but her fingers curled around his involuntarily. He wasn't wearing his ring. She glanced down at the other hand, but all his fingers were bare.

"I have some issues with a lot of things," she admitted. "I'm kind of a mess. You have no idea what you're getting yourself into."

Oliver's brow lifted hopefully. "Am I? Getting in?"

Lucy's heart gave a little involuntary leap. "I think you already have."

He kissed her, and this time Lucy didn't feel that sense of panic, the urge to flee, that usually accompanied emotional intimacy. There was just the heat of his lips and his tongue, and that sexy just-rained scent on his skin—even though it was snowing—and the rightness of his body as it fit around hers when his arms enveloped her.

The tie had slipped loose on her robe, and Oliver stepped back slightly, his hands on the lapels. "Close it? Or open it?"

"Open," she said. He took that invitation as far as he could.

As they spooned together under her blankets later, Oliver kissed her neck sleepily. "I brought you a Christmas present. I don't know if you do Christmas."

"It's a little early for Christmas presents, isn't it?"

"It's Christmas Eve."

"It's what?" Lucy turned toward him, incredulous.

Oliver laughed. "Lost track, did you?"

"I… But I came home after talking to you and went straight to bed. That was the twenty-third."

"You've been asleep for more than a day? I thought you were just ignoring my calls."

"My phone was off."

"I thought you didn't sleep."

"I guess I was saving it up. I took a sleeping pill—it was kind of a heavy dose. One of Smok Biotech's special formulae." Lucy lay back against the pillow and closed her eyes. "I guess that's Darkrock's special formulae now."

"Oh, that's the other present. I forgot to tell you." Oliver turned and propped his elbow on the bed. "All records of your statement, your demonstration of the wyvern shift, have been destroyed."

Lucy's eyes opened in surprise. "It's what? How do you know they hadn't backed it up to the cloud somewhere?"

"Darkrock protocol. Nothing is stored remotely via internet connection, not even over a VPN. They would have taken the SD card off-site and made a backup at one of their hubs, but they never had the chance. I burned the card myself."

Lucy breathed a sigh of relief. "Thank you. I was sure my career was over and Smok stock was going to be in the toilet." She kissed him gratefully. "So, what's this other present? I didn't get you anything."

Oliver threw off the covers, letting the shock of cold roll over them. "Come on. Get dressed. Wear something warm."

With an ivory cashmere coat over her jeans and long-sleeved thermal T—along with boots, gloves, hat and a scarf at Oliver's suggestion—Lucy followed him outside.

"They should be arriving…" Oliver looked at his smart watch. "Right about now."

"Who?"

Oliver put his index finger and his thumb between his teeth and whistled sharply. A Christmas sleigh appeared promptly from around the corner…driven by four young white wolves with red-tipped ears.

Lucy threw him an amused glance. "I thought you said they'd gone home."

"They did. But apparently I can call them for the Hunt whenever I need to. They love pulling this thing. Trust me."

Oliver helped her into the sleigh and climbed in beside her, laying a blanket over their laps before he took the reins. "Let's go, boys. Mush!" He grinned and put his arm around Lucy as the hellhounds took off.

Despite their size and the weight of the conveyance, the hounds seemed to have no trouble navigating the still-falling powder as the sleigh skimmed through the parking lot toward the private hiking trail behind the villas. On the trail, the hounds drew them at a brisk pace between sparkling snow-covered acacia bushes and desert broom, the powder-dusted domes of Thunder Mountain and Coffee Pot Rock rising in the distance.

"So, what are we hunting?" Lucy murmured against Oliver's side.

"Nothing," said Oliver. "I've already found you."

* * * * *

COMING SOON!

We really hope you enjoyed reading this book. If you're looking for more romance, be sure to head to the shops when new books are available on

Thursday
9th August

To see which titles are coming soon, please visit
millsandboon.co.uk

LET'S TALK
Romance

For exclusive extracts, competitions
and special offers, find us online:

f facebook.com/millsandboon

◎ @millsandboonuk

🐦 @millsandboon

Or get in touch on 0844 844 1351*

For all the latest titles coming soon, visit
millsandboon.co.uk/nextmonth